SACRIFICED

More Books by Suzan Harden
(Each series is in suggested reading order)

Bloodlines
Blood Magick
Zombie Love
Zombie Confidential
Zombie Wedding
Amish, Vamps & Thieves
Blood Sacrifice
Love, War & a Bulldog
Zombie Goddess
Ravaged
Sacrificed
Reality Bites
Ghouls in the Grocery Store
Resurrected
Bloodlines Shorts Anthology
Bloodlines: The First Boxed Set

Seasons of Magick
Spring
Summer
Autumn
Winter
The Seasons of Magick Anthology

Tales of the Twelve
*The Trickster Priestess
and the Demon*

Justice
Sword and Sorceress 28
("Justice")
Sword and Sorceress 30
("Diplomacy in the Dark")
Justice: The Beginning
A Question of Balance
A Modicum of Truth
A Matter of Death
A Touch of Mother
A Twist of Love
A Virtue of Child
A Hand of Father
A Measure of Knowledge
A Hint of Thief
A Cup of Conflict
A Barrel of Vintner
A Sprout of Wild
A Glimmer of Light

The Justice Thalia Stories
Snowfall
Murder Most Fowl
The Sweetest Poison
A Granddaughter of Mine
Too Many Fish in the Sea

Crossover Worlds
Invasion!

888-555-HERO

Hero De Facto
Hero Ad Hoc
Hero De Novo
A Very Hero Christmas
Hero De Jure
Hero In Camera
Hero Amicus Curiae
A Very Hero Wedding
A Very Hero New Year
Hero Ad Litem
Queer Eye for the Super Guy

Solar System Services, Inc.

Alone Is Not Lonely
Halloween Harvest
("A Place at the Table")
A Place at the Table

Millersburg Magick Mysteries

Spells and Sleuths
Fae and Felonies
Magick and Murder
Feline Navidad

Soccer Moms of the Apocalypse

Pestilence in Pumpkin Spice
Famine in French Vanilla
War in White Chocolate
Death in Double Mocha
Demons Run at Halloween

The Enchanted Bakery

Chefs, Shrooms, and Sherry
Cakes, Cookies, and Conjuring

Miscellaneous

Sword and Sorceress 31
("Pig-Headed")
Sword and Sorceress 32
("Unexpected")
Practical Witches
Revenge Served Hot
The Yule Switch
Chocolate for Dinner
Silver Shoes and Pigs' Ears
Snipe Hunt

For updates, news, and giveaways, join Suzan's mailing list at suzanharden.blogspot.com/p/contact-me.html, or visit her website at www.suzanharden.com. You can also check her out on Facebook @SuzanHardenWriter.

BLOODLINES #8

SUZAN HARDEN

SACRIFICED
(Bloodlines #8)

This is a work of fiction. All characters, organizations and events in this novel are products of the author's imagination and are not to be construed as real. Any resemblance to persons, living or dead, is entirely coincidental.

ISBN - 978-1-938745-41-6

Published by Angry Sheep Publishing LLC
Findlay, Ohio

Cover Design by For the Muse Design
Interior Design by JW Manuss

To my own Genius Kid

Prologue

Duncan

Eight months ago . . .

It was movie night. Samantha wanted the latest version of the Expendables franchise. I wanted the new Sandra Bullock-Melissa McCarthy comedy. We compromised with *Shakespeare in Love,* my wife's favorite method of torturing me.

Thankfully, my head of security, Mai Osaka, rang me before the end of the first act.

"Thad's out with Leslie and the kids northwest of the city. They found a body. Female. Possibly demon related from the damage to the abdomen."

Of course, Samantha could hear the entire exchange without benefit of activating the speaker phone feature. She stiffened, and her eyes glowed silver. Her appearance still bothered me. On the surface, my discomfort was ridiculous. As a vampire, my eyes did something similar, but it was a reminder I had failed to keep her safe when I had the chance. When she had still been alive.

"We are on our way," I said to Mai.

Our private elevator to our penthouse whined to life. "I'm still here in the Karnak. Please tell Sam to wait for me, Master St. James. I'll be there momentarily."

"Of course." I ended the call and rose from the couch.

"I wouldn't have left without her," my wife grumbled. Ozone tainted the air. Samantha's powers manifested further, changing her clothing from shorts and a t-shirt advocating a fictional character for president to a solid black coat with matching slacks and boots.

I had discovered I could not look at her directly too long when she was in this state. Not without risking my sanity. I focused on a spot on the couch next to her left ear. "Of course not, darling. However, I need to change my clothing if we will be traipsing through the desert." I gestured at the black sweatpants and t-shirt I wore.

She jumped up from the couch. "I could—"

I held up my index finger. "No!" At her stricken expression, I softened the tone of my voice. "I appreciate your offer, but I can dress myself through conventional methods. Thank you."

Samantha crossed her arms. "Just because I screwed up once—"

"If Thaddeus and the werecoyotes found evidence of a demon, arguing about my dress now is not a productive use of our time." I left the living room before either of us could say something else. Otherwise, she would continue to use the issue of my clothing to mask her anxiety of a possible demon incident so near our home.

A few seconds later, I returned to the living room to find my wife and my chief of security whispering furiously at each other. Perhaps they forgot I could hear every word from our master bedroom, but they dropped their argument of whether or not I should go to the crime scene the moment I stepped into the hallway.

And they both consistently accused *me* of being overprotective.

"I am ready unless you two wish to continue your debate concerning my delicate masculine sensibilities," I said as I strode into the living room.

Mai's cheeks flushed a bright pink. At the sweet scent of her blood, I had to clamp down on my instincts, but there was nothing I could do about the lengthening of my eyeteeth or the emerald glow of my own eyes. I hoped the women would interpret my slip as concern over Thaddeus's discovery.

Samantha glared at me as she seized Mai's hand. Unfortunately, her telepathic powers had been growing along with her other abilities as a goddess.

Goddess. As much as I tried, I still had problems accepting the concept.

"Get your ass over here if you're coming," she snapped.

"Yes, my lady." I crossed the floor and clasped her warm hand in mine. Everything went black and the floor tilted from under my feet.

Then the full moon shone directly overhead, and sandy loam cushioned my boots. Two high-pitched yips of dismay rent the cool desert air.

"Booker, Deanna, get your butts over here now," barked a deep voice. "I told you two not to wander off."

The female werecoyote pup toddled back to the Normal enforcer sitting on a nearby waist-high boulder. The male, however, crouched down and growled at us.

I scooped him up. The little bugger tried to nip my fingers while I strode to where Thaddeus Wolford waited. A shot gun lay beside the enforcer. He cuddled the whimpering female pup.

"Where is the corpse?" I handed Thaddeus's grandson back to him.

His head jerked in the direction of more boulders. "Back there. Leslie and the kids have been sniffing around, trying to pick up a scent." He turned in the direction he had indicated. "Staci! Need you to watch the babies for a few minutes!"

My wife's secretary trotted from between the two closest towering rock formations. Brimstone and ash radiated from the werecoyote. Thad set down her children, and they immediately began wrestling in the dirt. A sharp bark from their mother ended the tussle.

Samantha, Mai, and I followed Thaddeus through the maze of rocks to a shallow depression. Two flat slabs leaned against each other, forming a lean-to of sorts. From the run-off tracks in the soil, the corpse had originally been placed under the slight cover.

"In all my years as a sheriff back in Ohio, I never saw this much weird shit." Thaddeus paused at the edge of the depression. Four werecoyotes prowled around the area. The female padded over to the sheriff.

Her gray-brown fur faded. Muscles and bones flexed and twisted until Leslie Warner Wolford stood beside her husband. "Body's been here for at least a week. We were out here running last Thursday so somebody dropped the body soon after we left." She shook her head and her graying dirty blonde hair flew. "No scavengers have touched it. Not even insects." She shuddered. "Fucking creepy as hell. Boys!"

The three male werecoyotes, her sons by her ex-husband, backed away from the corpse, and Samantha took up their prowling behavior. Her eyes flared silvery-white. The glow provided enough illumination for Mai and Thaddeus that their flashlights were not needed.

Samantha crouched next to the body. "Honeyed apple. It's Sharon Tyson all right."

One of the two women who could not be accounted for after the Battle of Tuttle Creek. Sharon was the one woman we had discovered was supernatural. The poor lady had not known she was part fae. However, no one deserved her fate. If I did not feel the wash of my wife's rage, the rocks around us humming would have given us fair warning.

"Darling, you need to control yourself before someone is harmed."

Her attention focused on me. "Haight used her, Duncan. This is my fault." She jabbed her index finger in the direction of the corpse. A fissure appeared in a boulder with a sharp *crack*. "There's another demon running loose because I didn't find her in time." She rose in a motion that was unnaturally smooth even by my vampiric standards. "And they left Sharon's body here to make sure I knew."

Mai stepped a little closer to my wife, but I noticed not any closer to the corpse. "Sam, you can't let them rattle you—"

"Shut up, Mai. Just—" Her gulping inhalation meant she was trying not to let loose her tears. Or her power. "Just shut up, okay? I've heard it all." Samantha pushed past my chief of security.

"Darling—" I reached for her, but she evaded my touch.

A strong hand grasped my arm as I turned to follow her. "Let her go, Duncan. The kid needs some time alone," Leslie murmured.

"She is taking this personally." I glanced down at Leslie's hand but she didn't release me.

"The bastards meant it to be personal," the werecoyote said. "It's the reason they left the lady's body so close to Las Vegas."

"Leslie's right, sir," Mai said before she turned to Thaddeus. "You have any extra gasoline in your truck? We need to burn the corpse."

He frowned. "Don't you want one the witches to take a look at it first?"

Mai looked at me for confirmation, and I shook my head.

Thaddeus shrugged and trudged off to retrieve the fuel. Leslie released me and shifted back to her canine form. She and her sons followed the enforcer.

Mai clasped her hands behind her back. "May I ask why you don't want Quinn's people, or even Bebe, to check out the body?"

"Because its purpose was exactly as Leslie said." I stared at the thing that had been a living breathing woman until a demon had clawed its way out of her abdomen. "To taunt us."

"But why would the demons do such a thing?" Mai gestured at the remains. Remains not even bacteria would touch.

"This was not the demon's idea," I replied. "This was Marcus's."

Chapter 1

Max

Max Howell tossed ten M&Ms on the pile in the middle of the kitchen table. "See your five and raise you five, Caesar." The vampire master's left eyebrow twitched, but he said nothing. Max turned and watched the players on his other side.

Duncan held up his cards to consult with his partner sitting in his lap. "What do you think, Ellie?"

Max tried not to smile at his daughter's serious expression while she examined her uncle's hand. She'd inherited the St. James blue-black hair, but somehow ended up with the Howell blue eyes.

"Hey, that's cheating!" Alex said. His protest emphasized the Texas accent he'd kept for over a century and a half.

"You had the opportunity to obtain your own partner, Stanton." Caesar smiled over the top of his cards.

"At least Phillippa plays poker," Colin grumbled. "You should have heard the lecture I got about gambling." The last scion of the famed Fitzgerald political family scowled at his own hand.

"Auntie Anne is right. You're not very good at poker, Uncle Colin," Ellie's sweet voice piped in. She tossed twenty brown M&Ms on the kitty. "Raise you by another ten, Daddy." She popped a blue one from her prodigious pile into her mouth.

Colin glared at her in mock outrage. "Did you talk Duncan into reading my mind? Because that's cheating, too."

"Dude," Jake Wong drawled. "In case you hadn't noticed, two mere Normals are kicking your supernatural ass, and one of them isn't even in kindergarten yet." He tossed the requisite number of M&M's into the pot.

Max checked his two cards again. Did the four vampires realize how obvious their tells were? Only the really crappy hands he'd drawn had kept his pile from being as big as Jake's or Ellie's.

Alex pushed his cards aside. "Too rich for me."

After a bit of grumbling, Colin folded as well.

"I'm out." Caesar laid down his hand.

Max made a show of checking his cards again. He'd played with Jake long enough to know his sister's ex was bluffing. However, his sister's husband couldn't bluff to save his life even with Ellie as his partner. "I match your bet and raise you another five." He added more candy to the growing pile.

Sure enough, Duncan whispered into Ellie's ear, and she tossed the necessary amount of M&M's into the kitty. "Raise you ten, Daddy."

Jake tossed his cards face down on the table. "Mazel tov, kid. Maybe your mom and dad will let you come to Vegas with me next weekend." He winked at Ellie.

"Can I, Daddy?" She bounced in her excitement. "Uncle Duncan and Aunt Sam will let us stay with them." She batted her big blue eyes at her poker partner. "Won't you, Uncle Duncan?"

"Of course, you may visit." He glared at Jake. "But you need to ask your mother first." Silently, Duncan mouthed over Ellie's head, "And you are not taking her on the casino floor, Wong."

That didn't mean Duncan wouldn't set up a private room for Ellie with staff to play with her. Hopefully, her presence would get Sam to . . .

Max clenched his jaw at the disturbing thoughts. To what? Relax? Rejoin the human race?

Except his baby sister wasn't human. Not anymore. And she'd become obsessed with hunting down the rest of the saurian demons who'd managed to escape the Battle of Tuttle Creek last year. Even Duncan had admitted Ellie was the only thing linking Sam to the mortal plane these days.

Max stared at the flimsy cardboard in his hand. Duncan would totally lose it if Sam simply didn't come home from one of her hunting trips one day.

"Daddy!"

Max realized with a start Ellie had been calling him more than once. "Sorry, sweetie. Just thinking about what I should do." He tossed his matching bet on the pile. "I call."

Ellie squealed in glee. "Three kings!" She laid down her cards.

Max smiled. He may not be able to save his sister, but he could damn well make his daughter happy. He laid his full house face down. "You win, sweetie."

She clapped her hands. "Another hand."

"No. I said this was the last one for tonight." At her pout, he added, "But we can play more this weekend when we go visit Duncan and Sam." Tiffany wouldn't argue too much about a father-daughter weekend road trip. With the class load she was taking, she needed some serious study time.

"Can Uncle Jake come, too?"

Max hesitated for a moment. Jake and Sam's ancient engagement was a sore point with Duncan even though Sam was long over the stunt man turned enforcer.

"Yes, he may," Duncan said.

"Yay!" Ellie jumped off his lap and ran around the table, singing, "We're goin' to Vegas!"

Max rose and stretched, only to have Jake grab his arm and pull him into the foyer of Caesar's mansion.

"You sure this is a good idea?" Jake's brown eyes reflected Max's concern. "I was joking about Vegas. I won't come if it'll cause problems."

Max glanced at the vampires, who were studiously ignoring him and Jake. He knew damn well they could hear everything they said, but he was grateful they kept Ellie entertained while they cleared drinks and snacks so he and Jake could talk.

"Actually, yeah, it would be good if you came. Nothing against Duncan—"

"I am glad to know you bear me no ill will."

Max jerked and glared up at his brother-in-law. How could someone with his bulk and height sneak up on anyone? "I really need to put a bell on you."

Duncan's smile didn't quite reach his eyes. He turned his attention to Jake. "You are most definitely welcome to visit the Karnak. I think it would do Samantha some good."

A sick feeling filled Max's gut. Duncan wanting Jake at the hotel/casino he ran said volumes. "Are things getting worse?"

"Define 'worse.'" Duncan grimaced.

"She's been coming home, hasn't she?"

"It is not the coming home that disturbs me."

Alex joined them. "My father-in-law isn't trying to put the moves on her again, is he?"

Max leaned around the three men to check on Ellie. Caesar galloped down the main hallway of his mansion with her on his back. Max shook his head. If he filmed the vampire master, and former prince of Egypt, playing horsey with his daughter, he could make a mint. He just wouldn't live long enough to enjoy it.

"No, she has made her wishes in the matter quite clear to Ares. We have not had any more issues with unwanted suitors." Duncan looked perplexed. "She has taken to playing bridge with some of the goddesses when she is home."

Max took off his glasses and cleaned them on the hem of his button-down shirt to cover his own unease. He'd met some of Sam's new friends, all of them death deities from various world religions. It was creepy as hell, but what could he say when Sam was one of them? "She's not ignoring the baby zombies, is she?"

Duncan shook his head. "No, and please stop calling them 'baby zombies'. They are restored humans, and they have been for nearly five years now." Lines creased the alabaster skin of his forehead. "Frankly, they are doing better than she. And they are worried about her obsession with the Old Ones' acolytes as well."

Max put his glasses back on and rocked on his heels. "Guess we're coming out to Vegas this weekend."

As Max had figured, Ellie was out cold by the time they pulled into their Tarzana ranch house's driveway. When he lifted her out of her safety seat, her little arms automatically wrapped around his neck and baby snores filled his ear.

The living room lights weren't on. That was odd. Was Tiffany still at the university?

No, it wasn't just the main lights. Even the little antique lamp Grandma Neel had sent them as a wedding present was out, and he was pretty sure he'd turned it on before he and Ellie left for Caesar's this evening.

Crap. One burnt out bulb meant tripping over whatever toys Ellie left scattered in the living room. He really didn't want to set her down on the couch. If he did, she'd be wide awake, hyper about the trip to Las Vegas.

Then he'd get an earful from Tiffany for allowing their daughter to stay up so late.

Maybe if he shuffled along the carpet, he'd be okay.

Max twisted the key and nudged the front door open. The hairs on the back of his neck rose before he consciously recognized the scent of sandalwood.

Vampire. Fresh vampire. Except it had been two weeks since the last time Duncan had dropped by, much less any of the rest of Augustine Coven.

The odor was followed by the equally distinctive scent of unwashed human.

Intruders.

Max pivoted back toward his Volvo, but something grabbed him from behind at the same time his daughter was ripped from his arms.

"Ellie!"

Pain exploded at the back of his head. He couldn't make his arms work. The second punch landed on the side of his face and sent his glasses flying.

"Daddy!"

He struck out blindly in the direction of his daughter's terrified shriek. There was a muffled grunt before a blow to his back drove him to his knees.

"Ellie!"

Her screams grew fainter. Someone was taking her away. He lashed out, but fists pounded him, boots kicked him until he couldn't take a breath. A sharp crack and his jaw broke along with a couple of teeth. More bones broke until all he felt was agony.

But it didn't match the agony in his heart. Someone took his daughter. *Ellie!*

A voice whispered through his mind. *Your daughter is ours. Make sure you remember that when your world burns.*

The fire in Max's brain consumed him until everything he'd ever been burned to ash.

Chapter 2

Sam

I 'ported to Duncan before he finished his sentence.

He blinked and lowered his cell phone. "Someday, someone will capture you on camera," he muttered.

I glanced around me. We were in a private conference room in the Laura Lannigan wing of Good Samaritan hospital in Los Angeles. Just the two of us. "Where's Max?"

"In surgery."

I charged for the closed door, but Duncan grabbed my arm. I halted before I accidentally ripped his offending limb off. To say things between me and my husband were strained was the understatement of the century.

"Ellie is missing."

"Why didn't you say—" I cut off my words at his irritated look. Because I hadn't given him a chance to tell me, that's why. I cleared my throat. "What happened?"

"We were at Caesar's home for dinner."

I frowned. "Tonight's poker night."

Duncan pressed his lips in a straight line, but his gaze focused on a point near my left ear. The fact that my husband could barely look at me bothered me more than I cared to admit. But this wasn't the time to hash out our marital issues.

I raised my hands. "Sorry. I won't interrupt again." It would have been easier to read his mind, but part of our current problems was due to my becoming exponentially more powerful than him. Rifling through his thoughts would not help the situation.

"Thank you." He sucked in a large gulp of air. "From the preliminary evidence, whoever attacked Max was waiting in the house when he and Ellie arrived home. Tiffany found him on the living room floor."

All the energy seemed to rush out of Duncan. "He has broken bones, severe internal injuries, and—" His voice hitched. "Bebe is mostly concerned about the bleeding near his brain stem."

"She'll call in a healer or two from Silver Bear. Her grandmother's the high priestess of the coven for crying out loud."

"She has," he said tightly.

Duncan's attitude was really starting to piss me off. "Then what's the issue?"

"You do not seem to be taking this seriously."

"Of course, I'm taking this seriously." I threw up my hands. "But this isn't the first time one of us has been in the hospital."

His eyes flashed neon green. "Nor is it the first time you have forgotten the rest of us are not immortal." He pivoted on his boot heel, whipped open the door, and stalked out of the room.

Well . . . crap. Ever since he found out the damn nanites were turning my original human DNA into god DNA, his panties had been in a wad. I knew his ego was still firmly planted in the sixteenth century, but I was getting pretty fucking tired of his resentment that goddess trumped vampire in the power department. It wasn't like he didn't know what I was when we actually tied the knot.

So I did what any irritated wife did when her husband walks out in the middle of an argument. I followed him.

"What are you saying?" I asked when I caught up with Duncan at the elevator bank. "Bebe and her people can't help Max?"

"They do not know yet," he said softly.

My stomach lurched at the sadness in his tone. "Come on, my big brother's too tough to kill."

Duncan didn't even acknowledge my smartass comment. The elevator dinged. I followed him into the car.

So I tried to be as grim as he wanted me to be. "Have you called my parents yet?"

Duncan stared straight ahead. "They are upstairs in the waiting room."

His statement felt like a punch in the gut. "You called Mom and Dad before you called me?"

His jaw muscle twitched. "I tried you first, but as usual, you did not answer."

I opened my mouth to rip him a new one . . .

And shut it before I did. I hated that he was right.

I'd taken one fucking mental health day. I went to Paris for lunch after spending the morning exploring the Apollo 11 landing site on the moon. After a delicious meal on the Seine, I headed out to Pluto to check out its heart-shaped formation. It was such a thrill not to need travel money, or oxygen tanks, to visit all the places I dreamed of as a kid. I just kept forgetting that my cell service didn't extend past the International Space Station.

I stared at the elevator doors. "You're right. I'm sorry."

"I do not want to fight, darling," he said softly.

The fact that it'd been forever since he called me "darling" hit me even harder than the fact that he'd reached my parents first. Maybe we needed to look into marriage counseling.

The elevator doors parted, and we exited. Only Mom and Dad sat in the surgical waiting room.

I learned in and whispered, "Where's Tiffany?"

An exasperated sigh issued from Duncan. "At the moment, irritating the hell out of the enforcers looking into her daughter's kidnapping."

Chapter 3

Tiffany

Standing in my own living room, I glared at Alex Stanton. Yeah, technically he was my boss, but I couldn't believe what he'd done. "My daughter is missing, my husband had the shit beat out of him, and you called my mommy on me?"

He crossed his arms. "No, but you're are making me wish I had."

I glanced over at my foster mom, Phillippa Mann-Stanton, who stood at the entryway to the rest of our house. She spoke in low tones with Siobhan Sifuentes, the beta of the Lannigan werewolves, probably comparing scents or some other supernatural bullshit. I did my best to ignore the gigantic bloodstain amidst the scattered toys on my beige carpet.

Max's blood.

I tried to shove the memory of finding the nearly unrecognizable body of my husband on the living room floor into a deep, dark hole in the back of my brain. If I thought about it too much, if I thought about what some stranger may be doing to my precious little girl . . .

Work the problem, Tiffany!

Somehow, Max managed to text 9-1-1 to me when I was driving home from my quantum theory class. I'd been running late because I stayed to ask the professor a couple of questions. Max could have been trying to dial emergency services for all I knew. And I wouldn't know until he woke up.

If he woke up. I didn't need a medical degree to understand how bad his injuries were. And if I thought about the broken body of the man I loved too much, I would be useless to Ellie.

Stop it!

I took a deep breath. I had to focus on what I could control—the search for my missing daughter. So far, we hadn't found any evidence my baby had been hurt. But that didn't mean—

From the expression on Alex's face, he'd seen that awful thought in my head.

"You're implying I can't do my job," I said through gritted teeth.

He lowered his voice. "You're too close, and we both know it. Go be with your husband. We've got this. You know we will do everything we can to find her. Between Phil, Siobhan, and your grandfather, we have this covered."

"Duncan and my in-laws are at the hospital," I ground out. "Duncan will let me know when Max is awake. And if I have to listen to that bitch tell me how this is my fault one more time, so help me, I will stake her."

"I'll hold her for you," said a familiar feminine voice behind us.

Alex and I both jumped and whirled to find my sister-in-law dressed in her goddess clothes. In other words, she resembled Neo if Keanu Reeves had a blond ponytail and boobs.

"How many times have I told you to cut the creepy crap, Sam?" I holstered my gun. A little part of me was pleased Alex had to do the same. Someone catching a Normal like me off guard was one thing. A goddess of death getting the jump on any vampire, especially him as the Augustine chief enforcer, had to be embarrassing as shit.

"I've already been to the hospital." she shrugged. "There's nothing I can do there. I figured you could use my help." She closed her eyes, but they quickly popped open. "What the fuck! I can't sense Ellie."

"Try expanding your search outside of my neighborhood," I snapped. And the gods only knew what the neighbors thought with the extra vehicles parked in front of our house. Hopefully, they thought the werewolves were police dogs. I sure as hell couldn't contact Normal police in the assault on my husband and the disappearance of my daughter.

Sam glared at me. "I searched the whole solar system. Unless you're suggesting she was taken by Klingons."

Ice formed in my stomach. As much as I ragged on Sam about the deity stuff, I figured between her and Phil's dad being Ares, the Greek god of war, Ellie would be home within a couple of hours. The only other time I'd been this scared, the psycho bitch who had killed my parents had me by the short and curlies.

But her grandson was still running around causing trouble—

Rage roared through me as I realized what my boss had been hiding, the real reason he didn't want me inside my own home. I whirled and poked Alex's chest with my index finger. "Marcus Giovanni was here. You knew, and you didn't tell me!"

My fist clenched of its own accord and launched itself at Alex's face. Phil's tight grip stopped the blow millimeters from his nose. I glared at her.

Her expression held the same fierceness it had when I was twelve and had nearly gotten myself killed by rogue vampires when I skipped school. The one that said she wasn't tolerating any more of my bullshit. It didn't matter that we all knew hitting Alex would hurt me far more than it would him.

Which was probably why he was going to let himself be my punching bag. Better I take it out on him than some innocent Normal.

Well, if my foster mom wanted in the middle of this, I could turn my impotent wrath on her. "I promise not to try to deck Stepdaddy anymore—tonight."

Phil released me and turned to Sam. "I'm glad you're here. There's something Father and I want your opinion on."

"If you mean the lizard people scent, I picked it up the moment I 'ported in here." Sam had none of her usual snarkalicious attitude which scared me more than I wanted to admit. In fact, she was as all icy seriousness as Phil.

I folded my arms over my chest. "Is this the first sign you've had since the Las Vegas incident?"

"Yes." She drew the word out, like how dare I question her.

"Then maybe we need to pool our resources."

"I don't need your help."

Maybe Ellie's terrible twos had taught me some patience. When my sister-in-law and I first met, we snapped at each other like rabid dogs before settling down and getting the job done. But now . . .

"What's the problem? You afraid I have more skills than your new buddies?" Okay, maybe I did snap after all.

Sam's eyes started to glow. Not blue neon like they should if she were a vampire, but the reflective silver of liquid mercury.

And her pissy attitude just made me tired. I shook my head. "That intimidation shit isn't going to fly with me. I was raised by vampires and a demigoddess. Either be part of the team and help me find my daughter, or get the fuck out of my house."

Both Alex and Phil held their breath, but I calmly returned Sam's gaze.

Hell, if she smote me, Duncan would know for sure she was a danger to the human race and the sidhe.

After a long, tense moment, Sam's eyes slowly faded to their normal, human blue. "Sorry," she muttered. "I can't always control it sometimes." Her attention flicked to someone behind me. "Don't fucking say it."

I turned to find Grandpa Ares standing next to Siobhan in the entryway to the rest of the house, looking like a male supermodel as usual in his jeans, t-shirt, and boots. He ignored Sam's temper tantrum, and Sam herself. "I discovered how the lizard got in, Cherry Blossom. In turn, it opened the door for Giovanni and the rest."

Grandpa Ares's nickname for me should have made me feel all warm and gushy. Instead, my fingers clenched with the need for my favorite vampire weapon. "Bastard didn't learn anything from his previous experience with you, did he?"

"Apparently not, Cherry Blossom." He grinned, but it was one that would have scared the piss out of most people. Especially with the literal flames in his eye sockets. It reassured me to know if anything happened to my daughter, he'd hold the fuckers down while I peeled the skin off their bodies.

Like any other Normal Family, Max and I took precautions against not-so-friendly supernaturals. But how do you protect your loved ones against what were basically sentient velociraptors?

I wasn't dumb enough to cry "Why me?" either. I knew damn well why they'd invaded my home. They wanted to take Sam down before their boss tore into our dimension since she was the only one who could supposedly stop him. My family was simply the most convenient bait.

And I would be dead or in the hospital, too, if I hadn't had a night class this term. Thinking about how long Max would have been lying on the carpet bleeding if I'd gone out for coffee with some classmates instead coming straight home—

"It's not your fault." Alex rested a hand on my shoulder.

"I know that," I growled.

He didn't reprimand me for my lack of respect. He just clasped my shoulder briefly before we followed Ares back toward the bathroom.

I squeezed in beside the god. Our bathroom was too small for everyone, so they settled for watching from the doorway.

My foster grandfather pointed beneath the sink, and I crouched down to look. The access panel to the plumbing was loose. Three-toed scratches marred the Lovely Lavender paint Max had so carefully applied to the walls around the metal panel.

I held up my hand and compared the scratches against my spread fingers. "These are awfully small for even a lizard bred through a supernatural."

"It would have to be small to get through the crawl space beneath the house and gain entry to the pipe conduit," Ares said.

Sam ripped through more than George Carlin's seven words, though I noticed she left out anything referring to a deity. "The bastard's set up another nest."

"Let it go, Sam," Phil said. "If the baby got in here, it's already too late for the mother."

I'd seen the crime scene photos from Seattle, Tuttle Creek in Montana, and Las Vegas. The Normals in Washington never had a chance. As far as we knew, only one of the supernaturals survived the breeding attempt in Montana last year, and that was because Alyson's alpha Logan had been there to save her ass and call in the cavalry. Marcus and his rogues had dumped the body of a part-fae woman after she'd died during delivery somewhere they knew the Vegas werecoyotes ran during the full moon.

Something else bothered me though. "So they're immune to silver and garlic. It doesn't explain how the baby lizard didn't trip off the motion sensors."

"Because you don't have them in here, and they don't point at the ceiling in the rest of the house, Cherry Blossom," Ares said.

I followed his index finger. Tiny pin-pricks marred the wall paint from the panel under the sink with a detour around the hamper before reaching the top of the door frame. You couldn't see it unless you knew what you were looking for. The damn thing could have been clinging to the ceiling while I was showering this morning for all I knew.

"Shit." I ducked back into the hallway and followed the pinpricks along the wall near the ceiling. They ended by diving straight down to the security pad. I popped the cover. Sure enough, the circuitry had been bypassed.

Alex was right. I made a rookie mistake because I was too involved. I had assumed my husband had turned off the alarm when he got home.

"You think you can keep it together when you get the ransom call?" Alex asked.

Calls. I needed to call Jessie and let her know Ellie and I wouldn't make tomorrow's play date.

My cousin Jessie. A doomsday cult called the Sunshine Believers had kidnapped her five years ago, intending to sacrifice her unborn son to the Old Ones, the ancient gods of the dinosaurs. Just like they'd tried to sacrifice Grandpa Ares a little over four years ago. Not to mention, Siobhan's husband Jorge, a Normal detective with the Los Angeles Sheriff's Office, had discovered Jessie wasn't the first woman connected to the Augustine Vampire Coven those assholes had kidnapped with the intent to kill.

I couldn't suppress the sick feeling in my gut any longer as everything clicked into place. "We're not going to get a ransom call. They plan on sacrificing Ellie to summon an Old One."

Chapter 4

Tiffany

"That doesn't make sense," Alex said once I laid out my reasoning.

I jammed my hands on my hips. "Why?"

"Ellie is nearly four years old. Not an innocent fetus in utero. All the other women they've abducted were pregnant, or they were impregnated by a full dino demon. And she's definitely not a god."

"You're right. She's not any of those things." Sam actually looked worried, which fed the fear in my gut. "What she has is my DNA."

Phil stepped closer to me and wrapped an arm around my shoulders even as she stared at my sister-in-law. "But Bebe said the nanites were rewriting your DNA."

"No." I shook my head. "It's more like expanding it." Everyone stared at me. For all their various talents, no one, not even Alex, who had a year of medical school back in the 1800's, really understood Bebe's explanation of non-human genetics.

I rolled my eyes. "You all understand the basic double-helix, right?"

Everyone gave me dirty looks, except Siobhan who laughed and said, "The twisted ladder, right? It's the same regardless of whether we're Norm, were or witch."

"Yeah." I didn't want to admit how reassuring Phil's hug was. "Vamps, too. In their case, the V-virus replaces sections of the ladder. It doesn't change the basic shape. Because of the changes the nanites are making, Sam's DNA resembles a snowflake just like Grandpa Ares's."

My sister-in-law scowled and crossed her arms. "My precious little snowflakes don't change the fact that Ellie's my blood relative."

"No, it doesn't." The hard lump in my belly grew. "Like I said, it's also the fact that she's an innocent."

Alex snorted. "Innocent my ass. Not the way she took me in poker tonight—"

"Poker?" I glared at him. My fingers twitched next to the pocket where I kept sharpened number two pencils. Dammit, I told Max dinner only. The guys' poker nights often went into the wee hours, far too late for my daughter to be staying up. Ellie would be cranky and impossible in the morning—

The tightening of my throat threatened to choke me as I realized I may never see her again.

"Tiffany's right. They need a virgin," Siobhan said. "And Ellie would be the only one within Sam's lineage."

"Why would a dinosaur god get hung up on virginity? Wouldn't her relationship to me be enough?" Sam interrupted. She saved Alex from a staking and Siobhan from a shooting. And me from charging off half-cocked.

"Because our society is hung up on a woman's lack of sexual experience." I hugged myself again. "The dino demon has to play by our rules, magickally speaking."

Phil leaned back to face me. "Are you trying to replace Bebe as our resident magick expert?"

I knew she was trying to lighten the mood by teasing, but I was too worried for it to do any good. "I've been studying everything I could get my hands on since we found out what Sam was becoming."

"So what do you expect me to do?" My sister-in-law didn't look very happy. "I can't conjure Ellie out of thin air if I can't find her."

"Odds are they're only hiding Ellie from you and Grandpa Ares," I pointed out.

"That doesn't help us . . ." Ares's expression shifted from irritation to confusion as Sam's shit-ass grin grew to match mine.

"Marcus is one stupid son of a bitch," she said.

"You can do it, right?" I didn't like doubting Sam. It had nothing to do with her smiting me, and everything to do with my fear I was grasping at straws.

Her smile darkened. "Oh, I can do the tracking spell. I just can't guarantee the results."

Chapter 5

Sam

I chased everyone out of Max and Tiffany's house. For the first time, I truly understood why Duncan, and now Alex, got cranked about crime scene contamination. I was going to have to sort out everyone's DNA to find what I needed for this tracking spell.

I ignored the huge scarlet stain that was my brother's blood. I had to trust Bebe would find a way to save him. For all my new powers, I couldn't. At least, not without killing him first. And then, there was no guarantee I could resurrect him like I accidentally did with my three baby zombies.

I'd been practicing my powers, but animals and demons were one thing. I wasn't about to try with another human being. Especially not my big brother.

Even with my new abilities, separating DNA took time, and I wasn't the most patient person before the damn nanites rewrote my genetic code. These days, I made Ares of the Short Fuse look like a Normal on a weed binge.

The soft gray, amorphous head of Flopsy poked out from under my long, black coat. She wheaked a question in rabbit language.

"No, I've got this," I said. "I just need you two to stay out of the way for a bit." I could feel the ghost bunny curled up with her partner in my pocket again.

I'd been training my ghosts on intelligence gathering. We'd started by playing hide-and-seek with Ellie and progressed from there. However, I wasn't about to put Flopsy and Peter's little bunny souls at risk with a demon in play.

And having two dead souls in our penthouse was just one more issue between me and my husband, even if they were rabbits. I was still learning my skills and my limits, so I hadn't yet built the paradise I'd promised Flopsy and Peter in return for their sacrifice in dealing with the dino demons in Montana.

But one problem at a time. First, I needed to find my niece before Marcus

Giovanni and his demon friends did anything stupid. Or permanent. Because I wasn't going to practice my death powers on my niece.

Not unless I absolutely had to.

Standing in the middle of the living room, I sucked in a deep breath. I tasted the sweet familiarity of Max, Tiffany, and Ellie in the dust. My efforts focused on them first.

Ebony energy swirled through the ranch house, drawing a cloud of debris to the living room. It surrounded me, a mini gray tornado. I never realized how much crap humans sloughed off in their lives. Skin flakes, strands of hair, dried saliva, fingernail and toenail chips.

Max and Ellie's fragments were easy since we shared the same base code. I was a little surprised how much of my own modified DNA remained in the Howell-Stephens dwelling. From examining Ellie's DNA, I could separate out Tiffany and Duncan's genetic material. Five piles collected on the floor.

As my sister-in-law pointed out, Ares's snowflakes glowed, little red beacons of power compared to my black diamond ones. Phil's weren't quite as bright since her mom was an air nymph, but still an obvious neon compared to the other samples.

I shoved Siobhan and the rest of the were-stamped DNA into another pile. There was more than I would have thought until I remembered Tiffany and Siobhan were instrumental in hammering out the truce between the fae and the vampires. Their own homes would have been preferable for the two moms' meetings since both of their houses were already childproofed. Business had turned into friendship since their kids were close in age, and voila! A hell of a lot of wolf hair.

Also, were kind hadn't been involved in any of the dino demon business over the last four years unless I counted the poor, unwilling females kidnapped, raped, and impregnated by the demons. I'd give the weres a pass for now and ignored that pile of detritus.

That left Normals, non-Duncan vamps, and—BINGO! I grinned. The dino demons really shouldn't have interbred with us. The mixture of saurian and homo sapien stood out among the rest. Just microscopic fragments of scales and claws, not enough to fill the hand of the proverbial angel dancing on the head of a pin, but I had the little bastard.

Dropping out the remaining DNA, I built a tracking spell around Tiffany's little visitor and launched it. Unlike the fae and the witches, I could track someone even if they were dead. One second went by. Two.

A black sparkling ribbon flared to life. Shit. I was too late. I'd have to resurrect the little bastard to question it. That was going to be fun.

Not.

I frowned and double-checked the termination point. La Brea Tar Pits.

The location's counterpart in Otherwhere had been the site of my initiation as a death deity, though Baron Samedi had tried to turn it into a trial. Here in mortal reality, the park surrounding the prehistoric animal grave had been the meeting site for the were-brokered truce between the vampires and the fae. Morrigan had promised me she'd keep her people in check as long as I did the same with the vampires.

The difference was the fae were her people's descendants, and their courts regarded her as the goddess she was. The Vampire Nation tolerated me as a necessary evil.

And they feared rather than respected me.

So why was the demon's body at La Brea? A twisted message from Giovanni since his grandmother's hand in the creation of my nanites ignited the cold war between the fae and the vampires into a hot mess?

"Sam? You done?" Alex called from the front door.

"Not yet," I yelled. "Give me a couple of minutes."

I wanted to know how stupid Giovanni decided to be. Rebelling against his uncle Caesar was one thing. Selling out the entire planet was another.

It took me a few seconds to filter the Normal/vampire pile. Longer to separate out the three particles of Giovanni's bio material. The bastard had been careful, but not careful enough for someone like me. I cast the tracking spell.

A blood red energy ribbon snapped into place. It also terminated at La Brea. I wasn't cocky enough to ignore the obvious trap.

I strode out of Max and Tiffany's house. "The lizard's dead." I grinned at Alex. "But Giovanni's alive, and both are waiting for us at La Brea. Wanna spring his trap?"

The chief enforcer's return grin was absolutely feral. He liked Giovanni even less than I did and had for a hell of a lot longer. "Try and stop me."

Chapter 6

Tiffany

I insisted we drive to La Brea instead of using the gods to teleport. I trusted Sam and Ares's abilities to a point, but the dino demons had trapped my foster grandfather once before. Nor did I want my sister-in-law to take off in pursuit of the velociraptor wannabes and leave the rest of us stranded this late at night with who knows what lurking around the tar pits.

Sam rode shotgun with me, calling out turns even though it wasn't needed. I let it go because her attention was focused on her tracking spells, which meant she wasn't doing anything else monumentally stupid or risky for once. Siobhan's snickers in the back seat of my armored SUV didn't help my mood though.

"You wouldn't be laughing if it was one of your cubs," I muttered.

The werewolf immediately sobered. "You're right." She leaned between the two front seats and squeezed my shoulder. "I'm sorry."

If Siobhan offered an apology, she was just as scared as I was.

"De nada." I waved the fingers of one hand. "I know you're thinking, 'There but for the grace of God.'"

"Don't you have enough gods in your life?" Sam said dryly.

We all laughed, but it was forced.

"We'll get her back." Siobhan's fingers squeezed my shoulder again.

"Damn straight, we will," Sam added.

I hoped they were right. Given my family associations, I didn't think any other deity would listen to my prayers.

I'd like to say Augustine Coven had used its connections with the local politicians to get extra keys for the gates into the park. Truth was we'd stolen a set from a staff member and copied them some time ago.

Backup from Augustine, the Silver Bear witches, and the Lannigan Pack waited for us a couple of blocks from the park's main entrance. Over the last five years, Los Angeles's vampires, witches, and weres worked more as one unit. As much as I liked to think I'd developed marvelous diplomatic skills, I knew the truth came down to the various races' self-interest. Simple survival was now a matter of complete cooperation.

Since I, and thereby my daughter and husband, were members of Augustine Coven, Alex as our chief enforcer had the lead. He called out instructions and emphasized that the weres and vamps couldn't bite anyone they found. A vampire friend of his in Peru had found out the hard way the dino demons' blood was poisonous.

As teams split off to surround the park, I hadn't been given an assignment. So I pulled out my gun and followed Alex toward the main gate. He abruptly halted, whirled around to face me, and jabbed a finger in the direction of my vehicle.

"You're staying here with Sam."

"The fuck I am! This is my daughter—"

He softened his stance. "I know, Tiffany. But this isn't the first time Giovanni has targeted you and your family. Stay here with Sam. Please. For Duncan and Max's sake, if not yours and Ellie's."

I wanted to argue, but he made sense. Marcus Giovanni wouldn't hesitate to blow my brains out or suck me dry if it meant ending Duncan's mortal family line, all because my uncle refused to date Marcus's grandmother.

My fists clenched at the sick, twisted soap opera that was my life. Since Marcus the Asshole teamed up with the dino demons who wanted Sam dead, my poor baby was doubly damned.

Reluctantly, I nodded to Alex.

"Thank you," he whispered. Louder, he said, "Phil?"

She stepped closer. "I'll stay with them."

My shoulders slumped. "Seriously? You're playing the mommy card? Again?"

The overprotective expression on Alex's face reminded me too much of my uncle. "Until we clear the area, yes."

Knowing any further argument would result in me hogtied in the back of my own vehicle, I holstered my weapon, trudged back to the SUV, and leaned against the side, matching Sam's pissed-off, cross-armed stance. Alex had no problem taking Siobhan and Ares with him, but even I understood he was using me as an excuse to keep Phil out of harm's way as well. She dealt with the paradox by pacing around the vehicles, always remaining in visual range of us.

"At least, you haven't gone from totally ineffective to too valuable to risk," Sam muttered in a disgusted voice.

"That's because I pretend to be human," I shot back.

She unfolded her arms. "What's that supposed to mean?"

"Where were you when I called you tonight?" I said softly.

Her eyes started to glow silver which was how I could see her face turn beet red. "Out of cell range."

I wanted to get mad at her, but the fear for my family overrode any other emotion. So I did what I usually do when I was scared. I lashed out. "Define out of cell range."

Her eyes glowed even brighter. "You're not taking this out on me."

"Max and Ellie needed you tonight," I said.

"You weren't there either," she shot back.

"Stop it, you two," Phil snapped. "Dad and I didn't know what was happening either, so there's plenty of blame to share. But pointing fingers isn't going to help Ellie or Max."

"Fine," I muttered.

After a long moment, Sam said, "Mental health day. I was on Pluto, checking out the heart formation. I got Duncan's call when I stopped in Rome to pick up dinner."

"Bitch. And you didn't take me with you," I said. It was the closest either of us would come to apologizing.

"Every time I call you these days, you have class or homework or toddler gymnastics." She didn't sound angry. More like disappointed.

"You were on the whole get-an-education kick along with the rest of the family," I grumbled. "And I am a parent. The kid needs to come first."

"Yeah, but everyone knows I'm a selfish bitch. You got all . . . responsi-ble." Sam was silent for a moment before she added, "I was thinking about dying the ice hot pink before the Kuiper Explorer does its fly-by in a few months. Want to come with me?"

"I guess." Somehow I managed not to grin like a fool. "Do I need to provide my own spacesuit?"

"No, I got you covered."

"So we'll do it after we get Ellie back."

"After I slaughter some demons," Sam amended.

"And after Max is out of the hospital," I finished.

"Do you two need to hug it out?" Phil asked.

"Shut up, Phil," Sam and I said at the same time.

We both grinned like fools, and I raised my hand for a high-five when something hit it. A red circle blossomed below my middle finger right before the pain registered. I looked at Sam and gagged.

Silver goo ran from her left eye socket as she slid down the side of my SUV. It took a moment for me to register the smear following her down was bits of her own brains and skull.

Phil tackled me an instant before the next bullet hit the driver side window.

Chapter 7

Sam

Glass rained on me. I expected more bullets after the second one, but the night remained quiet. So quiet I couldn't block out Phil and Tiffany's thoughts. According to them, a high-powered sniper round had blown out my brains. But if that were true, I shouldn't be able to think at all.

If I were human.

What was worse was that I'd lost the threads of the tracking spells along with half my gray matter.

While the nanites repaired my brain and rebuilt the back of my skull, I needed to figure out how to bypass the damaged organ because whoever shot at us could resume any second. My little robots were fast, but I couldn't wait for the process to complete. Phil and Tiffany were in danger. Not to mention the not-breathing part was starting to get uncomfortable, too.

First, divert some nanites to my heart, and substitute their electrical charge for my missing autonomous reflex. Do something similar with their mechanical aspects for the lungs.

My body shuddered as the nanites kick-started the essential organs. Part two was the more difficult task.

Send a few of the buggers to where my brain and spine connected and wired them into the nerve strands.

Crap. This was more complicated than I thought. With a series of jerky motions, I climbed to my feet and lumbered forward two steps. I probably resembled a cross between Boris Karloff's Frankenstein and a Michael Jackson "Thriller" zombie. But if my weird behavior and appearance kept the sniper's attention on me, all the better.

"Sam," Phil hissed from somewhere to my right. "Get down."

I ignored her and focused on the direction the two shots had come from. Vampire. Female. Late twenties chronological age. She'd been turned less than a year ago for the sole purpose of taking me out from a distance.

Giovanni couldn't even shoot me himself.

Bastard.

I telekinetically yanked on my assailant. She was a former army ranger, so she didn't scream, but I could see the fear on her face with my one good eye as I drew her closer. I dropped her on the concrete. She landed on her knees. Hard. She still didn't cry out. In fact, she was fighting my telekinesis, so I superheated the rifle.

The stunt with the gun did make her scream, but it was pain, not fear. She tossed it aside and cradled her injured hands.

"Duhyuhneeebood?" I asked.

Her eyebrows scrunched. "What?"

I repeated my question.

She shook her head. "I don't understand."

Tiffany appeared in my peripheral vision, trodding slowly and carefully to a position between me and the sniper and to my right. She'd seen me lose control enough to know I was more dangerous to her than the vampire. "The goddess you were dumb enough to shoot in the head wants to know if you need blood for the burns on your hands."

The vampire did a slow blink as she tried to process my sister-in-law's words. She turned back to me. "Aren't you going to eat my soul?"

I tried to say, "No, you dumbass," but I still couldn't get my tongue to work right using the wired nanites. Talking was way harder than walking.

Once again, Tiffany translated for me. "Her preferred junk food is Twinkies." She snickered. "Or brains."

"Bitch," I said. Or I tried to say. It came out more like, "Ish."

Tiffany ignored my insult. "However, I'm the one whose daughter you and your friends kidnapped." She raised her gun. "You might want to worry about me instead of Brainless here."

"You're just a Normal." That punctuating sneer on the vampire's face was her big mistake.

Tiffany squeezed off a round. The vampire's left eye exploded. So did the back of her head.

"Thawashupid," I said. Or mumbled.

"I agree with Sam." Phil came and stood at my left. "That was stupid. How do you expect us to question her now?"

Blood ran down Tiffany's wrist and dripped onto the pavement. "How about I simply shoot her in the heart, and Sam can resurrect her?"

"How about you feed her your blood instead of wasting it on the ground?" I shot back. My words were a little more coherent this time.

Tiffany snorted, her disgust evident, but she holstered her sidearm before she stomped over and held her injured hand over the vamp's mouth. Scarlet liquid dripped between the sniper's lips.

The prone woman's fingers twitched, telegraphing the idiotic thought in her healing brain. She seized Tiffany by the throat and yanked her close. "Release me, or I snap her neck."

Phil and I exchanged looks.

"Your eye's growing back nicely," she said.

"Yeah, it's feeling better. I can see a little bit now, but everything is in gray-tone."

"What is wrong with you people?" the vampire shouted. "I will kill—" Blood bubbled out of her mouth. She slumped back to the pavement. An eraser tip poked out of her chest.

"Was that necessary?" Phil said.

"You weren't the one she was choking." Tiffany pushed away from the vampire and stood, an expression of royal disgust on her face while she rubbed her neck with her uninjured hand.

Phil frowned. "Why hasn't she melted?"

"Tiffany paid attention in anatomy class. She hit the aorta, not the heart," I said. Walking was much easier now that most of my brain had been repaired. I crossed over to the soon-to-be corpse and crouched beside her. "With a vampire's slower heartbeat, it takes them a minute longer to bleed out."

I stared at my assailant, knowing I looked a little worse than she did. Maybe my appearance would knock some sense into the baby vamp.

"Here's the deal. Stop acting like a douchebag and answer our questions, and I won't let my sister-in-law poke anymore holes in you." I smiled. "No matter what other people may have told you, vampires are alive. Once you die, your soul really is mine. You've got roughly forty-five seconds to decide."

It took her all of five seconds to telepathically say, *Yes*. Good to know I could still bluff with the best of them.

As a goddess of death, I couldn't heal her, but I could telekinetically seal the torn aorta until her virus could repair it. So I yanked out the No. 2 pencil in her chest and did just that.

"Blood." It was more of a moan than a word. She was super pale for a Latina, but I also knew how much was real and how much was an act.

"Really?" I said. "Like we're going to fall for that. You had your chance."

Her fingers twitched.

I smiled. "Go ahead and try drinking mine. It's a nastier and faster death than bleeding out if I release your aorta."

"No, it's not," Tiffany said. "You'll explode almost immediately."

"Don't tell her shit like that," Phil chided.

Tiffany shrugged. "Why not? Maybe I want her to make the stupid choice. Since Sam's really the vampires' goddess of death, it'll be easier for her to wring the answers out of the stupid asshat if she's dead."

My sister-in-law's veneer of nonchalance wasn't fooling me or her foster mom. It was, however, freaking the shit out of the baby vamp sniper.

"I'll talk," she whispered.

"What is Marcus Giovanni's plan?" I asked. "Why did he take my niece?"

"To set you up for me to take you out."

"Why does he think he can kill me?"

"He wasn't sure he could. He wasn't sure I could either." The vamp's voice shook, but her thoughts remained cottony clean. "I told him anything that was born could die. I had the kill shot. I took it."

"Where is my daughter?" Tiffany said. She was far too calm. She wasn't flavoring her words with obscenities. Even Phil gave her a funky look.

"I don't know." The vamp tried to shake her head, but she could barely move it.

"Then I guess we don't need you." Tiffany pulled out her gun and aimed it at the vamp's chest.

"Wait," Phil said, but she made no move to stop her foster daughter. "Sam, was she one of the vamps who beat Max?"

Maybe my dumbass sniper realized nothing she said would prevent her fate. She didn't say a word.

I didn't need to read her mind. I'd already checked her DNA. "No, she wasn't in their house. She may not be able to tell us anything of use, but I can use her strain of the virus to track down Giovanni since he's her maker."

I shrugged. "Then if she's dumb enough to run back to Giovanni, he'll will rip her apart himself. Payback for making me lose the tracking spells."

Tiffany didn't holster her gun, but she did lower it. "It's your lucky day."

"I'll grab a blood bag for her." Phil turned toward the SUV.

Light flashed a split second before the blast of hot air and sound knocked us all to the ground.

Chapter 8

Tiffany

My ears rang from the explosion. At least, that's what I thought it was. I raised my head despite the overwhelming dizziness. I'd landed on my back, half-way between the prone vampire and my SUV. An orange glow filled the night sky over the park.

The blast hadn't moved so much as a hair on Sam's head, though it had knocked her on her side and dust coated her. She pushed herself up and looked at me. "You still alive, Goth Girl?"

She knew how much I hated her pet name for me. I flipped her off before I rolled over to check on Phil behind me.

My foster mom was climbing to her feet, but I now had an Amazon-sized dent in the rear panel of my vehicle. She stared in the direction of the flames flickering above the trees. "Well, that blows. Sorry, Sam. I know you wanted to question the dino demon."

From her semi-mellow attitude, she must have heard from Alex that none of our people had been hurt in the blast. Otherwise, she would have charged off in the direction of the fire.

I looked back at my sister-in-law and our prisoner. "We still have some-one to question." When the vampire stared at me, I smiled at her. She shud-dered.

Smart girl.

I slowly and painfully stood as Phil joined me. A blur darted toward us, but when Sam didn't so much as twitch, I relaxed as well.

Tobias, one of my fellow vampire coven enforcers, stopped equidistant between the four of us. "C-4 took out the visitor's center. Alex wants us out of here before the fire trucks arrive." He glared at our sniper. "We're taking her to a safe house in case she's packed with explosives, too."

Siobhan trotted up to us as Tobias finished speaking. She shifted back to human form. It was worth the sniper's eyes bugging out.

"Next time, wait on me, asshole," Siobhan snarled.

Tobias's eyes went from a soft golden glow to full-out yellow neon at the reprimand. He started to open his mouth, so I stepped between them. Whatever insult he was about to hurl changed to "Yes, Beta."

Sometimes, being the niece of the Augustine second-in-command came in handy. Unfortunately, it was also why we were in this predicament.

I turned to my sister-in-law. "Sam, is there any way you can use the pieces of the demon?"

She frowned. "I can try, but we may have better luck attempting to track its compatriots from the remaining DNA fragments at your house if our NRA worshipper here—" She waved at our prisoner. "—doesn't work out."

"Let's see what we can do here before the first responders arrive." I didn't like her options. Not because she might not find anything more at our little ranch house, but because of Giovanni's relative sloppiness when it came to covering his tracks. He'd already been careless with DNA at our house, which wasn't like him, ergo the sniper and the C-4 traps. But we'd waste too much time backtracking to Tarzana if there were clues to find here.

The sooner we found Giovanni, the sooner we'd find Ellie. And if that rogue bastard hurt my little girl—

"But there's a better chance I can track Giovanni from your place," Sam said. "I can rebuild the tracking spell on him."

I shook my head. "He's too focused on self-preservation for us to waste more time at the house. I'm sure we'll find something at the blast site, and any trace here will be fresher." I glanced down at the sniper. "Contrary to what our new girlfriend thinks, we can still use her."

The sniper looked more unnerved.

"Ms. Stephens, the chief enforcer said—" Tobias snapped his jaw closed when I glared at him.

"Phil, you and Siobhan want to help Tobias here," I said. "Taking a newborn to a safe house is obviously too much for him to handle."

Neither woman contradicted me. Instead, they both wore amused expressions.

Tobias's jaw muscles twitched, but he remained silent. He may be a couple of centuries older than me, but I had more enforcer experience thanks to being raised by my uncle Duncan.

I walked over to Sam and took hold of her arm. "'Port us to the blast site."

"Excuse me?" She didn't exactly glare at me, but she didn't look pleased either.

I didn't need her holier-than-thou etiquette bullshit right now. "If anything happens to my daughter, you're going to have more holes than Giovanni's newborn."

Everything went black, and my ears popped.

Chapter 9

Sam

Tiffany and I re-entered mortal reality next to Alex, who jumped.

"For the love of—" Alex bit off whichever deity he was about to invoke. Between me, his father-in-law and a fun side trip to the Incan version of hell, he'd learned to be very careful who he called out to. "What the hell were you thinking bringing Tiffany here with her bleeding?"

I looked around. With the burning building and debris, there had to have been some injuries, but all the witches and weres had cleared the area. That left the vampires.

And the eyes of every single one of them glowed neon with bloodlust as they stared at Tiffany.

I turned my attention back to Alex. His eyes were a dull gold. "You're elected to not drink her and patch up her hand." I not-so-gently shoved my sister-in-law in his arms.

"I ordered you to clear out of here." He finally noticed the blood and other fluids on my face. Maybe because I didn't smell like a tasty treat. "What happened to you?"

"Giovanni had a sniper waiting for us." I waved at Tiffany. "That's how she got hurt. I lost both tracking spells thanks to the shooter." My scalp itched. I reached back. My fingertips met a sticky, jello-like substance. If it weren't for my cast-iron zombie stomach, I would have puked right then and there. No one should be able to touch their own brain.

Now, I was doubly-pissed at that rogue rat-bastard.

"Sam, the corpse is in burning chunks. It's not worth—"

"Shut up, Alex. I'll do what I have to. He has Ellie."

Through our exchange, Tiffany still hadn't said a word. That scared me almost as much as Giovanni kidnapping my niece. I didn't want to think about what she would do if we couldn't find her.

Or didn't find her in time.

I pivoted and stalked toward the inferno. Glass pinged as it succumbed to the heat. Wood crackled. The acrid smell of plastic tainted the night air as the toys in the gift shop melted. But over it all came the sizzle and scent of burnt flesh.

Concentrating on the rancid cooking meat, I pulled the bits together. The skeleton was complete since the fire wasn't hot enough to burn bone, but a decent amount of the flesh was ash. The worst part was how good it smelled to me.

As in mouth-watering.

However, something wasn't quite right. Something I couldn't quite put my finger on. I crouched next to the reconstructed corpse and held my palm over it.

The tail twitched, and the skull lifted up from the pavement. Blackened eye sockets focused on me as if they could see.

I screeched and awkwardly scrabbled back as the dino demon zombie snapped at my right boot, its teeth scratching the leather. A bullet whizzed past my ear and between two of the zombie's ribs. Bits of charred flesh and ash exited with the projectile.

More bullets whistled past while I scrambled to my feet. "Stop shooting, dammit! I've already had my brains blown out once tonight!"

I danced to the left in an effort to avoid the damn thing's bite. Thankfully, the vampires stopped firing at us.

Movement inside my coat warned me an instant before Flopsy and Peter flowed out. The two ghost rabbits darted around the resurrected demon in an obvious effort to distract it. And the dino demon could just as obviously see them.

It screamed at the three of us.

Or tried to. The noise it made was more reminiscent of cat gut sliding over bone.

"Put it down, Sam," Alex hollered.

"How?" I yelled back.

"You're the freakin' goddess of death!"

"I didn't resurrect it!"

"Do something!"

"What?" The gunfire started again when the demon snapped at Peter's ectoplasmic behind. Gunfire that was coming awfully close to my legs. One bullet through me tonight was enough. "And I said stop shooting at it!"

The barrage stopped. Alex's voice rang out. "You didn't raise the zombies at Max and Tiffany's wedding either, but you took them out!"

The demon gave up on the ghost bunnies since its teeth and claws passed right through their amorphous forms. Instead, it ran straight toward me.

Alex was right. For some reason, I didn't think taking a bite out of my flesh would kill this undead thing like it had my ghost bunnies. But it would explain why things went sideways when I tried to resurrect one of its cousins in Montana last year, and I was learning to trust my own undead sixth sense.

I stood still for a second, and the undead demon latched onto the heel of my boot and started gnawing. If I didn't do something soon, it would go after the living once it ate me.

The only problem was I couldn't remember how I took out the horde of zombies that had invaded my parents' backyard. People had been dying around me. I had been angry and scared.

No, not just scared. Terrified when I watched Tiffany collapse from a zombie punch her to the gut. She'd been nine or ten weeks along in her pregnancy that day. That's what it came down to. Ellie had been in danger then, just as she was now.

The black diamond beast within me roared to life. We grabbed the blackened little beast gnawing on our ankle. Hunger coursed within us, and the thing in our hand smelled so delicious. Better than steak. More scrumptious than chocolate.

Even more tempting than Twinkies.

We bit a chunk of it. So good. The burnt flesh tasted better than it smelled.

The enemy's minion screamed again. We ignored the sound and continued to devour our little feast. The crunch of its bones yielded hot, baked, and very succulent marrow. We missed the savory taste of its organs, but its frantic attempts to escape left our own blood to spice its flavor . . .

I blinked, and my belch broke the silence. I looked around the disaster area. The vamps and Tiffany stared at me. So did my ghost bunnies. Even the fire consuming what was left of the La Brea visitors' center quietly flared away from me.

With a muffled *pop*, Ares stood in front of me with three industrial-sized cardboard boxes marked with Hostess on the sides. He tilted his head with a quizzical expression. "Alexander, should I unwrap the snack cakes before I feed them to her or will she eat the plastic as well?"

Chapter 10

Tiffany

I jerked out of Alex's protective embrace and stomped over to my sister-in-law. Sam seemed to be still herself, which was a little better than the last few times I'd seen her after she tapped her death powers. On the other hand, she'd dismembered and crushed the zombies at my bachelorette party, the rehearsal dinner, and my wedding instead of eating them.

The wedding. The awful snap of Max's arm as he tried to get the zombie off of me. My stomach threatened to heave the two granola bars Phil insisted I eat after the ambulance left my house with my husband in the back of the vehicle.

Max.

Was he even still alive?

No, Duncan would have called if something had happened. Still, I'd like to hear the words. I needed that little bit of reassurance, or I would totally lose it.

Swallowing my fear, I eyed Sam. "You still coherent after your dino barbeque snack?"

She looked like she was about to upchuck herself. "Yeah." She belched again. "I'm not going to go Seymour on the enforcers if that's what you're worried about."

"So I retrieved the mortal food for nothing?" Grandpa Ares growled.

Sam thumped her chest a couple of times. "You wouldn't happen to have some antacid on you? That demon's causing some serious heartburn."

I crossed my arms so I wouldn't pull out my gun and shoot out her other eye. "You mind telling me why you ate our evidence? We can't question it if it's in your stomach."

She rubbed her abdomen. "Because Alex was yelling at me to kill it."

"Oh, no." The blond vampire stalked over to us. "I said stop it, not eat it. You are not blaming this on me! In Montana, you managed to question the damn thing before you ate it."

"I didn't eat it," Sam protested. "It happened to have a tentacle down my throat when I incinerated it."

"A tentacle?" I turned to Alex and stared at him. "Anything else you left out of the Tuttle Creek report?"

He scowled at me. "Caesar knows. We didn't need the rest of the coven panicking."

"Well, everyone knows now." I shook my head at the surrounding vampires. "If we'd known she ate the baby demons, we could have taken some precautions."

"I didn't eat it!" Sam yelled.

"If you want my job, you can have it," Alex growled.

"You can't pay me enough to take your job." I rubbed my forehead. The stress and fear of the last several hours caught up with me, and I tried think past the headache. "We still have Giovanni's offspring. Let's start with her."

"Phillippa has taken the newborn vampire to your safehouse as Alexander requested," Ares said.

"Well, I'm glad someone here listens to me," Alex grumbled.

I glared at him. "We listen when you make sense. Besides, you don't eat the evidence."

Sam held out her hand. "I'm sorry. Want a lift to the safehouse?"

"I can drive," I muttered. The need for some time alone was totally necessary, especially if I was going to start crying. I wasn't about to get all weepy in front of a bunch of supernaturals, even if they were family.

I pivoted to head back to my SUV when my grandfather called out, "Phillippa took your vehicle, Cherry Blossom."

"That's just fucking peachy," I muttered. I brought my own transportation to this fiasco, and I still managed to lose it.

A cold hand touched my shoulder. So cold it penetrated my jean jacket. "When was the last time you ate?" Sam asked. Another belch punctuated her question.

I shrugged out of her hold. "I don't remember. Besides, you scarfed all the barbeque just now."

She turned back to my boss/stepdad. "Alex, I'll take her to get something to eat, then we'll meet everyone at the safehouse," she said.

I jabbed a finger in her chest, only to end up with the tip covered in eye goop. "I don't need you babysitting me, any more than I need my foster mother to do it," I snarled.

"You need to take care of yourself." Sam's demeanor was eerily calm. "You're no good to Ellie if you don't. Besides, we'll still be at the safehouse before Phil."

I hated it when Sam was right. I hadn't eaten anything since breakfast, other than those two granola bars Phil had fed me. "Fine, but you're buying."

"Excuse me? I'm not the one with the trust fund." Her follow-up scowl was even less intimidating.

"I'm not the one with the real estate empire in Nevada," I shot back.

"Would you prefer I go on an eating rampage through the Midwest?"

"Hey! Find the dino demons, and have yourself another fucking barbeque! And wipe your face off before we go." I dug in my bag and handed her a wad of tissues.

She took them and scrubbed at the half-dried blood and vitreous humor on her cheek and nose. "I suppose I should be glad you didn't do the mommy spit thing first."

I looked around as sirens wailed nearby. "Where'd Grandpa Ares and the vampires go?"

"They left while you had your tantrum. Now, shut up or I'm taking you to McDonald's." Sam shoved the dirty tissues in her pocket and held out her hand again.

"You wouldn't." I took her hand because I knew she was bluffing. A visit to McDonald's and a particularly nasty round of morning sickness, or in my case early evening to late night sickness, had left a stench in her car so bad that I had to destroy the vehicle and buy her a new one. It left us both swearing off the fast-food joint.

I blinked, and we were no longer at the burning La Brea visitor's center. A huge glowing yellow and red sign blinded me. Traffic roared nearby. I looked around us. "Where are we?"

"Don't panic." Sam grinned and pointed. "That's the 101."

Recognition clicked, and I breathed a sigh of relief. The Delancey Street Foundation. CHP. Vermont Street off the Hollywood Freeway. Sometimes, I half-expected her to dump me in the middle of Mecca or Tiananmen Square just for kicks. My stomach growled at the nearby odor of fried foods, so I headed for Denny's main entrance. "I need some pumpkin pancakes, and we need to brainstorm. Giovanni was never at La Brea, was he?"

"I don't think so," Sam said as she followed me into the diner. "He probably placed a vial of blood or a hunk of his flesh inside the dead demon along with the explosives. Probably used a little magick to amp the signature. It wasn't like we didn't know it was a trap."

I held up two fingers, and the hostess waved at us to follow her with the menus in her hand. Once we were seated in a booth and she left with our drink orders, I stared at my sister-in-law. She looked perfectly normal. Her ponytail was straight, and blood didn't soak her clothes. It was probably an illusion for the comfort of the staff and guests.

Or she'd used her powers to clean herself up. It really didn't matter, so I didn't ask, which went to show how fucked up my life was.

"So what was the point of the booby-trapped corpse?" I said. "The other dino demons had to know all it would do is delay us."

"Maybe that was the point." She grimaced. "Look, I'm not trying to freak you out, but why delay sacrificing Ellie? Why not do it now at one of the weak points between dimensions?"

Thankfully, the waitress set down my coffee and Sam's cola. I shoved aside my own fear at the situation and tried to analyze it objectively. Again, I waited until the waitress left after taking our food orders before I answered.

I took a sip of java before I started. "When the Sunshine Believers kidnapped Jessie, they planned to sacrifice her on the Winter Solstice. For Grandpa Ares, Lizard Girl calculated for the Summer Solstice, but Alex and Phil messed that up. They have to use our human concepts of magick, which were adopted from the fae. So the next major magickal holiday is Samhain."

"Halloween." Sam grimaced. "And it would doubly amp their spell since it's both mine and Ellie's birthdays."

"Probably more than triple considering what you are," I muttered. I pulled out my phone and checked the time. "Halloween's now officially twenty-five hours away. That doesn't give us long to find her, so—" I set the device face down on the paper place mat.

"Giovanni will fuck with us as long as he has to in order to keep us out of the way."

Something else that had happened at the park troubled me, and now I wondered if my daughter's active imagination was truly that active. "Sam, I'm going to ask you a question, and I need you to be straight with me."

"Okay." Her expression turned worried, so even if she hadn't read my mind, she had picked up my scent.

"What's living in your coat?"

Relief spread across her face. "That's what you're concerned about? Shit, I thought this was something serious." She glanced around the diner, but no one was paying attention to us. Sam opened the left side of her coat and whispered, "Come out and say hi to Tiffany, you two."

Something stirred in the inner breast pocket. First one, then a second grayish-silver translucent head popped out.

"Bunnies?" I clapped my hand over my mouth to keep from laughing.

One of them looked up at Sam and squeaked. Its head turned back toward me, and I would have sworn it glared.

"Please call them 'rabbits.'" Sam rolled her eyes. "They get a little pissy when you call them the b-word. Flopsy and Peter, this is Ellie's mom, Tiffany."

Once I was sure I wouldn't bust out in guffaws, I lowered my hand and nodded to them. "Pleased to meet you, Flopsy and Peter."

The ghost rabbits inclined their heads and squeaked something to Sam.

"No, not now," she muttered. "Later." She let the coat drop.

I couldn't stop the shit-ass grin that spread across my face. "You have ghost rabbits haunting your coat? How'd that happen?"

"Long story concerning the Tuttle Creek incident." She grabbed the dessert menu from its holder.

"Ghost rabbits weren't in the enforcer report I saw."

Her cheeks turned bright pink. "Alex didn't put it in on purpose. It's bad enough Duncan freaked out when he discovered them. What do you think the rest of the enforcers would do?"

"What happened with my uncle? They leave little ectoplasmic pellets all over the penthouse?"

"No. Can we just drop it?"

"Oh, hell, no. Max was starting to talk—" All the pain rushed out of the mental hole I'd shoved it into. I couldn't breathe.

Sam reached over and covered my hand with one of hers. "Max talked about what?"

"He thought we should consult with a psychiatrist when Ellie told us about your bunnies." I gulped air past my tight throat. "Her word for them, not mine."

Sam's grip on my hand tightened. "Call Duncan. He should know something by now."

I needed to know my husband was okay. I was scared to know I'd lost him. My fingers shook as I thumbed the controls of my phone.

The device launched into the theme of the old TV show *Angel*, and I jerked, juggling the damn device. It started to fall into my cup of coffee when it hovered in mid-air.

Glancing around the diner, Sam snatched it and handed it to me.

"Thanks," I mouthed and hit the "Answer" icon. "How's Max?"

"He is out of surgery." Duncan hesitated before he added, "Bebe and her team have reduced the swelling to his brain, but his recovery may take a very long time. He may need to learn how to walk and talk again. You will need to be patient with Max."

A sliver of relief pierced my wall of fear. Max was still alive. That was all that really mattered.

I glanced at Sam. She smiled back. Of course, she was listening to the conversation. With most of my extended family having superpowers, it was a wonder I had any privacy at all.

"Have you found Ellie?"

My uncle's question drew me back to my present disaster. "Duncan, before you see this on the news tonight, neither Sam nor I started the blaze at La Brea."

Sam and I shared a mutual rolling of the eyes at the groan that filtered through the speaker.

"What happened?" he finally asked.

"Giovanni rigged a demon corpse with explosives as a trap for Sam, but you'll have to ask Alex which one of the enforcers actually set it off. My boss made Sam and me wait with the vehicles."

My eyes burned, and I needed to get the next words out before I started blubbering. "Will you please stay with Max until we get Ellie back? I'm worried that asshole may try something at the hospital."

"You know I will," he said.

"Call in whoever you need to. T-tell Caesar I-I'll cover the c-costs—"

My hand was shaking again, and Sam carefully took the phone from my tenuous grip.

"Hey, honey, it's me." She slid out of the booth and stalked toward the main doors. "I'm making her eat something while we plan our next step . . ."

I laid my head in my palms and let the tears fall. The waitress sat down our plates without a word, and she surreptitiously placed extra napkins beside my pumpkin pancakes.

Chapter 11

Max

"You shouldn't have lied to her, Duncan." Mom's voice. She sounded . . . sad. Tired.

"What benefit would have been obtained by telling her the truth?"

Through the buzz in his head, Max recognized his brother-in-law's voice. He tried to open his eyes, say something, anything. His body wouldn't respond.

"You're already planning to do it, aren't you? I-I was going to ask . . ."

"I presumed that was why you sent Ted for more coffee." Duncan's dry wit carried a heaviness with it. "But I will not, so do not bother making the request."

"I can ask Caesar—"

"Really? You would do that to your own son? Against his wishes?"

Aw, hell. Mom couldn't seriously be suggesting that the coven Turn him, could she?

"If Turning him is the only way to save him—"

"No." Max silently screamed the word at the same time Duncan said it.

"Listen to me, Elizabeth," Duncan continued. "Bebe is unsure how much brain damage Max has suffered. Yes, the V-virus can heal most physical injuries, but it cannot heal a damaged mind. In fact, it often leaves the victim insane in the best of circumstances."

The attackers in the house. The beating. The *hiss-click* of a ventilator. Oh, god, Ellie! Had the coven rescued his daughter? Had Tiffany gotten home only to be—

No, if his wife was hurt, Duncan would be with her, not here. Was Tiffany the one Duncan had lied to?

"What about my granddaughter? You'd let her grow up without a father?"

"That has never been my choice with any of my nieces or nephews." Pain and anger coated Duncan's words. The emotions sent a throb of agony through Max.

And he couldn't do a damn thing to get them to shut up.

"You should be out looking for Ellie, too," Mom snapped.

"No, Tiffany is correct," Duncan said. "Someone needs to stay here and protect Max while she and the rest of the enforcers search for Ellie. I strongly suggest you and Ted stay here as well."

"Like you could make us leave before Max wakes up." Mom snorted, which shocked him. Anytime his baby sister made that same sound of derision, Mom would give Sam a lecture on how unladylike that sounded.

Mom sniffed some more, and he realized she was crying. "I've already lost my daughter. I can't lose my son, too."

"You have not lost Samantha."

"She's drifting away from all of us, including you." The delicate noise Mom made when she blew her nose. "Even I can see that."

"She is in Los Angeles, and she is helping Tiffany look for Ellie," Duncan said.

"And she should be here at Good Samaritan, saving her brother's life," Mom snapped.

"How do you propose she do that, Elizabeth? Max is in a coma."

Please, don't go there, Mom. All those articles about people hearing their loved ones and medical personnel were true. Max tried to open his eyes again, lift a finger. No such luck. Finding their daughter had to be his wife's priority, but God, how he wished Tiffany were there. They had the talk, one of the coven attorneys, Ronnie Munroe, had helped them with the end-of-life forms, and here he was, as he'd always feared. In bed. Unable to communicate.

And Mom so desperate to save him she'd turn him into an undead freak. "Samantha could—"

"Do. Not. Even. Think. About. It." Duncan's enunciated words in his English accent sounded scary.

"Don't you try the fangs-and-glowing-eyes shit with me." Mom's voice lowered an octave and sounded equally threatening. "You don't have a say in this."

"Samantha does."

"She brought people back to life once before."

"Max is not dead!"

It was the first time he'd ever heard Duncan shout when it didn't involve Sam doing something incredibly stupid.

"Any change—" Dad's voice. "What's going on?"

Silence stretched for what seemed like forever until Duncan said, "Why do you not tell him, Elizabeth?"

There was a slight thump and a splash. "You didn't." Not a question, but a statement filled with profound disappointment. "Dammit, Elizabeth. We talked about this."

"No. You issued his death sentence. I refuse to accept it." The angry click of her heels faded.

"Did you talk to Tiffany?" Dad said quietly. The tail end of his question was muffled, but it was quickly followed by the distinctive crinkle of industrial-issue paper towels.

"Yes, and to Sam. A bomb was set to interrupt the primary tracking spells," Duncan said. "However, they captured one of Marcus Giovanni's newborns. Sam said she will call me after they have questioned her."

"Damn," Dad muttered. "I thought between Sam and Ares, they'd have found Ellie by now."

"They are up against demons that have existed for millions of years and a rogue vampire who would rather watch the world burn than admit his grandmother was psychotic."

Someone clapped their hands. "You two need to get out for a bit." Bebe's voice. "We need to take another scan."

There were footsteps and the rumble of something heavy with wheels. The voices of his family disappeared in a hum of activity.

"Good evening, Mr. Howell." He didn't recognize the woman's voice. Someone was touching him, but it felt vague, like his entire head was numb. "I'm Alisha, and I'll be your portrait photographer."

"I don't know why you bother," a gruff male voice said. "Dude's in a fucking coma."

"Because I've had too many patients come out of comas, saying they could hear every word," Alisha said primly. "You'll have to excuse Randy, Mr. Howell. You know how grumpy werewolves can be."

"I'm not grumpy," Randy muttered.

"Just to let you know, Mr. Howell," Alisha said, ignoring her co-worker. "I'm a Normal."

"Like he gives a shit," Randy muttered.

"Tonight, I'll be taking pictures of your brain," Alisha continued blithely. "Someone hit you pretty hard, and Doctor Zachary needs to make sure things are working properly for when you wake up."

Max wanted to laugh at the woman's upbeat demeanor. Despite the circumstances, her patter was relaxing. She kept up a steady stream of commentary on current events, ranging from American sports teams to a recent earthquake in Italy.

"What's wrong?" Randy asked.

"Oh, nothing." But there was an edge underlying Alisha's tone.

"You're lying," Randy said.

"Okay, Mr. Howell, we're done for right now. You try to get some rest."

The sound of something heavy being rolled away rumbled in his head. It added to the strange buzzing in his mind. And he understood why he felt so disconnected.

He was dying. That would be the only reason Duncan would ever lie to Tiffany. And it would explain Alisha's forced cheerfulness at Randy's accusation.

Ellie was still missing, and there wasn't a goddamn thing Max could do to help, lying in a bed and trapped inside his swollen brain. He couldn't leave without knowing his baby girl was safe. Without saying good-bye to her and Tiffany.

No. He wasn't leaving. He'd give the Angel of Death hell if he showed up now. Because dammit, Max needed to know there was, at least, part of a happy ending to his story. He had to know that Ellie lived.

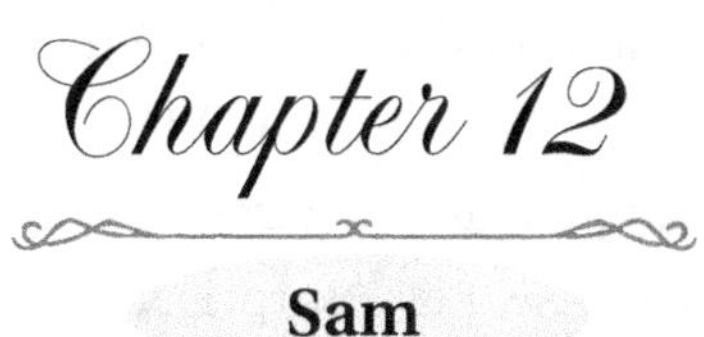

Chapter 12

Sam

I ignored the mascara and tear streaks on Tiffany's cheeks when I returned to our table. After handing back her phone, I methodically ate the two Grand Slam meals I'd ordered. Real food seemed to settle my stomach after what I had done at La Brea.

Losing control like that was only part of what bothered me. What would have happened if the beast inside me hadn't been satisfied with the token demon? Sure, just a tentacle had been enough to sate my unnatural hunger for a few weeks last year. But the hunger had been getting worse since then, not better. The thought of eating my friends and family during that loss of control scared the crap out of me.

My sniper proved tonight a single headshot wouldn't keep me down for long.

As I finished the last plate of my pancakes, I noticed Tiffany was only poking at hers. "We're not leaving until you finish at least one."

She glared at me before she forked a couple of pieces into her mouth. For her to not even make an obscene gesture, much less tell me off in equally colorful language, showed how close to the edge she was.

Or had she seen through Duncan's bullshit like I had? I didn't call my husband on it as I normally would have. He was doing what he felt he had to in order to keep Tiffany and me going.

But if anything happened to my big brother before we found Ellie, there would be hell to pay. And Giovanni and his followers would be the ones to pay it.

Between Tiffany's slow devouring of her seasonal pancakes and the third Grand Slam plus the desserts I ordered, Phil, Siobhan, and Tobias actually beat us to the canyon safehouse with their prisoner.

It had been nearly five years since the first time Duncan had brought me to this particular safehouse. It had been quite literally the day after I'd died. Giovanni and his grandmother knew too much about Augustine Coven, having been former members. They hadn't known about this particular property since Caesar bought it after their rebellion.

When we entered the house, I was surprised to find Caesar already pacing the living room. Scott Epstein, one of Bebe's step-cousins, glued himself to a corner by the kitchen pass-thru and watched the vampire master. A definite giveaway about how bad things were with Max if our resident witch doctor wasn't leaving the hospital.

Even worse, Caesar's eyes glowed red, not gold, which meant he was even more pissed about the situation than I was. I didn't blame Scott for staying as far away as possible from a vampire master in a blood rage.

"Where is she?" I asked.

"Downstairs." Caesar's attention focused on Tiffany. "I want to hear your report before we begin."

My sister-in-law's recitation to the vampire master was short, sweet, and succinct, without a trace of emotion in her voice. Maybe she'd gotten everything out of her system at the diner.

Those eerie red eyes targeted me. "Do you have anything to add, Sam?"

"Only that I apologize for eating the evidence, sir."

Phil and Siobhan smirked at my words, but only because they stood behind Caesar.

"Try to restrain yourself in the future." His eyes shifted to a bright orange before glowing blood red again. He found my statement amusing, and I hadn't been trying to be a smartass. He was deliberately keeping himself enraged in preparation for questioning our prisoner.

I wondered if I could pull off his trick now that my eyes had started mimicking that particular vampire trait.

"The rogue is waiting for us," Caesar stated before he marched toward a door in a hallway off the living room.

The last time I was here, I hadn't been in the basement. When we entered one of the downstairs rooms and I saw my shooter, it finally dawned on me how much Caesar relied on my husband's judgment as his second-in-command. It could have been me hanging by the silver and titanium chains the first time I was brought here. Somehow, I managed to squelch a shiver at the stained concrete walls and the drain in the middle of the sloping floor.

Giovanni's spawn watched us through swollen eyes. The skin on her wrists and ankles sizzled with each micro-shift of her body. The odor of burnt flesh filled the air, and my mouth watered at her suffering.

Caesar dragged a chair in front of her and straddled it. He simply stared at her, not trying to read her mind or anything.

She licked her cracked lips. "Sergeant Constanza Torres, serial number RA70665832."

The vampire master chuckled. "My dear Constanza, the Vampire Nation isn't at war with the United States of America."

"Then why am I here?"

He smiled, showing his full fangs. "When you agreed to become one of us, your Normal titles and rules no longer applied. You are subject to our laws. Or didn't your maker tell you that?"

"He told me you and she—" She glared at me for an instant before her attention returned to Caesar. "—were trying to take over the world."

Another chuckle from Caesar. "And who is your maker, Ms. Torres?"

"Sergeant," she snarled.

Attitude despite her predicament. I almost admired her.

"The name of your maker, Sergeant Torres."

"Sergeant Constanza Torres, serial number RA70665832," she repeated.

"And did he tell you what he was trying to do?" Caesar asked.

Once again, she gave her name, rank, and serial number. This was going to take forever, and Ellie didn't have that kind of time.

Caesar, mind if I take a stab?

Curiosity poured out of him, but he didn't take his gaze from our prisoner. *Of course.*

I crossed my arms and paced in front of the newborn vampire. "Remember what I said earlier tonight about not acting like a douchebag, or were your brains still growing back at the time?"

She remained silent.

"Well, here's a reminder." I stopped and stared into her big brown eyes from a few inches away. "First of all, we already know you're one of Marcus Giovanni's spawn. Do you know how I know? I can read your DNA. It's like reading the fine print on a legal contract. Or a deal with the devil, which is what you did by agreeing to let that asshole bite you."

Her face reddened, and she squirmed. That led to more of her skin getting burned off by the silver. And I didn't need to read her mind to know what had really happened.

I shook my head. "Really? You fucked him? Did you read *Twilight* too many times when you were growing up?"

She squirmed some more, and her breath hissed at the pain.

"Do you even realize what you've given up?" I stared at her in disbelief. "Or did he just tell you to spread your legs, and you jumped at the chance?"

"You're one to talk, *puta*. You're nothing more than a lab experiment gone wrong." Her sneer punctuated her insult.

I sighed. "You know something. You were a lot more cooperative when Tiffany was poking holes in you. But I'm sure you're expecting more torture. That's what Marcus told you would happen if you were caught, right?"

She didn't say a word, but the determination in her expression said I'd hit the nail on the head.

I opened my coat and whispered to my ghosts. They hopped out and shook themselves. I made sure everyone in the room could see them, not just Scott and Siobhan. "Well, Sergeant, there's torture, and then there's torture."

Constanza stared at them, then at me, disbelief written all over her face. "Bunnies? You're threatening me with glowing bunnies?!"

At the b-word, Peter charged across the room and bit her bare foot. Or tried to. His ectoplasmic teeth didn't do any actual damage to her flesh. She shrieked, not from pain, but from the stab of cold when a ghost goes through a body.

"Scott, would you mind setting a circle for me?" I smiled at the witch. "Around both my rabbits and our prisoner?"

He eyed me suspiciously, but nodded.

I telekinetically unchained Constanza while Scott drew a circle around her with silver-laced chalk. I held my sniper until the split second when Scott activated the magickal shielding. I spoke in rabbit language before the sergeant could do anything more than collapse to the concrete. She writhed and shrieked with laughter as Flopsy and Peter tickled her with their ghost fur.

How long will this go on? Caesar asked silently.

I grinned at him. *Ellie lasts roughly five minutes.*

Apparently, Constanza was even more ticklish than my niece. She lasted three minutes and twenty-six seconds before she begged for mercy.

I ordered Flopsy and Peter away from her. They stayed within the circle, waiting patiently for my command. It wasn't like they could leave without Scott dropping his circle.

But they were hoping I'd sic them on the vampire again. I couldn't blame them. They were happy to be out of my coat and running for a bit.

Caesar kept his gaze on Constanza as he questioned her. Tiffany pulled a pad of paper out of her bag, and took notes. Scott examined her aura, looking for the change in color if she lied. Siobhan had shifted back to her wolf form and used the newborn's scent to confirm Scott's analysis. Tobias stood quietly by the only exit and watched the proceedings.

Phil, on the other hand, looked perturbed, like she was pissed she hadn't thought of something so ridiculously simple as tickle torture.

The sergeant didn't know where Marcus had taken Ellie, though she gave us a few possible places. She couldn't tell the difference between Normals and the dino demons, so we still didn't have an accurate number of how many damned minions were running around. However, she could give us the number of rogue vampires she'd met and most of their names.

Finally, Caesar asked the most damning question of all. "Have you drank human blood?"

Constanza's expression became confused. Her glance flicked to each of us before settling on Caesar again. "Of course. How else are we supposed to survive?"

Oh crap.

Both Tiffany and Tobias turned to Caesar, waiting quietly for the execution order. But from the quick flex and release of his right hand, he wasn't going to dump the task on one of the enforcers. That was one of the many reasons I actually respected the man.

"May I speak on behalf of the newborn, Master Augustine?" I said.

He looked up at me and his eyes narrowed. I had to give him credit for not trying to read my mind. Not that he could without my cooperation these days.

"Under Article Sixteen of the Vampire Nation Accords, if a Normal is

Turned without being given full knowledge of her rights and obligations under the Accords, she is given a grace period to redeem herself."

He nodded. From the fading of the slight crinkle between his eyebrows, he understood where I was going with this. He didn't want to chop off the sergeant's head any more than I did. Marcus had set her up as his fall guy.

"Whoa, whoa, whoa." Tiffany dropped her pad and pen on top of her bag at her feet. "According to Article Twenty, she did agree to the Turn, and from her own testimony, she knew Giovanni was at war with the current master of this territory."

"You're just pissed she choked you," I said.

Tiffany's incredulous expression would have been funny if the situation weren't so serious. "And you're not pissed she blew out most of your brain?"

"Oh, it was the highlight of my night," I said, letting the sarcasm drip. "But the reason she did it is because her maker lied his ass off. She could have read his mind if she knew how—"

"A newborn can't read their maker's mind," Constanza said.

"You were wrong about *Twilight*, Sam." The red glow in Caesar's eyes had died to a dull gold. "She's read too much Anne Rice."

I covered my mouth to hide my smile at the disgust in his voice. Obviously, Duncan wasn't the only one Tiffany had tortured with vampire fiction.

Once I had myself under control, I looked at our prisoner. "Giovanni also told you that you could only survive on human blood, right?"

"*Hijo de puta,*" she spat, but the insult wasn't aimed at any of us. She looked at Tiffany. "Why did you give me your blood, then?"

My sister-in-law rocked back on her heels. "Well, I did shoot you in the head." If I didn't know better, I would say there was a hint of guilt in her voice.

"You can have human blood if it's an emergency situation, the donor is willing, and you don't kill her," I said. "Otherwise, it's a capital offense."

Constanza wrapped her arms around her knees. "It doesn't matter if I killed and drank a pedophile, does it?"

"No." Now, I understood the weariness Caesar felt in his position. "If a Normal has committed a crime, we turn him and the evidence over to Normal authorities. We don't judge and execute them because we are not technically Normal law enforcement." I sucked in a huge breath and blew it out. "Your fate is, of course, ultimately Master Augustine's decision since you committed the crime of drinking and killing an unwilling Normal in Augustine territory."

"We shall deliberate the matter before we pronounce your sentence," he said. Not "we" as in the group, but the royal "We". It wasn't too often Caesar reminded everyone he was the son of one of the most powerful rulers in the ancient world.

I looked at the sergeant. No attitude or fear in her expression. She almost seemed relived at the possibility of her death. I felt sorry for her. What the hell had Giovanni really told her to make her take the plunge? Or had the dino demons cast a spell on her to make her act so stupid?

"Peter, Flopsy, keep an eye on her, please," I said. "We'll be back in a few minutes."

We trudged up the stairs after Caesar and back to the living room. Ares waited there with Anne Levy, the head of the vampire master's personal security, and a man in an U.S. Army uniform. Taller than the vampire master, with silver hair, a matching full and thick moustache, and sharp brown eyes. From the tiny eagles on his coat, he was a full colonel.

I breathed deeply. Granny Smith. He was definitely a Normal.

"Gregory." Caesar's face split into a grin.

The colonel's smile was a weird combination of weary and happy. "It's been a long time, old man."

They did the man-hug thing. Embrace, two slaps on the back, and step away.

The officer took off his cap and toyed with the brim. "Ms. Levy says you found my missing soldier."

Caesar repeated the prisoner-of-war information the sergeant had given him earlier. "She's been illegally Turned, Gregory."

"Shit. That's her, all right." He raked a hand through his full head of hair. "Her lieutenant said she had a promising career."

"There's more to it," Caesar said. "She admitted to killing and drinking a Normal."

From the way the colonel's face paled and the ashy scent of fear rolling off him, he had to have been Family. "You sure?"

Caesar nodded.

"There's mitigating circumstances," I interjected.

"Colonel Gregory Smith, Samantha Ridgeway." The vampire master waved a hand in my direction. "Ms. Ridgeway has taken an interest in your Sergeant Torres, despite the sergeant's attempt to kill her tonight."

"Damn it, Caesar! She was set up, and you know it," I said.

"She's also affiliated with the same assholes who beat my husband and kidnapped my daughter!" Tiffany was back to being pissed. "You know, your brother and your niece, or have you forgotten those facts?"

"No, I haven't, but Giovanni and his groupies also killed a lot of innocents, including your parents," I snapped back. "Why are we helping them add to the pile?"

She jabbed a finger at the floor. "Because we'd have to waste resources guarding her that would be better spent tracking down the rogues and the demons. She's already admitted to a murder. She shot you tonight with the intent to kill. Why the hell are you defending her?"

"Because it's not—"

"Fair?" Caesar finished. "Samantha, you of all people, should know that fair doesn't enter into the equation."

He was right. We both knew it. Every time either of us had tried to do the right thing, it blew up in our faces.

"I'm not willing to give up on her just yet, Master Augustine," I said softly. "She may be of some use to us."

"Are you willing to teach Sergeant Torres and accept responsibility for her behavior, Ms. Ridgeway?" His voice was equally calm and quiet.

Nearly five years ago, Duncan had gone out on a limb for me. From my point of view, Constanza was in the same damn boat I had been. "Yes."

"Thank you for giving her a chance, Ms. Ridgeway," Colonel Smith said. His smile looked a little more tired than when he arrived. "I'd like to speak with Sergeant Torres before I leave if you don't mind, Caesar."

"Of course." Caesar eyed me. "Sam, would you please escort him downstairs?" *And for the love of Hades, don't let him see your rabbits.*

I returned his perturbed expression. *Dude, it's not like they're Head's zombie bunnies.*

I gestured for the colonel to follow me and I led him to the basement door. I waited until we were at the bottom of the steps before I asked, "You're one of his nephews, aren't you?"

Smith nodded. "Does that bother you?"

I laughed. "Nah. I like you a lot better than some of your cousins."

We entered the basement room. Constanza still huddled on the concrete floor with Flopsy and Peter standing guard.

The sergeant lifted her head, and her eyes widened. She tried to scramble to her feet, only to hit her head on the witch's shield. The shock tore a yelp from her throat.

"At ease, soldier." Smith's moustache twitched. "Trust me. It's safer for you."

She sat cross-legged. "What are you doing here, sir?"

"You were reported missing." He straddled the same chair Caesar had been using. "Got a call from my uncle that his people found you."

"Y-your uncle?" Ashy fear rolled off of her.

"Young lady, I can trace my ancestry back to Mark Antony and Cleopatra. The man who questioned you is their last surviving child, so yes, my uncle." Smith rubbed his chin. "I get why you did this. Losing your squad was a terrible thing, but it wasn't your fault, Constanza."

"I needed to pay. I should have paid." Tears streamed down her face. "I should be in the stockade."

"It wasn't your fault," he said again. "I just wish you had talked to someone at the base. Now . . ."

He looked up at me. "Did you mean what you said about taking responsibility for her?"

I blinked. "Yes."

"Then you need to tell her exactly what you are, Ms. Ridgeway, if you're going to make a full disclosure like it says in the vampire regs."

He knew. Why would Caesar tell him . . . ?

At my recognition of Caesar's reason, I also realized how thin the ice I had skated when I first met him had been. Almost as thin as the ice Constanza now perched on.

"Your uncle consulted with you about how to destroy me if I lost control," I said flatly.

"Yes, ma'am, he did." No apologies. No remorse. A simple statement of fact.

I crossed my arms and stared at the tips of my boots. Where the hell to begin?

Finally, I sucked in a deep breath, released it, and met Constanza's curious gaze. "Giovanni was part of a group of rogues led by his and Colonel Smith's grandmother, many generations removed. In our case, rogues are vampires who refuse to acknowledge any master or the Vampire Nation Accords.

"He did tell you one truth. I am a lab experiment gone wrong. The rogues were trying to develop a way for vampires to walk in daylight. For them to no longer be susceptible to silver or garlic. I was their guinea pig, and their experiment backfired big time. In trying to play god, they accidentally created one. Me."

Constanza stared at me for a good five seconds before she started laughing hysterically. We let her go until she wiped the pink tears from her face.

"It doesn't matter if you believe her, Sergeant," Smith said. "But you'd better listen to her. Ms. Ridgeway has agreed to vouch for you and train you. She'll be the one to kill you if you fuck up again 'cause you can't come back to the Army."

That statement sobered Constanza faster than a bucket of cold water. "Why not? Think of what we could do with a whole unit of vampires."

"Because there are rules, Sergeant Torres," I said. "And when a supernatural breaks the rules, the human race ends up with concentration camps and atom bombs. That same bitch tried to break the rules again, and ended up with me."

Constanza looked at Flopsy and then at me. "And I'm supposed to believe someone who claims they're a goddess?"

Maybe I was wrong about Constanza Torres. Maybe she was as irredeemable as Tiffany believed. Maybe it would be better if I simply staked her now.

"Connie," Smith said, his voice so full of sorrow I could barely stand it. "You told your lieutenant you wanted your life to have meaning. That you wanted to make a difference in people's lives. How much more of a difference can you make than getting a little girl back to her mother?"

The sergeant wrapped her arms around her knees again and rocked herself. "You don't understand, sir."

"He may not, but I do," I said. At least, Constanza looked up at me and listened as I spoke. "I know what it's like to have an uncontrollable hunger inside of you. And I know what it's like to accidentally kill someone because you have no fucking control over your new body."

I crouched down next to her and stared at her through the greenish cast of the shield. "But I learned. So can you. If you're willing to try."

"If you're a goddess, why can't you find the kid?" She was trying to understand. I had to give her credit for that.

"Because we're not dealing with just vampires. Some of the people with Giovanni you thought were human, aren't. They're demons from another dimension, and they're planning to sacrifice my niece to bring back one of their gods. An ancient being, who frankly makes Cthulhu look like an undersea octopus buddy of SpongeBob Squarepants."

Constanza stopped rocking. Her gaze swept from Flopsy to Peter before back to me. "Let me guess. You're the goddess of cute, furry things, and you can't handle this dude by yourself."

Wearily, I stood and scraped my boot across the silvered chalk. The protective sphere faded. "No, Ms. Torres, I'm not the goddess of bunnies. When a new pantheon is born, death always comes first."

Chapter 13

Tiffany

While Sam and Colonel Smith were talking with our prisoner, I pulled out my phone and called Alex. He made a disgusted sound after I read off the list of places our prisoner had given us.

"Either she's fucking with us, or Giovanni is fucking with her," he muttered. "None of them correspond to a holy place, a geographic hot spot, or a fault line." Good to know he had been reading my research reports based on any information Sam could pry out of her fellow death gods concerning their battles with Old Ones.

"But Alcatraz is a spiritual and magickal hot spot on a ley line," I said. "Can you at least have Stan send someone in to check it out?"

"Tiffany, I'll have all of the places you listed investigated. There ain't a stone I'll leave unturned, but I got the feeling that yellow-bellied son of a bitch is leading us on the proverbial wild goose chase."

I sighed. "Sam and I were thinking the same thing. Halloween is in two days. It would be the p-perfect—" My vision blurred and I blinked the wetness away. "Um, perfect time to sacrifice Ellie. Giovanni only needs to stall us until then."

Caesar signaled he wanted in on the conversation.

I nodded. "Alex, the big boss wants to talk to you. I'm putting you on speaker." Anne and Tobias edged closer to hear as well when I tapped the icon on my phone. Siobhan, Phil, and Grandpa Ares were listening to the conversation, too, without making it obvious. Scott made a point of heading toward the bathroom, which was a little weird. He'd always been a nosy fucker when we were kids.

"Alex, make sure all enforcers are reporting in every hour whether they are involved in the search for Ellie or not," Caesar said. "Unfortunately, Marcus has picked up some bad habits involving misdirection."

"Should I send out a coven wide alert, master?"

My attention jerked from the phone to Caesar. While such an alert would be a prudent move in Normal law enforcement, the vampires loathed to do anything that would make them look weak. From his expression, Caesar fought a mental war over the well-being of my daughter versus thousands of innocents.

I caught his gaze and gave a slight shake of my head. Sam and I would pull some idiotic plan out of our asses to save Ellie. We had done something similar the last time the rogues had tried to take over the coven.

Even though our stupid ass plan hadn't just fallen apart, but epically failed, it had given the cavalry time to arrive.

"Not yet," Caesar finally said. "Sam and Gregory are still questioning our captive."

"Anything else then, sir?" Alex said.

"Not at the moment. Thank you." Caesar's focus remained on me as I thumbed the control to end the call. "You have an idea."

"You know how I feel about that mind-reading shit." I shoved my phone into my jeans pocket.

His wry smile matched mine. "It was the change in your scent that gave you away."

Grandpa Ares strode over to me. "Take this." He held out a ginormous knife in a sheath. The damn thing was large enough it would be practically a sword in my hands.

I looked at him and frowned. "Should I ask?"

"It took Phillippa and Alexander funneling her power and our southern cousins' to kill the Old Ones' demons in Peru. If you find one without me or Samantha around, you will need a weapon of power as well. Therefore, I loan this to you until Ellie is recovered."

I took the knife from him expecting it to be heavy as hell. Instead, it felt light, balanced, in my grip. I pulled it out of its sheath. The knife appeared to be bronze with a bone handle. Despite its apparent fragility, it practically hummed with pent-up energy. I sheathed it and bowed. "Thank you, Grandfather."

When I straightened, he laid one of his huge palms on my shoulder. "Good hunting."

As I buckled my belt after ditching my knife's sheath for the loaned one, the door to the basement opened. This time, our Army sniper accompanied Sam and Colonel Smith.

"Hey, Sam, you up to running an errand with Siobhan and me?" I said.

My sister-in-law scowled. "I need to find a babysitter first."

"Bring the new kid." I aimed a vicious grin at the newborn. "We're going to need her."

"You will need more than a newborn's assistance." Anne stepped toward me.

"No." I shook my head. "You need to do your job, and watch the master's back. Marcus is trying to finish what Selene started." At Caesar's grimace, I said, "It's true, and we all know it."

"That doesn't negate your need for assistance, Cherry Blossom," Grandpa Ares said.

Again, I shook my head. "The fewer people with me, and the fewer that know what I'm doing, the better. I'm assuming you brought the colonel here?"

My foster grandfather nodded.

"Then please take him home first before transporting Phil and Tobias back to Alex. He's going to need you guys."

"Any other orders, Master Stephens?" Caesar smirked.

I scowled at him. "Yeah, where the fuck is Scott?"

"Here." The witch strolled into the living room.

I stomped over to him and glared up at him. "What's your job right now?"

His jaw opened and closed a few times before he stammered, "Th-the high priestess said I-I'm s-supposed to stay with M-master Augustine while Doctor Zachary is at the hospital."

"That means he doesn't leave your sight. If you need a potty break, you clear it with Enforcer Levy first." I poked him in the chest. "Understood?"

He blinked rapidly. "Y-yes, ma'am."

I turned to Smith. "Colonel, you got an explanation for Sergeant Torres's death?"

"Wait a minute—"

At Sam's raised index finger, our sniper abruptly shut up. She made muffled sounds and her eyes bulged as she continued to try to speak.

Smith rubbed his chin. "Yeah, I can come up with something so her family gets full benefits. But I'm going to need a body."

I yanked my phone back out and texted my ME contact at the morgue. Two seconds later, the device buzzed with an answer.

"Grandpa Ares, can you make a detour to the Los Angeles County Morgue? Ask for Dr. Ray Xavier. He has a Jane Doe who can pass for the sergeant here."

"You can't do that—" Once again, Sam raised her index finger, and the sniper's jaw audibly snapped shut.

I glared at them. "Sam, keep your bitch quiet, or I will fucking stake her." I returned my attention to Ares.

"Of course, I will gladly transport a corpse for you, Cherry Blossom." My foster grandfather grinned. He was enjoying this situation way too much.

"Thank you." I turned back to Caesar. "Anything else before we leave, Master Augustine?"

"No, I believe you've covered everything." His expression was impassive. Good. Because with everything else happening, I was ready to shove a number two pencil into the next person who fucked with me.

"We'll contact you once we know something. Siobhan, you're with us." I pivoted and marched out the front door.

Siobhan, still in wolf form, trotted at my side. Sam and the sniper followed us out to my SUV.

"Do you want me to drive?" Sam asked.

"Why?" I snapped.

"So you have both hands free to shoot, stab, and mutilate people," she responded dryly.

"I think it's best I keep my hands on the steering wheel so I don't do just that," I said.

We put the newborn in the backseat so Siobhan could keep an eye on her. Sam rode shotgun in the front with me. Surprisingly, my sister-in-law kept her mouth shut until we were halfway between the canyon safehouse and Los Angeles proper.

"You gonna tell us what your plan is?"

"It's actually partly yours. We'll use the newborn's blood to try another tracking spell on Giovanni." I glanced at Sam. "When her usefulness is done, we really should get rid of her."

"I'm in the vehicle," the sniper said. "I can hear what you're saying."

Sam looked over her shoulder. "Do I have to gag you again?"

Silence reigned in the SUV until I said, "This is what I mean."

"You think I'm in over my head," Sam said sourly.

"Three baby zombies, two ghost bunnies, and a vampire up a shit creek," I replied. "Yeah, that's on my all-time favorite Halloween song list."

A soft huffing sounded in my ear.

"Glad you think this is funny, Siobhan," I snapped. "My Glock is still loaded with silver bullets." The huffing sound stopped.

"So where are we going?" Sam said.

"Duke Miller's." In my peripheral vision, my sister-in-law's eyes started to glow silver, but she said nothing. Either she figured out my reasoning herself or she read my mind. Either way, she wasn't happy about dealing with him.

"May I ask a question?" The badass sniper sounded a little less sure of herself.

"Go ahead," I said.

"Why are we going to some pop star's place?"

I glanced at her in the rearview mirror. "Not a fan?"

She shrugged. "Not my first choice in music, but what can he possibly do?"

"He's the power behind the Seelie throne," I said.

"He's the what?"

Sam looked over her shoulder again. "He's a fucking fairy."

Chapter 14

Sam

I chuckled and faced the road again. "Time for your education to start, Constanza Torres. Rule number one as a vampire and as my new protégé: Fairies won't like you, so keep your mouth shut while we talk to him."

"You shouldn't open your mouth either," Tiffany said. I ignored her.

"Fairies don't like any vampires or just you in particular?" Constanza asked.

Joints popped and bones crackled from the backseat when Siobhan shifted back to human form. "Don't call them the f-word," she said. "Especially in front of them. They'll stab you with silver for the insult. If you think Tiffany's bullet stung, an elf-forged blade is worse. It can kill you."

"Wait." Constanza tapped my shoulder. "If Tiffany shot me with a silver bullet, why am I still alive?"

"Because it exited your skull, taking the gray matter it touched with it," I said. "Not enough time for anaphylactic shock to kick in. If she'd actually been trying to kill you, she would have shot you in the heart or beheaded you."

"Are there any other ways for me to die?" the former sergeant asked meekly.

"Dirty nukes. Nuclear meltdown. The jury's still out on a wood chipper, mainly because no one's been sick enough to try it," I said.

"Good to know." Constanza made an odd burping sound, as if she were trying very hard not to throw up.

"Rule number two," I continued. "You are alive. You are not dead, un-dead, or any other shit. You have a chronic disease, which is why the fairies don't like you. If you're sick in their culture, you would be put down like a rabid dog.

"As for why they don't like me, they react to iron the same way you react to silver. Watching them die by iron poisoning ain't pretty, any more than watching a vamp die of silver poisoning. In my case, your boyfriend and his grandma's mad scientists rewrote my DNA using nanites, which are little robots. I still have a fuck-ton of them inside me, and guess what they are made of?"

"Steel, of which iron is the primary component," Constanza said dryly. If she stayed this smart, I could forgive her for the whole blowing-out-my-brains stunt.

"Maybe she is trainable after all," Tiffany commented.

I ignored my sister-in-law and continued my lecture. "Rule number three: Not only are folks with the V-virus allergic to silver, they often develop an allergy to garlic. The severity can vary from mild discomfort to death, just like any other allergy."

"So what can Duke Miller do to help us find your niece?" Constanza's voice no longer held that military-lifer self-assured quality.

I glanced at Tiffany, but she kept her eyes on the road and her mouth firmly shut. I really couldn't blame her. I was worried about Ellie, too.

And because of Ellie, I didn't want to reveal Tiffany's plan just yet. Despite what I said to Caesar and my own examination of Constanza's thoughts, there was the slight possibility she was playing us.

I sighed. "Giovanni sent you to La Brea to shoot me."

"Yeah, um, I guess I should apologize for that," Constanza said.

"You think?" Tiffany muttered.

"You're not helping," I said.

"Um, Tiffany, do you have an emergency pack?" Siobhan said. "Connie's eyes are starting to glow."

"Yeah, behind your seat under the floor panel," Tiffany said. "The combination is eight-four-seven-two."

"Oh, come on!" Constanza protested. "I don't need naked chick ass in my face."

"You wish, bitch, but I'm married," Siobhan's muffled voice shot back.

"We don't need to be pulled over thanks to your full moon," Tiffany snapped.

I looked over my shoulder and concentrated. Siobhan's jeans and t-shirt materialized around her. She slid back into her seat with a disguised blood bag and a straw. I got an ugly glare from the were as she handed them to my protégé.

"Thanks, Mom. I was planning to shift back," she said.

"We're in a Normal city," I reminded her.

"Typical one-form thinking," she sneered.

"Oh, my god! Stop it, you two!" Tiffany's knuckles stood out on the steering wheel, her skin nearly bone white. "And Max wonders why I don't want another kid."

I caught the catch in her throat and glanced over my shoulder at Siobhan. From her abashed expression, she had, too.

"We're sorry," I said.

"Let's get this over with," Tiffany said. "The same thing you said to Torres applies to you, too. Keep your trap shut, and let Siobhan and me do the talking."

If Ellie's life wasn't on the line, I probably would have argued with Tiffany. But in this case, she was right. "I'll behave. I swear on myself."

"Do you have any idea how conceited that sounds?"

"What?"

"'I swear on myself'?" Tiffany shot a nasty look at me before her attention returned to the road.

I tried to keep my voice calm. "I can swear by whoever's name you would like as long as you realize that particular deity might actually show up in your SUV. And I won't be responsible for the damage they cause."

"You are so arrogant—"

"Tiffany, all she did was promise to let us handle the duke," Siobhan interjected. "Let it go."

The passenger compartment was quiet except for the sound of liquid being sucked through a straw. Constanza slurped the last of her blood before she said, "Y'all are pretty fucked up if you ask me."

"No one did," Tiffany growled.

Thankfully, we passed the Beverly Hills sign, which meant we weren't far from our destination. It would be the second time I actually stepped foot on fairy territory since I died. The first time, I hadn't known what I was getting into. All other quasi-cordial meetings since then had been on neutral territory.

Gray stone walls tinged with green marked the beginning of the fae property. Tiffany turned into the driveway. A dark purple metal gate protected the estate. Now that I knew about the fae, I realized it couldn't possibly be steel or iron, and it definitely had been there when Duncan and I had crashed a party here four and a half years ago. I'd always assumed the pop singer I knew as Duke Miller had the gate painted his signature color, and the paint had reacted with the metal.

I looked at the gate more closely while Tiffany dealt with the guard. The alloy was a mix of copper, gold and silver with the distinctive green signature of fairy magick threaded through the molecules.

Fae security must have gotten clearance from the main house. The guard waved us through.

As Tiffany guided her SUV up the long drive, I asked, "Is that gate made of hepatizon?"

"Beg your pardon?"

My history degree was showing itself. "It's an alloy also called Black Corinthian bronze. The formula for it was lost in antiquity, but its color is pretty distinctive."

"I have no clue," Tiffany said. "I always figured they powder coated the gate so the sidhe could touch it."

Security had been stepped up since the last time I'd been here. I was on assignment to snap some photos of the King of Funk, or so I'd thought. It had been a couple of months after my death, when I was still getting a handle on what had happened to me. Instead, I was bait so Caesar and his people could see exactly what the damn fairies would do.

But rumors about me had already been flying since the vampires had taken over the lab where I'd been the guinea pig. The fae queens viewed me and my nanites as weapons of mass destruction. In trying to take me out, the fae had killed a lot of innocent people, both Normal and supernatural, before their goddess of death had enforced a truce.

And here I was, waltzing in the fairies' front door.

Tiffany parked in front of the mansion. Ostentatious didn't begin to cover the description. Bushes were trimmed into erotic and decadent designs. The statuary followed the same themes. But nothing was more obvious than the guards hidden in the trees, on the rooftop, and beneath trapdoors in the grounds.

I did my best to not make any sudden movements that would spook them.

I may be immortal, but the rest of the women with me weren't. Thankfully, Constanza imitated my behavior. And we let Tiffany do all the talking.

The honey scent was overwhelming as we were ushered into what was obviously a receiving room. Surprisingly, we didn't wait long. Duke Millanthropas of the Seelie Court swept through the door like the world power he truly was.

His bodyguard Sapphire strode a hair behind him. She glared at me. The bitch could blame me for her sister Ruby's death all she wanted, but I wasn't the one stupid enough to strike a bargain with a necromancer, then try to kill him.

Curiosity sparkled in Millanthropas's eyes as he held out a hand to Tiffany. "What may I do for you this fiery evening, Ambassador Stephens?"

So, he already knew about the explosion at La Brea. I bit my tongue to keep from asking how.

She shook his hand. "It's a matter that concerns all of our peoples, Your Grace. The Old Ones' demons abducted my daughter tonight and left my husband in a coma."

"And what do you wish us to do?" Sapphire bit out. "Die for your spawn?"

Despite the rise of her blood pressure, Tiffany ignored the bodyguard. "Samhain is just over a day away, Your Grace."

The implications clicked with both Millanthropas and Sapphire from the sudden concern in their expressions. The duke pressed his palms together and rested the tips of his index fingers against his bearded chin. "I presume you have a plan."

"The demons are being advised by Selene Antonius's surviving rogues. I ask that you perform a tracking spell with this woman's blood." Tiffany indicated Constanza. "She's the deceived spawn of one of the rogues and is assisting me in my quest."

"Why haven't the witches or your abomination—" Sapphire inclined her head toward me. "—tried their own tracking spells?"

"They did," Siobhan said, entering the conversation for the first time. "The demons anticipated those would be the first things we would try. They have the child shielded so well not even her grandfather Ares of Olympus can find her. Given that rogue vampires are involved, we reasoned that they would not anticipate we would approach you for assistance."

"Very well, then." Millanthropas dropped his arms to his sides and nodded. "That leaves the matter of payment." His gaze settled on me, and with the slight lift of his eyebrow, he made his terms known.

"You have got to be fucking me."

"I'd like to." His salacious grin sent willies down my back.

"Aren't you afraid of iron poisoning? That's been your previous queen's excuse for trying to take my head."

"If we survive any bedplay, we'll both be assured neither of us is a danger to the other."

I rolled my eyes. "Look, Morrigan already approached me about spouse swapping. I said no then. What makes you think I'd agree now?"

His smile turned totally smarmy. "Because your blood's at stake, my dear Samantha."

"I'll do it," Constanza blurted.

"No," Tiffany, Siobhan and I shouted at once.

I grabbed the vampire's arms. "He tortured my husband for the sheer fun of it. If he doesn't agree to help us, we'll find another way."

"Sam's right." Tiffany glared at the fae duke. "We *will* find another way."

"By midnight, Ambassador?" Millanthropas practically purred. He had us over the proverbial barrel, and he knew it.

"The colonel's right. I fucked up." Constanza looked at Tiffany. "You need your daughter back." The former sergeant sauntered over to the duke. "He's an honorable man. And attractive. I don't mind paying the price."

"An intelligent decision." There was a sick touch to the way he leered at her.

The former sergeant's next moves were so fast Sapphire couldn't stop her, much less Siobhan or me. Her leg swept Millanthropas's feet out from under him. He landed face first on the plush wool carpet with Constanza's knee planted in the middle of his spine and his arm wrenched back at such an awkward angle it hurt to look at it.

"But no play time for you until after the spell is cast," she murmured in his ear. "The spell needs to be done right. Otherwise, Sam will tell me if you deliberately fuck it up. And we find Ellie alive, or the deal's off. *Comprende, mi amigo*?"

To my shock, he started laughing. "Oh, my dear. How I wish I'd met you before you were Turned. However, I cannot guarantee the life of the ambassador's daughter. If I cast the spell properly, and the child is already dead, it will fail anyway. Nor can I guarantee that you will reach her in time."

Constanza looked at me. I looked at Tiffany. She gave a slight nod.

"I agree to your amendments," Constanza said.

Millanthropas smiled. "I swear by Morrigan and Lugh I agree to your terms."

She released him and held out a hand to help him up. I expected Sapphire to try to slit the newborn's throat, but she looked Constanza with a sexual hunger in her eyes. It was no secret Millanthropas and Sapphire were a thing. I fervently hoped my new protégé knew what she was getting herself into by having a ménage with those two.

Five minutes later, the four of us were deep in the wooded area at the rear of the fae estate with Millanthropas and Sapphire. Their water bill had to be insane for the amount of greenery this place contained. In the small clearing, a literal fairy ring of mushrooms encompassed a good three quarters of the mossy ground.

Once again, I felt more than saw the sidhe guarding the duke. Millanthropas himself had changed from the tight pants and loose shirt of his pop star persona. Now, he wore the gossamer white silk and the black and silver armor of a fae noble. Sapphire's outfit was even simpler. A sheer deep blue gown of the same silk that left nothing to the imagination and a silver belt to hold her dagger and its sheath.

You don't have to do this, Constanza.

She looked at me while Sapphire set lamps at the cardinal points of their fairy circle. *Why are you being nice to me?*

I'm not being nice. I don't trust the fae.

Her eyes shifted from brown to gold. *Who did you kill?*

Figured that now of all times I leaked my thoughts. I didn't want to talk about the night I woke up after the bad guys injected me with the nanites. The night I accidentally killed two people because I had no idea what had been done to me. Didn't know my new strength. It didn't matter how many times Duncan told me it had been self-defense. Constanza's steady gaze made me squirm.

She tilted her head as she regarded me. *No, I didn't hear your inner thoughts. I recognize that look of guilt. I see it in the mirror every morning. Now, unless you have a plan for tracking down Tiffany's little girl, shut the fuck up.*

I glared at her. *Do you have any idea who you're talking to?*

Yeah. An odd smile tilted her mouth. *My dad always said I liked to court Death.*

Holy crap! Was she making a pass at me?

"Constanza Abril Torres," Millanthropas called out. "Come." He beckoned her with a two-fingered gesture. She entered the circle and stood by him.

His eyes met mine. "You will need to take Ms. Torres with you to track her maker, Lady Samantha. Do I have your word that you will return her to me to complete our bargain?"

My attention flicked to Constanza. "Last chance to back out."

She shrugged. "Consider it my contribution to vampire-fae relations."

I looked at Millanthropas again. "What do you consider an adequate timespan for her to return for your personal encounter after we recover my niece, Your Grace?" I cocked my head. "For instance, is she allowed to shower or change clothes before presenting herself to you? Or would you prefer her covered in vampire slime and demon guts?"

Millanthropas chuckled. "If you fail in completing your quest and the Old One devours you and your companions, the point is moot, isn't it?" He ran his thumb and forefinger across his moustache and down to meet at his chin. "At dawn on Samhain, clean or dirty. However—" He held up an index finger. "If my playmate gets herself killed in this rescue attempt, and you do recover Ambassador Stephens's spawn, you will resurrect Constanza Abril Torres to complete our bargain."

"Oh, my—" I stopped myself just in time. "Eeeewwww! Did you also fuck Ruby after Head killed and resurrected her?"

Sapphire drew her dagger and charged toward me, but Millanthropas grabbed her arm and jerked her to a halt. For an instant, the cloak of humanness dropped from them both. The odd colors of skin and hair and the elongated limbs weren't nearly as unnerving as the quick flash of their very pointy teeth.

He whispered something in his bodyguard's ear. She sheathed her knife, but the nasty look she gave me said this wasn't over by a long shot.

"This is what happens when you don't listen to me," Tiffany muttered. "I told you to keep quiet."

"You want Ellie back?" I whispered in return.

She pursed her lips, but she kept her hand close to her holster. Good to know she was as leery of the fae as I was.

When Sapphire retreated back to the other side of Constanza, Millanthropas turned to me. "Well? Do we have a deal?"

I knew exactly the stunt he was trying to pull, but I would make sure my protégé knew as well. "Constanza, who is your allegiance to?"

She blinked as she tried to process my question. "To Master Augustine."

"No," I said. "Who do you pray to?"

She held out her spread hands and shook her head. "What does that matter?"

I kicked one of the little mushrooms. It immediately turned black and shriveled. A little reminder to the duke of who he was dealing with. "Because I can't resurrect you unless you pray to me. If I do, I'm in trouble with whoever you've sworn yourself to."

I smiled at Millanthropas. "And since he's materially changing our deal, negotiations must start again. It means, according to the International Council's treaty, I can call an arbitrator."

His eyebrow rose and he smirked. "Really, Samantha? You're going to waste more time calling in one of the other races? What about your precious niece?"

I smiled right back at him. "You're right, Your Grace. We need someone who can speed up the process. Yo, Morrigan!"

A shudder went through the little woods at my shout. Not a California quake sensation. More like the wake that disrupts smaller craft when a large ship powers out to sea. Millanthropas's eyes widened, and both he and Sapphire dropped to their knees.

"Does this mean you're reinstating bridge night, Lady Samantha?" a voice behind me said, and I turned. The woman who strode into the clearing could have been an extra in a horror movie. Blood soaked her hair and the shift she wore. More of the scarlet fluid coated her face and arms. Two wolves trotted beside her as she approached me.

Siobhan dropped to her knees and bowed as well.

I inclined my head. "I beg your pardon for disturbing you this evening, Lady Morrigan."

Her attention flicked over the people present. "I assume there's a good reason for one of your vampires to be in a circle with two of my fae."

"Under the terms of the treaty between the vampires and the fae, I am allowed to call for an arbitrator when the other side wishes to revise a nego-tiated contract." I quickly laid out what had happened earlier in the night, including mine and Ares's efforts to find Ellie.

"Do you have any recent pictures?" Morrigan asked.

I pulled out my phone and swiped to the latest photo, Ellie proudly show-ing off her brand-new pink tights and tutu. Mom had insisted on the ballet class, and Max had smoothed Tiffany's ruffled feathers over the activity by pointing out it developed strength, flexibility, and discipline.

Morrigan grabbed the phone out of my hand. I tried not to wince at the blood she smeared over the casing. Her wolves remained beside me as she marched across the ring of mushrooms. A hundred little capped fungi grew in her wake.

She shoved the phone under Millanthropas's nose. "Explain why you would further endanger a mortal child under my protection."

If the Seelie duke was an old Warner Brothers cartoon, his eyes would have been popping out of his skull. "I-I didn't know."

Her gaze swept over Constanza before turning back to Millanthropas. "One of the night children offers herself freely to you, and you cannot honor her gift?"

"It was no gift," he spat. "It was a bargain."

Morrigan grabbed his chin and forced him to look up at her. Blood welled on his cheeks where her nails dug in his skin. "A bargain which you tried to change at the last moment out of spite. You deposed the Summer Queen because you understood the cycle of things. Yet, here you are, making the same prideful mistake both she and her sister of Winter did."

She released him and sighed. "You will honor the original bargain."

"But if she dies—" Millanthropas started to protest.

A low chuckle came from the goddess as she examined Constanza once again. "She was a warrior when she was a mortal, and she is still a warrior now she is vampire." Morrigan looked down at the fae at her feet. "If you were wise, you would ask me to make sure she doesn't come back from Death's grip. You may not survive a night with her, my would-be king."

She strode out of the circle and back to me. I tried to gracefully accept my now gross and tacky phone from her.

"Your daughter is beautiful," she said to Tiffany. "I will ensure my children assist you properly in finding her."

"Thank you, Lady Morrigan." My sister-in-law bowed to the goddess.

Morrigan turned to me. "Has Kali seen this picture?" she asked.

"Not yet."

"Good." The smile on her face was pure mean girl malice. There was a bizarre sort of rivalry between the other death goddesses about who got to see pictures of Ellie first.

I glanced at Tiffany. Her lips were pressed shut, but from the glitter in her eyes, there would be hell to pay later.

Chapter 15

Tiffany

Rage had overtaken my fear. Rage at Giovanni for kidnapping my daughter. Rage at his minions for hurting Max. And rage at my sister-in-law for not keeping her mouth shut and endangering not only one of the vampires I was charged with protecting, but my daughter as well.

Once Millanthropas found his balls from where Morrigan tossed them, he cast the damn spell that turned the stupid-ass sniper into our very own magickal compass. We thanked Morrigan and the sidhe and got the hell off the duke's estate before anything else could go wrong.

I tossed my SUV keys to Torres. "Drive since you know where we're going. I'll navigate."

"It would be easier if I—" Sam started.

I whirled and nearly jabbed my index finger through her right nostril. "I am not talking to you. You have no idea how bad you fucked up in there!"

"I didn't—"

"Shut up and get in the back seat!" I didn't care if she teleported out now. I whirled and stomped to the passenger side door, imagining Sam's smug face with every step. We were going to be fucking lucky to get Torres back alive once Millanthropas was done with her after Sam's holier-than-thou shit.

And I was going to be damn lucky if I ever saw my daughter alive again.

The four of us climbed into the SUV. Torres peeled down the street like her ass was on fire.

"Direction?" I asked.

She glanced at the brightly lit compass on the dash. "South."

I punched up the map app on my phone and called off turns and routes to keep us in a general southerly direction.

"Tiffany, would you at least tell me what I did to piss you off?" Sam said. She actually sounded contrite.

"What part of keeping your mouth shut did you not understand?" I snapped.

"How can I apologize if I don't know what I'm apologizing for?" she shot back.

"Tiffany means with the fae," Siobhan said quietly. "She may be Normal, but her job is keeping coven members safe. Even from themselves."

"But we're out and we're intact."

I twisted in my seat to look at Sam. "Torres has to go back because of you!"

"Hey, I volunteered!" The former sergeant actually had the vagina to look offended.

I glared at the woman. "Did you not hear what Sam said about the fae torturing her husband, who, by the way, happens to be my uncle and a vampire?"

"Wait a minute. I thought you were married to Sam's brother?"

Siobhan leaned forward. "The squirt's related to half of the vampires in Augustine in some way, shape or form. Don't think for one moment you will ever outrank her."

I yanked out my sidearm and aimed it between the were's eyes. "Don't call me squirt!"

In my peripheral vision, Torres's face muscles twitched, which meant Sam was talking silently about me in front of me.

Siobhan didn't move, but she had the were expression of accepting a challenge. "Do you have any kids, Constanza?"

"No."

"Significant other?"

There was a slight hiss of air between the vampire's teeth before she said, "Not anymore."

"This is how a Normal freaks out about her family." Siobhan didn't take her eyes off me. "Now, imagine me furry and pissed if someone touched my mate or cubs."

Shit. I lowered my gun and took a deep breath. "Sorry," I muttered. I relaxed back in my seat and holstered my weapon. Siobhan was right. I was out of control if I even thought to put a bullet in my best friend.

The were turned back to Sam. "Tiffany's right though. The other stupid thing you did was getting Mother Wolf involved. You essentially tattled on

Millanthropas, and he can't touch you directly. Who do you think he's going to take his embarrassment and general pissy attitude out on?"

"I'm sorry." Sam let out a long, gusty sigh. "I didn't mean to screw up all the work you two have done. It's just the lady in red said if the fae gave me anymore trouble or violated the treaty, I was to call her directly. Millanthropas changing the terms like that qualifies."

A dull ache started right between my eyes, and I rubbed my forehead. "So what are you saying? Siobhan and I didn't actually do anything? You two had already ordained the outcome?"

"No! Oh, Je—" An angry sound caught her voice. "One of these days, I'm going to say the wrong damn name." She cleared her throat. "No," she said more firmly. "You guys did all the real work. She just told them no more bullshit like when the fae sabotaged our phones and computer network a few years ago."

"Has it occurred to any of you that I know exactly what I'm getting myself into?" Torres asked.

"No. You don't," I said. "This isn't some billionaire BDSM Cinderella fantasy."

An odd smile crossed Torres's face. "It can't be any worse than a dungeon I went to in Brooklyn."

I sat up straighter and stared at the woman. "You can't be serious."

"Totally." She glanced at me and her eyes glowed a dull gold. "You've never done any kink?"

I looked over my shoulder. "Siobhan, the newborn needs more blood."

"Avoiding the subject, Tiffany?" Torres flashed her fangs in a wide grin.

"No." I grabbed my bag from between my legs and started checking weapons and stuffing clips in my jacket pockets. "I've seen too much pain and death to find sadism fun."

I was also too damn tired to argue with Torres anymore. I checked in with Alex via text because I couldn't deal talking with him either.

My phone buzzed five minutes later. The other enforcers had checked half of the facilities in Augustine territory from Torres's list. So far nothing. The San Francisco enforcers along with the White Rose witches had even cleared Alcatraz.

The vehicle was quiet as the SUV aimed for some unknown destination. My fear for Ellie escalated, as did my worry over Max. Duncan hadn't called or texted since we'd been at Denny's, which meant there was no change in my husband's condition.

I also began to worry about timing. Dawn was still a few hours away, but if we didn't find Giovanni soon, we would need to get Torres to shelter for the day.

"What are you planning for backup, Tiffany?" Sam finally asked.

"Depends on how soon we get there," I said. "If we need to get Torres under cover, Siobhan and I can scout the area and have the cavalry there before noon."

"Yeah, but we're almost in Orange County."

"And?" I looked over my shoulder at Sam. "You saying you want to hit Disneyland?"

Her eyes silvered in the oncoming headlights. "How do you hide vampires and demons in Orange County?"

I couldn't stop my wry chuckle. "The same way you hide nymphs in a demigoddess's antique shop." I faced forward again. Thankfully, it wasn't early enough for morning rush hour yet.

"Yeah," Sam drawled. "And how many times has Phil's shop been trashed?"

"I seem to recall one of those times was your fault," I said.

"Excuse me, but your uncle did his fair share that time," she replied.

"We need to go more southwest," Torres said.

I checked my map app. "Take the next freeway exit."

"I'm serious," Sam said softly. "They'd have to take over an entire neighborhood."

"Or just a block," I answered. "Send just enough people out to make everything seem normal like they did at Tuttle Creek."

Torres shot a look at me before returning her attention to the road. "Tuttle Creek?"

"Augustine Coven has been killing the original demons," Siobhan explained. "The surviving one tried to breed with humans four years ago. When that didn't work, he tried with supernaturals at a ranch outside of Tuttle Creek, Montana."

"Torres, didn't you find some of Giovanni's people weird even by supernatural standards?" I asked.

"I . . ." She swallowed hard. "Oh, my god. I had the weirdest dream when I was being Turned that I was pregnant. But vampires can't get pregnant, right? Or did he lie to me about that, too?"

"No. Vampires are sterile thanks to the V-virus," Siobhan said.

"Aw, shit," Sam muttered in my ear. "We should have taken her to Bebe."

"We didn't have time," I murmured. I didn't need telepathy to know what my sister-in-law was thinking. My brain had already gone there, and it was worse than any of my beloved horror movies. The bastards had impregnated Torres, then Marcus Turned her after the baby had torn its way out of her womb.

A shiver ran down my spine. My little girl was with those sick fucks. I needed to find her.

Before they did God knew what to her.

Chapter 16

Max

Max tried to move again. Still no luck.

Duncan had either sat from the squeak of the chair or paced from the clip of his shoe heels for who knew how long. Once in a while, his phone rang, but he spoke so softly Max couldn't hear what was going on. Bad enough the strange buzzing in his head was getting worse. The fuzzy noise made it difficult to concentrate.

The rich aroma of coffee penetrated the blanket covering his mind. The delicious smell preceded the *whoosh* of the door. "Tea. Earl Grey. Hot." Jake's voice.

"Very funny," Duncan muttered. "But thank you. Did you get Ted and Elizabeth to go home for some rest?"

"Actually, you can thank Doctor Zachary for that one. She threatened to throw Elizabeth into the biohazard shower if she didn't go home and freshen up." Jake slurped his coffee. "And don't worry. Enforcers from Silver Bear and Lannigan are with them and watching their house."

Max tried to remember how Jake took his coffee. He should know it, knew it long after Jake and Sam had broken up, but nothing in his head seemed to work right. Had they gone on the road trip to Vegas yet? No, they were still in Los Angeles.

Ellie! *Talk about her. Please talk about her.* How had he forgotten her? Had the coven found her? Was she safe?

"Any word from Tiffany or Sam?" Jake said.

"Not yet. Why are you not helping Alex and the search teams?"

"Because my boss sent me here to relieve you." Max could almost hear the smile in Jake's voice.

"I do not need to be relieved." Did Duncan realize his accent became more pronounced when he was offended?

Jake lowered his voice, probably to preserve the vampire's dignity. "You need to get some rest and some blood. So if Doctor Zachary stabs you in the ass with a needle full of downers, you can't say I didn't warn you."

"Very few drugs work on vampires," Duncan said, rather primly.

"Really?" Another slurp of liquid. "I heard she had some elephant tran-quilizers that took out a certain Olympian."

"Fine." A slight screech of metal on linoleum.

"The doc said you could use the couch in her office."

Another *whoosh* of the door, then the distinct impression of someone moving closer. "Just when I think he can't possibly get more dickish. Well, Max, I hope you get better soon because I don't know if I can keep your family from killing each other if you die."

Chapter 17

Sam

A bit of relief seeped through me when the scarlet line of energy connecting Constanza with her maker terminated at a house ahead of us. The Orange County neighborhood screamed expensive. Not exactly a subtle, out-of-the-way place to keep a kidnap victim or hide dino demons. Despite Morrigan's assurance and Constanza's belief in my powers of perception, I feared Duke Millanthropas had pulled a fast one on me.

And if he had, I deserved whatever Max and Tiffany did to me for not getting Ellie back safe and sound.

"It's the one on the right. Three houses ahead," the vampire said.

"Drive past, Torres," Tiffany ordered.

"Give me a little credit on knowing how to scout a location," Constanza grumbled. "I did three years overseas."

"Yeah, but that was human against human." I watched the windows, the bushes, and the fences as she drove past, but no one showed their beady little eyes. "These dino demons are a whole different matter." Not even my weird sixth sense could detect anything.

Was this another set-up? From Tiffany's thoughts, I had caught that Alex and the other enforcers hadn't found anything yet either. I didn't like dipping into her head, but if she'd talk to me instead of throwing a Tiffany tantrum, I wouldn't have.

And that was exactly the problem. I wasn't respecting anybody's space. Ares was right. I *was* starting to think the ends justified the means. And that realization chilled my soul.

I cleared my throat. "Tiffany, was the text from Alex? Have they found anything yet?"

"No. Why?"

"I'm not sensing anything inside or around the house marked by the spell."

She paused in her rapid-fire typing on her phone and looked over her shoulder at me. "How can you tell?"

"I can see the magick."

"Like a witch?" Siobhan asked.

"Yeah."

Constanza turned the corner at the end of the block. "How come I can't see it?"

Siobhan reached forward and patted the vampire's shoulder. "Did you notice the smell of ozone in here?"

"Yeah."

The were chuckled. "If you smell it again, and you don't know who's casting, duck and cover. It'll keep you alive, especially if the magick wielder tends toward fire talent."

"What she's trying to say is don't piss off Master Augustine's girlfriend," Tiffany added. "She *will* literally fry your ass. Pull into that driveway." She pointed at the next house.

"You trying to get the neighborhood watch to call this in?" I asked.

Tiffany held up her phone, and the garage door slid up, revealing an empty space next to a Porsche.

"Is this another safehouse?" I said.

"No." She made a derisive sound. "This is why I tell the entire fucking coven not to have social media accounts. The homeowners are in Barbados right now."

Constanza guided the SUV into the available slot. Tiffany tapped her phone again, and the garage door slid back down.

"Let me do the scouting," I said as I climbed out.

"No," Tiffany slammed her door shut to emphasize her point before she stomped toward the door into the house. "We go together."

"I'm the least vulnerable," I protested.

She whirled to face me. "No. You're the most vulnerable." The automatic light clicked out. I swear she picked up dramatic timing from Duncan.

"Am not," I muttered as I followed her into the mud room.

"This whole scheme is the dino demons' way to kill you." Tiffany added injury to insult by slapping my hand away from the light switch. "And you can fucking see in the dark!"

"We don't need you tripping over shit," I said. I followed her into the house and past a side door. I stopped and did a double-take. The half-bath's sink faucet was gold-plated. Good grief, not even Mom went that far during the last redecoration.

"Tiffany is what would happen if Tiny Tim's family were the Sopranos, isn't she?" Constanza said.

"Yep," Siobhan said. "And just as deadly, or didn't the bullet to your brain and the pencil embedded in your chest teach you anything?"

The house was typical twenty-first century McMansion. Past the half-bath and utility room was the kitchen. To the left was a formal dining room and straight ahead was a family room. The light on the alarm panel on the kitchen wall shone a steady green. Was there anything my sister-in-law couldn't hack?

When we reached the back door leading from the family room to the deck, Tiffany drew her gun. "If you two are finished mocking me, remember you can *not* bite anything we find."

"Why not?" Constanza said.

"Dino demon blood is poisonous," Tiffany said. "As in instantaneous. Don't let them bite you either. Sam found out the hard way."

I turned to the vampire and the were. "I don't recommend the experience. And no, you guys won't survive it." I looked Tiffany squarely in the eye. "Do you have an actual plan?"

She stiffened. "Kill Giovanni, grab Ellie, and get out before the cops show up."

I curled my fingers against the urge to slap some sense into her. "Really? That's all you got? I had a better plan when we went into Mallory Labs!"

"What? You're upset that I'm not blowing up the house?" She unlocked the door and wrapped her free hand around the latch. "Which, by the way, was the entire sum of *your* plan five years ago."

"I can scout the place without arousing their suspicion," Constanza offered.

"No," Tiffany and I both said.

"But—"

I put my index finger on the vampire's lips. "Do you want us to trust you, or would you prefer I rip off your head now?" Taking my irritation with Tiffany out on Constanza wasn't fair, but she needed to understand her place within the coven.

"Fine," she muttered around my finger. "But even my squad knew how to take orders."

"Then you'd better re-learn how to take them." Siobhan's voice was muffled for an instant as she stripped off her shirt. "Because right now, you're the omega of this pack. I'll take Fang Girl with me. That way we have a telepath in each team. We'll go in the back." She spoke while she shed her jeans. "First one to find Ellie grabs the kid and hightails it back here to the SUV." She stared at Tiffany. "Assuming she's here."

Siobhan's skin rippled, and she dropped to her hands and knees. A couple of seconds later, a huge she-wolf with red-tipped fur shook herself out.

Tiffany yanked open the sliding glass door. Siobhan shrugged past Tiffany and prowled across the deck. Constanza followed her across the yard and over the fence.

I clasped Tiffany's shoulder. "Ready?"

She sucked in a deep breath and released it. "Yeah. My eyes have adjusted now."

It figured she would know why Siobhan and I were stalling. I concentrated, and reality winked out.

Chapter 18

Tiffany

Action kicked my fear to the curb and cleared my mind. The scent of sandalwood was so thick even I couldn't miss it.

I'd assumed Sam would teleport us to the front door so she could dramatically kick it in and lay some witty banter on the bad guys before beating the shit out of them. Instead, we had materialized just inside and well to the right of the front door. Her body blocked mine from the motion detector.

Can you handle the security system? She pointed to a little box inside what appeared to be a home office.

I nodded and holstered my gun. Satisfaction flooded me at being able to turn the same tables on the rogues. People really shouldn't depend on the retail security firms. Their circuitry is all wired the same. The little light switched from red to green, and I gave Sam a thumbs-up gesture.

She glided deeper into the house. The way she looked and moved when she tapped her abilities was creepy as hell. It made my hindbrain whimper and want to hide. But no matter what eerie shit she did, my gut said she'd do her damnedest to get Ellie back.

I followed, checking the dining room as she did the same with the formal living room. The hairs on the back of my neck stood at attention, and it wasn't because of Sam. I drew my Glock again. Even vampires needed to breathe, and I couldn't hear a thing in the house.

Until the clicking ahead of us.

Sam turned and shook her head at me. Instead of glowing white this time, the entire orbs of her eyes were blacker than anything I could imagine. Siobhan entered the family room. The sound had been her nails on a harder flooring than the carpet.

Constanza appeared in the third doorway. *Nothing down here.*

Did you check the pool house? Sam asked.

Siobhan nodded. She started to trot past us, and I grabbed the ruff at her neck. She cocked her head and waited.

I released my friend's fur. With gestures more suited to my daughter,

I pointed to Sam's coat with my free hand, made a hopping bunny, and pointed upstairs.

My sister-in-law's laughter echoed in my mind. She pulled open her lapel. The silver-gray ghosts jumped to the floor and shook out their ectoplasmic fur. Sam crouched next to them and whispered to them in rabbit language.

I just hoped she was only letting our team see then, not everything else that may be in the house.

They took off down the short hallway to the foyer. We followed them to the foot of the stairs. They bounded up the steps and disappeared from sight. Part of me wondered why they didn't just float through the family room ceiling. Maybe they still thought of themselves as regular live rabbits.

An animal scream echoed against the cathedral ceiling of the foyer. One of the bunnies raced down the stairs and leapt into Sam's arms.

Siobhan and Torres beat me up the stairs, but not by much. To my surprise, Sam stayed behind me. Maybe something I said tonight had actually sunk into her rebuilt brain.

Giovanni stood in the middle of what appeared to be a gaming loft with a victorious smile on his face. He held the other rabbit by the throat, his fingers through the poor thing's neck.

Except a vampire shouldn't be able to hold a ghost.

I lifted my sidearm and fired.

Somehow, I missed the clear headshot. The fake vampire's tail whipped out and caught Torres in the midsection. She crashed through the wooden railing, and a sick *thump* came from the first floor. As long as none of the splinters pierced her heart, she would be fine. Thirsty, but fine.

If we killed the demon before he got to her.

Siobhan dived into his knees, driving him to the floor. She rolled out of the way, and I fired again. Unfortunately, he was already moving. The bullet caught the meat of his shoulder instead of his head, and he dropped the ghost rabbit. The bunny made a beeline for the stairs.

The dino demon gave up any pretense of being Giovanni. The human skin split and shredded. Greenish scales glistened underneath, punctuated by the appearance of huge slashing talons on its hands and feet. It looked like a Spielberg velociraptor, which from Alex's reports meant it was a demon-human mix.

That didn't make the creature that faced us any less dangerous.

Siobhan raced for him and leapt. He kicked out, a blow that should have sliced her gut open. She twisted and shifted in mid-air, and her claws raked across his eyes.

The instant she cleared him, my finger squeezed the trigger. The bullet hit his mid-section, and black liquid sprayed everywhere. Wood, leather, plastic, everything hit by the droplets began to sizzle.

Except I didn't have any of Alex's special bullets from Uku Pacha, the Incan version of hell. Plain old steel and silver rounds would eventually kill the half-breeds, but it was a question of whether I could inflict enough damage before one gutted me.

The demon finally decided I was a danger. His tail lashed at me. I dived. In the odd slow-motion feel of something bad and unavoidable, I watched the scaly appendage aim straight for my throat.

A cool silver hand grabbed the tip an instant before it struck me. I landed hard on the hardwood walkway and slid on my side.

Sam wasn't exactly Sam anymore. Her eyes gleamed and swirled like liquid mercury. Silvery metal coated her exposed skin. Hell, even her ponytail shone with a golden metallic finish under the ambient light from the pool-side lamps outside.

She swung the demon by its tail. He sailed above me and out into the empty space over the foyer before she smashed him into the shelves holding a massive collection of media and knick-knacks.

Siobhan rose, her form half-way between human and wolf, with some kind of trophy in her hand. She drove the pointed tip down into the middle of the bookshelf debris. A high-pitched screech rent the air, followed by more sizzling.

A foot shot out of the pile. Siobhan tried to duck the slashing talon. It cut a line down her furry chest. The demon's tail lashed out and caught her in her abdomen. The force of the second blow drove her backwards, and she crashed through a window. The tinkling of glass shards hitting something hard and a splash came from outside. I prayed the splash was Siobhan landing in the pool.

Sam grabbed the demon's tail once again and yanked. Her leverage tossed the demon into the computer monitor. He landed on all fours amid bits of plastic, motherboard, and wires. An angry shriek tore at my eardrums.

He whirled and charged Sam. They traded blows. The demon's claws scratched her metallic skin or armor or whatever the hell covered her, but she didn't stand still long enough for the claws to penetrate. The knife-like sharpness of her own nails damaged the demon's hide, but not enough to put him down permanently. I couldn't get a clear shot with the speed they moved.

And if I, a lowly Normal, jumped in the middle of their battle, I was a corpse. If this fight continued much longer, we'd have vulnerable and un-prepared police officers responding to the noise complaint.

An odd humming vibrated against my hip. Grandpa Ares's knife.

I'd done some dumbass things in my life. Most of them before my daughter was born. But this idea had to have been the stupidest of all.

I shoved my gun into its holster, pulled out the bronze blade, and crouched, waiting for an opening. The demon's tail whipped around Sam's neck. With a half-running step, I launched myself from a gaming chair and landed on the demon's back.

His shriek died abruptly when I plunged the knife into the base of his skull. I closed my eyes and dropped. From the burning along my cheek and forehead, I wasn't fast enough to avoid the blood spray.

My left foot hit something at an awkward angle. The ankle twisted, and pain shot up my leg. Keeping my eyes tightly closed, I rolled away from the demon and over broken chunks that jabbed my body and snagged my clothes.

Silence reigned for a couple of seconds before a massive *whoomp* vibrated the flooring beneath me.

"Oh, no, you don't," Sam said. Another metal-on-metal shriek, but this time the noise was in my head, not my ears. It died just as abruptly as the physical sound had when I stabbed the demon.

This time the silence was punctuated by heavy breathing, but no change of air pressure said something approached me. I slowly reached for a conventional blade.

Just in case.

"Tiffany? You okay?" Sam's voice.

"Is it dead?" I said.

"Yeah. Are you okay?" she repeated.

"I've got demon blood on my face," I grumbled. "I don't feel like melting my eyeballs."

"Oh, shit. Don't move," she ordered. Like I planned to blindly trip on all the broken crap and plummet off the ledge the way Torres had. With my luck, I'd impale myself on something below.

The soft rustling of her coat moved away and came back. "Hold still." A warm, wet cloth stroked my face. The touch stung portions of my skin, but it was better than letting the demon blood burn its way to the bone.

"Okay, it's safe to open your eyes," Sam said. "First and second degree burns. Nothing one of the water witches can't heal."

I blinked, ready for the burn of poisonous acid to fry my eyeballs. The odor of smoldering cotton hit me when she tossed the washcloth aside. I sat upright and examined the carnage.

The demon's body lay still in the wreckage of the room, except for the occasional twitch of the tail tip. Nothing worse than the last neurons struggling to keep the dead thing going. It's why I secretly loved vampires' tendency to melt.

"If it isn't life-threatening, I'll stick with aloe vera." I climbed slowly to my feet, every joint and muscle protesting. My body shouldn't be this fucking sore at twenty-four.

Sam crossed back to the corpse and pulled out the bronze and bone knife. Her skin no longer had its silver metallic sheen, but her eyes still glowed. She carefully cleaned the demon blood off on her sleeve before she handed it back to me.

"That crap is going to ruin your coat," I said.

"No, it won't." She smiled. "Technically, it's not a coat." Her expression grew down right wicked. "And now I can trace the demons."

Chapter 19

Sam

Before I could deal with the dead though, Tiffany and I needed to deal with the living.

Not to mention the sirens I could hear in the distance.

I crossed to the smashed window and looked down. Siobhan was climbing out of the pool, human and very naked. That should give the neighbors something to report to the police. I scanned the area. Especially the asshole with the binoculars on the second floor of the house next to the one where we parked.

"Siobhan," I called as quietly as I could.

The were looked up and signaled she was all right. She had some scrapes and a large cut down the center of her chest, but nothing that wouldn't heal with time, rest and food.

I pivoted and headed for the stairs. "Police are on their way. Tell me everything you can about the owners."

Tiffany didn't question me for once, but then she'd been doing the supernatural cover-up and clean-up thing all her life. She rattled off the essentials while she followed me down the staircase.

Constanza lay in the middle of the foyer, her head at an obscene angle. A broken neck wasn't life-threatening to a vamp, but it would take longer to heal. She groaned when we came into her field of vision.

"Let's settle her in the living room," I said.

"I'll take care of those chintzy decorative pillows." Tiffany shuffled down the hall, turning on lights as she went. She was seriously trying to hide her limp, which meant she hit the floor harder than she wanted to admit.

I could have teleported her to Good Samaritan and had Bebe take a look, but timing worked against us. We couldn't get what we needed from the dead demon and out before the cops showed up, much less take care of the injured vampire, so we were going to have to pretend we were the home owners when the police arrived.

I crouched next to Constanza. "Sorry, lady, but this is going to hurt." I picked her up as carefully as I could, cradling her head like I did when Ellie was an infant, but the vampire cried out anyway. Tiffany had cleared the couch as she promised.

My sister-in-law grimaced. "I'll get her aligned if you can grab a bathrobe for Siobhan."

"Where is she?"

Tiffany gave me an are-you-that-stupid look. "In the kitchen raiding the refrigerator so she can heal before the cops get here."

I teleported upstairs and snagged a bathrobe from the husband's closet. I tried not to think about the family that lived here. Knowing the rogues and their demon allies, the Normals were probably dead. I stopped for a second and concentrated on the rest of the McMansion, the yard, the pool house. Nope, the fake Giovanni was the only corpse in the immediate vicinity.

However, that didn't mean the homeowners hadn't been eaten.

I popped back downstairs and handed the thick robe to the still dripping were who was ploughing through a huge aluminum foil serving pan of brisket. The temporary kind of pan caterers used.

"I know who narced on us," she muttered around a mouthful of beef.

"Back neighbor? Binoculars? Yeah, I noticed him, but I don't know how much he really saw."

Siobhan shrugged. "We may be able to work it to our advantage."

With another teleport to Tiffany's SUV in the neighbors' garage, I collected the blood cooler and telekinetically summoned Siobhan's clothes from the family room. One last jump, and I was back in the trashed house where Tiffany had arranged Constanza so she didn't look quite so damaged.

"I can't find the residents of this house anywhere on the property. Dead or alive," I said as I handed my sister-in-law the package with the alcohol wipes, needles and line.

"As much as it pisses me off, that's a good thing." She cleaned the inside skin of Constanza's elbow. "Their bodies will turn up eventually. Okay, Torres, we're starting a blood IV. It'll speed your healing and alleviate your hunger until you can swallow."

I grabbed an ugly candelabra off the fireplace mantel, set it on the table behind the couch, and hung the blood bag from it. Tiffany handed me one end of the line, and I connected it to the bag. She connected her end and started the fluid flow.

Siobhan sauntered into the living room, dressed in the bathrobe I'd given her and carrying a plate with a large slab of chocolate cake decorated in bright pink and green frosting. "What's the story we're giving the cops," she said around a mouthful of the confection.

"Did you finish the brisket?" I asked. A faint gurgle rippled through my stomach at the sight of the food.

The were nodded and shoveled another forkful of cake between her lips.

Tiffany eyed the cake before she looked at me. "Birthday party and friend got too drunk?"

"That'll work." I wiped a hand over my face. "They'll never believe the body upstairs is real. Can you conjure up a picture of who lives here?"

She pulled out her phone and thumbed the controls. A couple of seconds later, she held up the phone so I could see the screen. The family was very white, very upper middle-class, and very average.

I concentrated on the image of the wife. The feeling of shrinking and plumping and bones rearranging made me nauseated. When the movement under my skin stopped, I looked at Tiffany. "Well?"

"Please don't make me watch that ever again."

I looked down at myself. I'd even managed to create the same clothes the wife wore on her social media page. "Hey, I have boobs for once."

"Whoopee for you." Tiffany shoved her phone back into her pocket. "What are you going to do about the mess in the foyer?"

"Leaving it." I turned the were. "Siobhan, there were a couple of throws in the family room. Would you grab them while I work on an illusion?"

She headed back the way she came. I should have asked her to slice some cake for me, too.

Tiffany cocked her head. "Wait a minute. You just said we were leaving the mess."

Outside, the sirens cut off abruptly. We were out of time. "The damage can be explained by a drunk friend. The IV cannot." I concentrated on the IV bag and exposed line. They shimmered before they faded from view. "Can you see anything?"

"Nope." She flicked at the spot where the bag hung. Her finger hitting the plastic made a *splooch* sound. "Nice glamour, but the cops can still touch it."

Red and blue lights flashed at the front of the house. I shook my head. "Just make sure the police don't knock into the table and candelabra."

Siobhan appeared with the light blankets in one hand and more cake in the other as the pounding on the front door started. I left Tiffany to arrange the blankets over Constanza while I answered the door.

It felt a little weird looking *up* at an officer who was about my natural height. "Is there a problem, sir?"

He frowned and his attention immediately darted to the broken railing on the floor. "We received a complaint about a disturbance, Mrs. Ryan."

"Oh, dear." I did my best to channel my mom's fake Beverly Hills attitude. "I'm terribly sorry. I assure you it won't happen again." I started to close the door, but he shoved it open. He and his partner pushed past me, and I had to let them. They weren't Family, and I couldn't display my super-strength.

"Are you here alone, ma'am?" the second officer asked. He started up the staircase. I hoped he didn't stick a finger in the demon's blood.

I could argue the legalities of what they were doing, but it would only make them more suspicious. Messing with their memories wouldn't delete the 911 call, so I had to play along.

"Just me and three friends, sir."

The first officer strode down the short hallway to the rest of the house. I followed. Tiffany was going to have a field day in her mockery of my handling of the police when things got back to normal.

In the living room, Constanza pretended to be unconscious on the couch. Tiffany sat beside her on the ottoman, acting like a concerned friend. Siobhan lounged in a plush chair with her feet on another ottoman. The were made a point of showing her legs while she ate her cake. Thankfully, the cuts on her skin from where she'd gone through the window had healed. I couldn't begrudge her the brisket, though I was going to need some food myself.

Very, very soon from the hunger growing inside me.

"What were you ladies doing tonight?" He couldn't rip his gaze from Siobhan's bare skin. If he knew she was a cop's wife, he wouldn't be so blatant in his staring.

"It was supposed to be a birthday party," I grumbled.

"Where's your family, Mrs. Ryan?" he asked.

I primly folded my hands, a gesture I'd seen Mom do a million times. "My husband took the kids to Disneyland for the weekend so I could have some girltime."

He finally tore his attention from Siobhan and noticed Constanza on the couch. "What's wrong with her?"

"Hopefully, not alcohol poisoning," Tiffany said sourly. "She found out earlier tonight that her boyfriend had more than one side chick. We didn't realize how much she had to drink until she started ripping up shit upstairs."

"Did she have a gun?"

"A gun?" I splayed a hand across my chest. "She most certainly does not!"

The second officer sauntered into the living room. "The media room window is definitely smashed. Didn't find any bullet holes, but there's definitely a stab wound to the—" He turned to me. "What the hell is that thing lying on the carpet?"

"A life-size prop from one of those dinosaur movies that my husband insisted on buying for the kids," I said. "I hate it. Please tell me Connie damaged it enough I can throw it out."

He chuckled. "You might want to put plastic under it. It's leaking god-knows-what all over your floor."

The first officer moved closer and examined Tiffany's face. "How'd you get burned?"

"It's not a burn. It's an allergic reaction—oh, crap." She looked at the second officer. "You didn't stick your finger in the fluid coming out of the animatronic dinosaur, did you?"

He shook his head and rocked back on his heels. "Not after what I saw what it was doing to the carpet."

The first officer glared at me. "In addition to the gunshots, we got a report of someone getting pushed out of the game room window."

Siobhan started laughing. "Let me guess. The same yahoo with binoculars who was watching me skinny dip?"

The ears of both officers reddened. From their surface thoughts, this wasn't the first time Mrs. Ryan's neighbor had come up. What I saw in their heads made me queasy.

I crossed my arms. "So he's retaliating because I reported him for spying on my daughter and her friends?"

"I'm sorry, ma'am," the second officer said. "You know we can't divulge who called in a report."

The first officer stepped in front of his partner. "So where's the knife she stabbed the fake dinosaur with?"

"It wasn't a knife," Tiffany said. "It was a trophy. From the way it shattered when Connie threw it out the window and hit the patio, your forensics team is going to have a heyday putting it back together."

"Maybe I should take you in?" The first officer reached for his cuffs.

Tiffany shot to her feet. "How much do you love your job?"

I stepped between the two. "Stop it! Both of you." I turned to the officer. "If you need to ticket me for the disturbance, I understand. I should have locked the liquor cabinet." Hell, I'd even pay the damn ticket for the real Mrs. Ryan, and she'd be none the wiser.

Assuming she was still alive.

I turned to Tiffany. "And you are not going to threaten his job. Yes, I know you have more money than . . . me." That was close! "But I need them to take me seriously the next time that pervert is jacking off while watching my daughter sunbathe. You have a daughter. You, of all people, should understand!"

Fear flicked across Tiffany's face at my not-so-subtle reminder of our purpose for being here. Her shoulders sagged, and a wave of rancid meat mixed with ash hit my nose. She looked at the policeman. "I apologize, officer."

His posture relaxed a fraction, and he released the cuffs. "Apology accepted, ma'am." He nodded toward Constanza. "You sure you don't need an ambulance for your friend?"

"No," the vampire mumbled. "I just need everybody to stop yelling. My head hurts."

The second officer stared at Siobhan again. "Ma'am, did you want to press charges against the gentleman watching you?"

She chuckled. "No, a little visit from my husband will suffice."

"Ma'am, you know we can't condone vigilante—"

"He's a brother in blue." She smiled. "Let's leave it at that, shall we?" She followed up with a wink.

He touched the brim of his cap. "Understood, ma'am."

I escorted the officers out. I overheard the partners from the other car confirm the broken glass and the base of the statue Siobhan used as a weapon were scattered across the patio. I didn't really breathe until all four police were in their cars, the flashing lights stopped, and their vehicles headed away from the house.

When I walked back into the living room, Tiffany was trying to feel her way through changing blood bags. I dropped the glamour. "That better?"

"Yeah, thanks."

"I think I can drink now," Constanza protested.

"I'll give you one to drink, but let's get the second bag started first," Tiffany said. At Constanza's disgusted sound, Tiffany smiled and said, "I've been taking care of vampires since I was in kindergarten. Trust me, I want you back on your feet ASAP."

My stomach chose that moment to gurgle. Very loudly.

Tiffany glanced at Siobhan. "I've got Torres if you can feed Sam."

"On it," the were said, rising from her chair.

My vision was starting to get fuzzy as I followed her into the kitchen. Siobhan grabbed me under the arms before I hit the floor.

"Guess I used up more energy than I realized," I mumbled.

"You might want to drop Mrs. Ryan's form," Siobhan said as she settled me at the little table in the breakfast nook.

"Oh, I didn't realize . . ." I let go of the picture in my head. Muscle and bone contorted as my body sprung back to its original shape. It didn't hurt, but the mix of hunger and nausea set my head spinning.

"Here, start on the chicken." Siobhan set another aluminum caterer's pan in front of me. The scent of barbeque was overwhelming. I tore into the meat.

I was halfway through my third breast when I noticed the were staring at me. I swallowed. "What's wrong? Didn't your dad tell you what happened after the zombie attack at Tiffany and Max's rehearsal dinner?"

"Yeah, he did." She crossed her arms. "He didn't say anything about you eating the bones, too."

I looked down at the pan and the breast in my hand. She was right. There wasn't one bone left from my first two pieces. Just like there had been nothing left when I ate the resurrected dino demon earlier tonight.

An awful thought formed in my head, but I was slightly more in control now than I had been at La Brea. I put down the hunk of chicken I was working on. I didn't like the idea of testing my theory, but after what had happened tonight and in Montana last year, I needed to know for certain.

I stood, crossed to the counter, and snatched the butcher knife out of its block. As I strode out of the kitchen, Siobhan followed me, calling my name. My body shook as I climbed the steps.

The full-grown demon hybrid laid where we left it. No footprints marred the cooling blood. The faint scent of burning plastic tainted the air where the black fluid ate through games, video cases, and carpet.

I stepped over broken items and piles of debris and knelt next to the body. Tiffany joined Siobhan at the top of the staircase. I lifted the butcher knife and sawed off a bite-sized chunk of undamaged shoulder.

"Sam? What are you doing?" Tiffany whispered.

I closed my eyes and shoved the bit of flesh in my mouth. The black blood didn't burn my lips or tongue as I expected. The bite had the consistency of avocado, but with a slight cola taste. I forced myself to chew and swallow.

The dangerous hunger in my belly faded in a way the chicken couldn't fill. No wonder regular human food could never appease me for long. I dropped the knife, wrapped my arms around my legs, and rested my forehead on my knees.

I wasn't a god.

I was a monster.

Chapter 20

Tiffany

I watched Sam rock. She may even have been crying. Dammit, she couldn't break on me. Not now. Not until we found Ellie.

"What happened in the kitchen?" I whispered to Siobhan.

The were looked as freaked out as I felt. "I got out the pan of barbeque chicken. She was eating the bones, too, which I thought was weird after hearing yours and Dad's descriptions of her hunger binges. When I said something about it, she dropped the piece she'd been working on, grabbed the butcher knife and came up here. And, well—" She waved at Sam. "You saw the rest."

Sam ate everything, bones and all, of the reconstructed dead baby demon at the La Brea visitors' center. I figured it hadn't burned her because it had been cooked. But now, she just ate a hunk of raw, bloody demon with no ill effects.

Other than the sound of her either crying or hyperventilating.

It's just another change. Her abilities have been growing. Except I didn't believe my inner voice anymore. The one thing that had been constant over the years had been her insane appetite for regular food, especially when she used her powers.

Dammit, Sam couldn't do this to me. Not now. I needed her. A lot more than I wanted to admit out loud. Phil and Alex and Grandpa Ares and, well, every supernatural in California would help me, but no one else had a direct connection to the Old Ones' minions like Sam did. She was the key to finding Ellie.

They took Ellie because of Sam.

I picked my way through the smashed furniture and mounds of broken and chemically burnt cases. I crouched next to Sam and rested a hand on her shoulder.

"Bitch, I know you're scared, but I need you to pull yourself together," I said quietly.

She lifted her head and looked me. Her eyes were bloodshot and puffy.

Tear tracks on her cheeks glistened under the overhead track lighting. "Do you have any idea what's going on?"

"Yeah." I pointed my finger at the corpse. "Giovanni and the demon's siblings have my little girl. Your niece. I can't do this alone, Sam. I need you to help me find her. Tonight."

"You don't get it," she hissed.

"You're right. I don't." I squeezed her shoulder. "But we'll deal with it together. All of us. After we find Ellie."

Saying my baby's name seemed to shake Sam out of whatever she was freaking out about. And the issue was far more than eating fresh demon flesh. Even if it was the absolutely grossest thing I had seen her do to date.

She nodded. "You're right."

She wiped her eyes with the backs of her hands and took a deep breath. "You're right," she said again.

I stood, my legs reminding me of their earlier abuse. "I'll call Alex for a clean-up team."

Sam climbed to her feet as well. "Tell them we need to preserve the body."

"How?" Siobhan waved at the corpse. "His blood is going to dissolve through any container we put it in."

Sam rubbed her cheek as she looked at the body. "Not if he's frozen."

"Transportation to the freezer is still a problem," I said dryly.

"I'll do the tracking spell, and then freeze the body before the clean-up team arrives." Sam nodded as if that decided everything and looked at Siobhan and me. "You guys might want to go downstairs so I don't accidentally give you frostbite."

"What are we going to do about the nosy neighbor?" I asked. "The last thing we need is the police back out here tonight."

"I'll take care of him. Give me ten minutes." A vicious grin spread across Siobhan's face. "Because who's going to believe a werewolf attacked him?"

I followed Siobhan back down the stairs. She motioned for me to follow her to the kitchen. I held up my index finger and headed to the living room.

Torres looked up at me. "Can I have one to drink now? It doesn't feel like my head's going to fall off."

"You sure you can hold a bag?"

She held up her free hand, waggled her fingers, and nodded. I pulled the cooler out of the closet I had shoved it into when the cops arrived. One blood bag and a straw later, she was happily slurping away while I swapped out the second IV bag for a third. It was about like taking care of Ellie after a boo-boo.

My lungs seized at the thought of my baby girl, alone and terrified by the monsters who'd stolen her. I forced my hands to continue the task.

Torres released the straw and licked her lips. "We'll get her back for you."

"Yeah, we will." I blinked to keep my own tears from falling. "Sam's upstairs casting the tracking spell. Siobhan is going to deal with our witness. I'll be in the kitchen, making some phone calls." I tapped my temple. "Yell when you need more blood."

"No problem." She went back to happily sipping her drink.

I stalked into the kitchen where Siobhan waited for me. The expression on her face was a mix of worry and terror. I'd never seen her afraid of anything. Not even when we negotiated the fae-vampire treaty.

"What the hell is wrong with Sam?" she whispered.

"What do you mean?" I walked as nonchalantly as I could to the refrigerator. I opened the door and examined the contents. The need to do something drove me more than actual hunger. I pulled out a wrapped cheese plate and a cola.

"I mean, when did she start eating demons instead of Twinkies?" Siobhan slammed the fridge door shut before I could claim the white cake, with the same pink and green frosting as the chocolate one the were had devoured, that was on the top shelf.

I sighed and set down the cheese plate. How the hell did I answer this? I popped the soda top and took a sip before I replied. "Tonight was the first time I know of. At La Brea, she ate the baby demon that had been rigged with explosives after it had been resurrected by Giovanni's new friends."

"Are you telling me the truth?" She glared at me. "Did she eat the ones in Tuttle Creek, too?"

"No . . ." Would Alex or Sam have told me if she have devoured the Montana dino demons? Sam wouldn't, not if she were ashamed like she was tonight. Alex—

My boss had become very close-lipped since his and Phil's little trip to Peru four years ago. How much of the information he'd given me were tidbits to make me feel like I was in the loop? And how much was he with-holding?

"I don't think so," I amended. "But I don't have time to hack the coven network to make sure for you right now. I need to get my daughter back first."

The fain sheen of fur on her exposed skin faded. "I'm sorry. Sometimes—sometimes, I forget you're not pack."

"Look at it this way," I said softly. "If Sam's losing it, I don't want her around Ellie either. I *will* check into it." I took another drink of cola to dampen my suddenly dry mouth. "Later. Now, go take care of our witness while I call in a crew."

Siobhan nodded. She pivoted and practically bounced out of the house. The back door didn't quite slam shut behind her.

I folded back the plastic wrap on the platter and popped a cube of Swiss in my mouth. It hadn't been that long since Sam and I had eaten, but lord only knew how much longer I'd be—

Be what? A wife? A mother? Everything could come to an end before dawn. I sucked in a harsh breath. *Focus on what you can control, girl.*

I forced myself to swallow the cheese and thumbed Alex's number.

He answered before the first ring finished. "Whatcha got?"

"Another trap down in Orange County." I gave him the street address. "I need a clean-up team down here. We also need a truck big enough to carry a frozen full-grown demon."

"For the love of—what are you girls doing down there?" He hissed the last part under his breath. Grandpa Ares must be close by for Alex not to say a deity's name. Another reminder of Sam's arrogant attitude from earlier tonight.

You need her to find Ellie, remember? Besides Sam nearly had a mental breakdown just now.

"Like I said, they set a trap. We tried a spell based on Torres's blood link to Giovanni. Instead, we got an adult demon disguised to look like him." I took another sip of soda before I could finish. "We think the family who lives here may have been killed, but Sam can't find the bodies nearby."

"I'll run their IDs. See what we can find." He hesitated. I knew what was coming, but I closed my eyes anyway. "Two more teams have checked in, but so far, we've got nothing on our end. Has Torres given you any more to go on?"

"No, she—" My mind replayed what had happened upstairs. The demon's tail lashing out. Not at Sam. Not even at me to get to Sam. No, he'd focused on Constanza first.

"Tiffany? You still there?"

I told Alex the sequence of the attack and about Constanza's broken neck. "She may know something important and not realize it," I breathed.

"Or the demon could have just been pissed she'd switched sides," he said dryly.

"Maybe." I didn't feel like arguing with my boss over something I felt sure of in my gut. "Sam's trying another tracking spell with the demon blood here."

"I thought you said it was frozen?"

"It will be when the crew gets here. Otherwise, we can't transport it without the blood eating through the truck floor. There's a couple of more things, and for the first one, I really need you to be straight with me, Alex." I sucked in a deep breath. "Did Sam eat any of the demons in Montana?"

"Not exactly."

My boss's reticence frayed my last nerve, and I needed that nerve to keep it together in order to track down the asshole who took my daughter. "What do you mean 'not exactly'?"

Alex's breath whistled through the receiver. "The one that had gestated in Alyson Tribideaux shoved a tentacle down Sam's throat—"

"A what?"

"You heard me. Logan killed the baby demon, and when Sam resurrected it for questioning, its partially frozen body broke. Like an egg shell cracking. A mass of tentacles came out. The demon shoved a tentacle down Sam's throat. Trying to choke her, I think, but she let off this blast of power that incinerated the demon. She complained about an upset stomach like she did tonight when she ate the baby at La Brea, but she also said she was full . . ."

There was a very long pause before Alex asked, "She didn't start gnawing on the fresh demon meat, did she?"

"I wouldn't call it gnawing," I said. "According to Siobhan, Sam was eating roasted chicken, bones and everything, in the kitchen after our battle with the demon. She grabbed a knife. I followed Sam upstairs where she cut off one bite-sized piece of fresh demon shoulder. She popped it in her mouth, chewed and swallowed. Then she had what my psychology professor would call an emotional break-down."

"Tiffany, if you don't feel safe with her, grab Siobhan and get the fuck out of there." His tone matched my best friend's voice not five minutes ago.

"We're okay. The incident scared her more than it did us. This wasn't one of her usual out-of-control hunger binges. In fact, she hasn't touched normal food since that one bite." I tucked the phone between cheek and shoulder so I could carry the cheese platter and the soda can to the breakfast nook table. The pan of chicken sat where Sam had left it.

"All right, but don't take any chances," Alex warned. "Ellie doesn't need to lose two parents tonight."

I fell more than sat in the chair I had pulled out. "Max is—" I couldn't bring myself to say the final word.

"No, but since we're being totally straight with each other . . ." There was a soft rustling over the line. He was running his hand over his hair, a nervous habit he'd picked up long before my biological great-grandparents were born. "Look, Duncan's just trying to protect you, but Bebe's worried the swelling of Max's brain isn't going down."

Alex sighed. "Please, be careful tonight. For Ellie's sake, if not yours. If Sam's not reliable, then come home. We'll figure out another angle to tackle this. Now, what's the other thing you wanted to talk about?"

I twirled a cheddar cube between my thumb and forefinger. "Have you ever seen Sam's eyes turn black instead of silver or white?"

"That's a new one," he said.

I dropped the cheddar back on the platter. "Crap, I was hoping it had happened up in Montana."

"I'll ask Ares about it, but right now, I'm more worried about finding Ellie."

My blood boiled. "And you think I'm not!"

He chuckled. "There's my little Chihuahua. Now go find your daughter."

"Fuck off, Stanton!" I jabbed the icon to end the call. I barely resisted the urge to fling my phone across the room.

"Your step-daddy stick his boot in his mouth again?"

I looked up to find Sam leaning against the doorjamb. How much had she heard of our conversation?

"Not nearly as bad as he has in the past," I said.

She sauntered over to the table. "I checked on Constanza. I started another IV and gave her a second bag to drink. She's sitting up, reading a magazine."

"Siobhan should be back soon." I snatched the cheddar cube and popped it in my mouth.

Sam examined the platter. "Are there any you haven't played with?"

"I licked them all," I said around my mouthful.

"Bitch." She picked up a cube that may have been Edam. "I scare myself, too, you know."

"For the record, I'm not scared so much as concerned. I need you. I need your skills to help me find Ellie. You're no good to any of us if you lose your mind now." I took a drink of soda.

"He tasted like your cola."

My mouthful of caffeinated, carbonated beverage sprayed across the cheese, the tabletop and my clothes. Once I stopped coughing, I glared at her. "You did that on purpose."

She peeled the rest of the soda-spattered plastic wrap off the platter. "You can eat the ones with your spit on them."

Chapter 21

Max

So this is what dying is like. Max had given up on moving his extremities hours, days, weeks ago. His swollen brain tissue must be why the buzzing he heard was getting worse. He was having a harder time understanding the people in his room now.

The tech Alisha came back to take another scan of his head. At least, he thought it was her. The faint voice sounded chipper anyway.

Tiffany still hadn't visited him. He would know her voice, her touch, her scent no matter what. Ellie must still be missing. Their daughter would be the only reason Tiffany wasn't here.

Something flared behind his eyelids. Alarms drove spikes into his mind. He tried to scream at the pain, but something blocked the sound.

It would be so easy to let go.

Ellie.

No.

He couldn't leave.

Not yet.

Not until she was safe.

Chapter 22

Sam

Tiffany and I were eating our cheese in silence when Siobhan sauntered into the house. She didn't say a word either, simply shed the borrowed bathrobe and donned her own clothes.

The black diamond trail of my tracking spell sparkled, far more solid than the previous one that had led us to La Brea. Either a fresh kill worked better, or Giovanni and his pals were done playing games.

By the time Constanza was walking on her own, the clean-up crew and their trucks arrived. Tiffany reiterated her warning about keeping the demon's body frozen.

Duncan was going to be even more squicked than usual about something I'd done. But Bebe could analyze samples, and the rest I would . . . eat.

My husband couldn't bitch too much if dino demon carcass saved us on our astronomical grocery bill, especially since he didn't consume any of it.

I teleported us back to the garage where we'd left Tiffany's SUV. We climbed in, but Tiffany didn't turn the key. Instead, she slung her body around so she could see all of us.

"Constanza, we need to have a heart-to-heart."

The vampire's eyes brightened to gold. "What do you mean?"

"Anybody else notice something funny about the battle with the demon?" Tiffany asked.

Siobhan shook her head, a confused expression on her face.

I replayed the encounter in my mind and frowned when I noticed the same oddity my sister-in-law obviously already had. "It didn't come after me first. They always come after me first unless someone else gets in their way."

"And I was the one in the way," Tiffany added.

Siobhan's head slowly swiveled toward Constanza.

Ashy scent filled the vehicle. The vampire's eyes flashed from gold to neon yellow. "But it tried to kill me."

"And that's what I'm trying to figure out," Tiffany said. "Giovanni already intended to use you as his fall guy, which was why he didn't tell you much about his plans."

"Other than crap to lead us on a wild goose chase," I muttered.

"True." Tiffany inclined her head at my point. "But even if the demon was pissed at Torres's betrayal of them, why kill her? From what we know of them, the demons prefer torture for that kind of backstabbing, like they did with Phil's client. Or they would use a supernatural as an incubator, which they can't now that Constanza's a vamp. The only people they really care about killing are you or their sacrifices to open a portal."

"Incubator?" Constanza squeaked.

I rested my forearm against the back of the bucket seat and stared at our little newborn. "So what do you know that's so important the demon needed to take you out first?"

"I swear!" Her gaze swept to each of us in turn. "I told you everything I know."

"Calm down, Constanza," I said. "We're not angry with you. There's something you saw or heard. Something that you regarded as totally inconsequential."

"Or what if it was a memory Giovanni or the demons suppressed before sending her to shoot you?" Tiffany said.

"That's a possibility," I admitted.

"Go back! What do you mean 'incubator'?" Constanza had handled breaking her neck better than she did this conversation.

I didn't blame her one bit.

"The demons need supernaturals to breed with. When they tried with Normals, the baby demons died," Tiffany said. She was enjoying Constanza's freak-out a little too much.

I should be the one exacting revenge. Constanza had shot me in the head, not Tiffany.

"Mother Wolf!" Siobhan swore. "You two think the demon impregnated her, then Giovanni Turned her while she was pregnant?"

Tiffany and I exchanged guilty looks. "It's a possibility," I admitted. "It would be the only way for the baby demon to survive the birth from a Normal."

"I think I'm going to be sick," Constanza murmured.

"Don't you dare!" Tiffany had a pencil out and pointed at the vampire. "I'll have to replace the upholstery because you can't get half-digested blood out of the fabric."

"Deep breaths, Sergeant." I reached around the seat and took her hand. "We don't know anything for certain, other than that killing you was more of a priority for that demon than killing me, which is a major change in their behavior."

Tiffany slid the pencil back into her pocket. "It still doesn't make sense to kill her if they already wiped the memory we could use from her head."

"If the demons can change shape, look like anyone, it may not have been Marcus that I . . ." Constanza's voice trailed off as she really contemplated what Tiffany and I suspected.

"Maybe, but in the end, it doesn't matter who you slept with." I released her hand now that she had calmed down a bit. "Let's think about it on the drive. We need to get moving before they figure out I've cast another tracking spell." I turned around and faced forward again.

Tiffany used her phone to open the garage door. "How do we know this new target isn't another trap?" she said as she backed her vehicle out onto the drive.

"We don't, but given the games tonight, we need to keep playing until we figure things out." I inhaled and released a deep breath. Brimstone coated Tiffany's scent. It was a bit more tolerable than Constanza's ashy fear or Siobhan's wet-dog irritation.

"Then let's hit the mansion, and let Caesar sift through her mind," Tiffany muttered. We zipped past the house we'd trashed. The coven members were loading a large object under a white sheet into the refrigerated truck.

"If he could read my mind, why didn't Master Augustine do that earlier?" Suspicion laced the vampire's voice.

"Because he didn't have to. As a newborn, you broadcast as loud as a Los Angeles heavy metal station," I said. "The problem is you not consciously knowing whatever it is that your previous associates fear you know. And if anybody should be poking through your head, it's me as your trainer."

"What if I say no?" Constanza said.

Siobhan and Tiffany burst out laughing.

"I think that answers your question, Sergeant Torres," I said dryly.

"All right. No Caesar for now." Tiffany glanced at me. "So when are you going to do it because despite the roominess of my full-sized SUV, I'm not driving while you do a mind meld. Especially, if weird shit starts happening."

Despite what I'd just said, the last thing I wanted to do was to poke through Constanza Torres's mind. From the little both she and Colonel Smith leaked, she saw shit in Afghanistan that already left her with a tenuous grasp on her sanity. Even though my own telepathic skills had improved over the past four years, she didn't need to see my nightmares on top of hers.

"Let's follow the current tracking spell," I said.

Tiffany grunted her displeasure.

"Give Constanza a chance to remember on her own," I said. "The woman's been traumatized enough."

"Thanks," the vampire whispered.

"Which way are we going?" Tiffany asked as we neared the freeway once again.

I concentrated on the black diamond thread. "West on 91 then north on 15."

Tiffany stared at me. "Las Vegas? You have to be shitting me!"

I grabbed the wheel when we started to drift into the wrong lane. I felt the thread of magick again. She was almost right. "Not quite. Closer to Fort Irwin."

"We need fuel then," Tiffany muttered.

"It would be faster to teleport," Siobhan said.

"We'll do both." At Tiffany's harrumph, I added, "Just in case you lose me."

"We'd better not, bitch." She hit the turn signal and turned into the corner gas station. "And this better be the last damn stop."

Tiffany stomped into the convenience store to buy caffeine for us. Constanza tagged along, mainly because she hadn't been allowed to drink anything but human blood for nearly a year. She was curious to try her favorite beverage with her new taste buds.

Siobhan leaned against the dent Phil's ass had left on the side of the SUV while I pumped gas. "We're almost out of blood. We shouldn't take Torres out into the desert with us. Not this trip. Definitely not while she's this young."

"Colin had perfect control three months into—"

"There's a big difference between a willing and unwilling Turn, Sam," the were said softly. "I don't think she was totally willing. And that girl has been drinking human blood the entire time."

"She hasn't bitched about the cow blood we've been giving her," I pointed out. The handle clicked. I pulled the nozzle out, hung it up, and tapped "Yes" for the receipt.

"If you were captured by the enemy, what would you do?" Siobhan said.

I stared at her. "Do you really believe she's still working for Marcus?"

"She smells like she honestly believes she's helping us." Siobhan shrugged and pushed away from the SUV. "She smells like she's honestly pissed about what was done to her, and that her maker lied to her. That doesn't mean either Giovanni or the demons haven't planted a subconscious command."

I turned toward the convenience store's plate glass windows. Tiffany and Constanza were paying for the sodas and a buttload of Twinkies. And I understood that the vampire wasn't the only one Siobhan was worried about.

I looked at the were. "The fresh demon flesh appeased my hunger. It scares the hell out of me, too, but eating it means I won't lose control around the rest of you." I drew in a deep breath and released it. "I'm sucking up my own fear and disgust because what I've done tonight grosses the hell out of me."

Siobhan scowled. "That doesn't exactly make me feel better."

I grinned. "Welcome to my world."

Chapter 23

Tiffany

Once Constanza and I delivered the crap we'd bought to the SUV, I claimed I needed a pee break before we got back on the road. Thankfully, no one decided a trip to the restroom needed to be a group excursion.

However, Sam demanded the keys, claiming I needed to get some sleep while we were on the freeway. I didn't feel like arguing. Or trying to drive through a teleport.

I jogged to the ladies' room. Thankfully, it was one of those that was essentially a single half bath, and it was unusually clean. I could lock the door and not have someone walk in on my conversation.

It didn't mean the three supernaturals with me couldn't eavesdrop if they wanted to either. But I decided to take the chance anyway.

Uncle Duncan's phone rang twice before he answered. "Have you found Ellie?"

"Not yet," I whispered. The damn lump grew in my throat again. "I wanted to check on Max."

"I am sorry, but there is nothing new to report."

God, did he have any idea of how bad he sucked at lying? "Dammit, Duncan. I'm not a little kid, and I don't need any telepathy to know you aren't telling me everything."

The line was silent for a long moment except for what may have been footsteps. "He had a seizure a few moments ago. Bebe has him stabilized for now."

I leaned my head against the cool wall tile. I didn't need a medical degree to know this wasn't good. "Thank you for being straight with me."

His sigh whistled through the connection. "There is something else you should know. Elizabeth asked me to Turn him."

I straightened. "You didn't tell her yes, did you?"

"You know I would never—"

"I'm sorry, Duncan. I'm . . . sorry," I finished lamely. Despite my momentary panic, I should have known my uncle would never go against mine or Max's wishes. "It's been a very shitty night."

"I am aware." He cleared his throat. "Caesar said Samantha planned to use Giovanni's spawn to find him." The questioning note in his voice meant neither Caesar or Alex were giving him the full story either. A nasty part of me was glad. Now Duncan would know how it felt to be lied to for his own good.

"It was another set-up. We've got a new plan. I'll call you later."

"Tiff—"

I deliberately killed the connection. It wasn't fair to take my anger out on my uncle. The man was more than that. He'd essentially been my father, just as Phil had been my mother. I didn't remember my own parents because they'd died when I was a few months old.

If we didn't get Ellie back, if she and I died tonight, it would effectively wipe out Duncan's entire family line. We'd been systematically hunted for the last four and a half centuries by his maker. And her grandson was determined to finish not just what she started, but end the entire fucking human race.

I may lose my husband tonight, but I was not going to lose my daughter.

Maybe it was the lack of lights that jerked me awake, or maybe the desert quiet. Or maybe it was the faint nausea of a teleport.

I stretched as best I could with the damn seatbelt in the way. "Where are we?"

"We just got off the exit for Baker."

"That's past Fort Irwin," Torres said.

"Yep." Sam didn't take her eyes from the road.

I glanced at the dash. If Sam hadn't monkeyed with the compass, we were headed north. And the clock said it had been two hours since I'd fallen asleep. "We didn't drive the whole way, did we?"

"No." Sam grimaced. "But we were delayed. There was an accident before we got out of the Los Angeles area. Too many witnesses to risk a teleport."

"Well, you being all circumspect around the Normals is a first." I scrubbed my eyes. "We're still too close to dawn for my comfort."

"We'll be fine," she snapped.

"You've got a newborn you took responsibility for," I said.

Sam sighed. "If I have to, I can 'port us back to Los Angeles," she said. "And Ares is listening for you and me in case we run into problems."

"When did you talk to Grandpa Ares?"

Siobhan snickered. "You slept through Alex's call."

"Why didn't you wake me?"

"Because you needed the rest," Sam said. "You've been up nearly twenty-four hours."

I hated to admit she was right. The adrenaline surges from Constanza taking potshots at us and the fight with the demon pretending to be Giovanni weren't enough to keep me going. I popped the tab of an energy drink. Neither was all the caffeine I'd been drinking.

Fishing through the grocery bag, I found the beef jerky and handed a couple of sticks to Siobhan before I peeled off the wrapper of a third. I looked at Sam. "You need a Twinkie?"

"Not now, thanks." I hoped she was right about how her changed body metabolized fresh demon flesh. Otherwise, we were screwed out here in the middle of nowhere.

A canine shape with a bushy tail darted across the highway in front of us. "Anyone you know?" I quipped before I bit off a hunk of dry meat.

"Funny, ha-ha." Sam shot me a sour look.

"I don't get it," Constanza said.

"There's a werecoyote family that works for Sam and Duncan in Las Vegas," Siobhan mumbled around the mouthful of jerky she chewed.

"Is anybody but me questioning the demons' obsession with United States parks tonight?" Sam asked. "First, La Brea. Now, we're headed into Death Valley."

I swallowed my mouthful of jerky. "Both are ancient holy sites. The original tribes of North America didn't feel the need to erect monuments the way other societies have. Actually, so is Yellowstone, and Tuttle Creek isn't far from that park."

"That's not always true," Sam said. "Sometimes, their markers are a little more subtle."

"What do you mean?" Siobhan asked.

"The earthen works of the so-called Mound Builder tribes follow the New Madrid fault lines. I've been checking." She shot a glance at me. "Are you going to freak out like your uncle does?"

"Is this why you've been disappearing for weeks at a time?"

She shrugged. "Part of it. The other part is training."

"With my foster grandfather?" I asked.

"I'm way beyond what he can show me," Sam said. She wasn't boasting. She sounded . . . regretful.

It also meant she was spending more and more time with the other death gods. A shiver ran down my spine as I processed what she was telling us. "So most of the attempted incursions by the Old Ones into our dimension occurred at places with major cracks in the planet's crust."

"All of them. Including holes in the main plates, like Hawaii." Sam's voice was grim.

"As above, so below." Constanza's soft voice lent an eerie quality to her statement.

And my sister-in-law's plan clicked in my own head. Her original question had been rhetorical. Or maybe she needed someone she trusted to talk it through with. "You're narrowing down the possibilities of where the next one will break through."

"Trying to."

The glittering desert stars seemed to close in on my SUV. They were the only things between us and the unending, hungry darkness beyond the farthest galaxy.

"Has any Old One tried to come through a previous breach?" I asked.

"So far, no. And there's too much hominid power at La Brea for them to make another attempt there."

"But you think it'll be somewhere close to where you were created?" Siobhan said.

"That's the way the pattern seems to go," Sam said.

"These nests the demons make that you all have mentioned. Wouldn't the demon want to be close to where their masters come into this world?" Constanza asked.

Sam tapped on the brakes and guided the SUV onto the berm. She threw the gear into "Park" before she unsnapped her seatbelt and turn to look at the vampire. I did the same.

Constanza's eyes glowed dimly from the backseat. "I'm not going to let you tear my mind apart." She lifted her chin. The gesture made me admire her spirit.

And her defiance was totally futile compared to Sam's power.

My sister-in-law gave what I was sure she meant to be a reassuring smile. "Where did Giovanni first approach you, Constanza?"

Horror filled her face. "Here at Death Valley." Tears glistened as they rolled down her cheeks. "A year ago. I-I camped out here when I was on leave. I-I was about to eat a bullet."

"Where did he take you after you were infected?" I asked.

Constanza hugged herself. "I-I'm not sure. I was pretty out of it with fever hallucinations. Or that's what he said it was."

Sam and I looked at each other.

"We already know it's another trap," I said. "But if we don't trigger it, Giovanni's going to know we're on to him."

"If I don't trigger it, you mean," she said. "I can 'port you, Siobhan and Constanza back to the mansion, then come back here."

"Don't be an idiot," Siobhan spat. "You need backup going into the valley. Or do I need to remind you that it was Tiffany who actually killed the demon?"

Sam's initial anger turned to a wry smile. "She'd be right. I didn't say thank you, did I?"

I grinned. "Why start with good manners now, bitch?"

"Gold digger," she shot back.

"Hey! Leave your mom out of it." My humor died abruptly. "I'm going with you, though," I said to Sam before I jabbed a finger in Siobhan's direction. "No arguing. You didn't do much better than Sam did against the demon." I softened my voice. "Constanza is going to need a little support, and Sam and I together will give Giovanni a target he and his demon buddies can't resist."

"You're making a huge assumption," Siobhan growled.

But my gut said it was the right decision. "Have Alex put an extra detail on Duncan. If either of them argues, go to Caesar. If Giovanni can take out the three people he blames for his grandmother Selene's death, he won't hesitate."

"What about Max?" the were asked softly.

"If they wanted him dead, they would have done it at our house." I couldn't stop the bitterness in my voice. "Sam, I'll wait for you here."

All three women protested, but I held up a hand. "I'll be fine for five minutes. No sense teleporting the SUV all the way to Los Angeles and back again." I shrugged. "Besides, what can happen?"

"Famous last words," Siobhan muttered.

We climbed out of the vehicle. A thin wedge of moon climbed above the eastern mountains. My breath clouded in the night air, as did Siobhan's. Sam and Constanza? Well, it was just a reminder of how different we all were.

"Be smart," Constanza said. "If something shows up, run."

"Oh, running is one thing I'm very good at." I patted the pocket holding my supply of number two pencils. "I'm also very good at stabbing things."

The vampire absentmindedly rubbed the spot on her chest where I'd rammed a pencil in her earlier tonight.

"Okay, everybody grab their safety buddy's hand," Sam said. The three of them joined hands and popped out of sight.

A shooting star flared in the night sky. I climbed into the driver's seat, locked the doors, and counted the seconds before Sam returned.

Chapter 24

Sam

We popped back into conventional reality in the middle of Caesar and Bebe's living room. Out of habit, I immediately ducked. Siobhan followed suit.

A shot rang and Constanza cried out.

"I think you forgot to tell her something," Siobhan pseudo-whispered.

I slowly rose to my feet. The were who'd shot at us shivered under my glare, her face turning bright red. "Jesus Fucking Christ, Cara! How many times do we have to tell you—"

"My Lord is not currently available, Lady Samantha." Azrael materialized behind the embarrassed were. "How may I be of assistance?"

Cara screamed, jumped, and somehow pivoted in mid-air. I managed to jerk Cara's arms up and away as the second shot fired. It barely missed the archangel's head. And I really didn't want to find out what one of the specially-modified bullets would do to his kind.

Sucking in a deep breath, I decided to deal with the most pressing problem, which was the Angel of Death in a vampire and witch's living room. I bowed to him. "I sincerely apologize for taking your lord's name in vain, Azrael. My charge was injured, and in my anger, I was extremely careless in my words."

A faint smile appeared on his face, and his pale blue eyes twinkled. As he had the first time I saw him nearly five years ago, he wore blue jeans and a white t-shirt. His feet were bare. Thankfully, his wings weren't visible.

"While your . . . slips are more infrequent of late, they do divert me from my own duties."

I winced. "I know. I'm sorry. I am trying to break the habit. I really am. But we're talking thirty years of—"

"Calm down, Samantha." The twinkle disappeared, and his smile grew sad. "In thirty centuries, we will be able to talk about the events of this time. However, since you do not require me . . ." He bowed. A muffled *pop* of displaced air signaled his departure.

Anne Levy-Fitzgerald, the head of Caesar's household security, peered around the corner of the entryway, her big brown eyes wide in amazement. Or maybe it was awe. "Was that really—"

"Yeah, it was." I rubbed my eyes. "Remind me to stop summoning archangels accidentally." Generally, it was Azrael who showed up since he and I had similar roles, but on other occasions when he was busy, Michael, Gabriel, or Raphael had shown up. Two of them were like their brother, pretty tolerant of my fuck-ups. Michael threatened to shish kabob me with his flaming sword if he had to answer another one of my accidental calls.

I pinched the bridge of my nose. Four-letter words were one thing, and Tiffany had made it clear she thought I was being an arrogant bitch if I took my own name in vain, but I really needed to watch who I mentioned. Some actual deities were even less thrilled with me than one particular archangel.

But right now, my more immediate problems needed to be dealt with. I lowered my hand and turned to Constanza. She cupped her left ear. Blood trickled onto her borrowed shirt. A hint of burnt hair tickled my nose. "How bad is it?"

"Nothing a drink won't fix. It startled me more than anything." She glared at the were cowering in my grasp. "You owe me a decent salon cut, bitch."

"Anne?" I gave her my best puppy dog look. "Could you show Ms. Torres the kitchen and laundry facilities?"

"On it." The enforcer smiled at Constanza. "Follow me."

As the newborn passed me, I grabbed her arm. "Don't let the sweet little Amish act fool you. She can kick my ass. If you give her any shit, she can and will stake you. And she has my permission to do so." I raised my voice. "Got that, Anne?"

"Yes, ma'am." Anne's face remained serene, but I could hear her giggling in my head. "Master Augustine is waiting for you in the study." From their footsteps, Anne guided Constanza to the kitchen.

I turned to Cara. "What's with the trigger-happy bullshit? And it's always me." I threw up my hands. "You never do this to Ares!"

"I-I-I—" A heavy sheen of fur sprung from her skin.

"Dammit, Cara! If you pee on Caesar's expensive Persian carpet—"

"It's been almost five minutes, Sam," Siobhan said. Her not-so-subtle reminder of what we were facing.

"Fine, just . . . please talk to her." I stomped toward the doorway, but paused to face the two weres again. "Or better yet, take away her gun."

I didn't bother knocking on the study door. Caesar's expression wasn't exactly displeased, but it nevertheless let me know I was acting like a rude bitch. Alex stood at the other end of the room, probably updating Caesar on the latest news about the search for Ellie.

Scott Epstein stood between the huge desk and the only doorway. He relaxed a hair when he saw it was me. Apparently, he took my warning to keep Caesar safe to heart.

I bobbed my head. The power dichotomy with vampires could be a little touchy at times, especially when other supers were present, like they were now. "Pardon the interruption, Master Augustine, but time is of the essence."

"Please speak." He waved to indicate his guests sitting on the couch, Siobhan's dad John Lannigan who was the alpha of the Los Angeles werewolf pack and Bebe and Scott's grandmother Ziva Epstein who was the high priestess of the Silver Bear coven.

I eyed Alex. *How far did you get?*

His mouth twitched, but he didn't dare smile. *Up to the part where we have a frozen demon carcass in the walk-in freezer.*

I updated Caesar on what had happened since we left the site of the battle in Orange County. "The demon seemed determined to eliminate Constanza Torres. Tiffany believes she may have been held at the demons' nest while she was undergoing her Turn."

He stared at me over his steepled fingertips. "I don't like the idea of you and Tiffany alone in Death Valley."

"All we're doing is buying time for somebody here to go through Constanza's head." I wrapped my arms around myself. "The harder job is weeding through her fever dream memories to figure out where the rogues and the demons are really hiding. It has to be within driving distance. Ellie hasn't been missing for twelve hours yet."

"You're assuming they didn't have air transport ready and waiting," John said. The alpha werewolf had always made me nervous. It was the combination of tenderness and ferocity, and I was never sure which side would show itself.

"Maybe, but I don't think so." I didn't want to scare anybody, but they needed to know. "I've been talking to any of the death gods who will speak with me. The attempted break-thru of the Old One will be fairly close to where I was created and where I will be when the break occurs. There's a lot more to it, but a sacrifice only unlocks the door. They need me to wedge the door open."

"Then we need to kill you to keep that from happening," John said.

My arms dropped, and I glared at him. "Is that the real reason Cara takes potshots at me every chance she gets?"

The were's smile became enigmatic.

I decided to ignore him. Caesar would be pissed if I fricasseed his friend. Besides, I might accidentally give John more ideas for killing me. My attention shifted to the vampire master. "I need to leave soon if we're doing this. Not to mention Tiffany's waiting on the road into the park—"

My phone rang as if on cue. I pulled it out of my pants' pocket. Sure enough, it was my sister-in-law. I looked at the vampire master.

He rolled his eyes. "Put her on speaker."

Maybe Tiffany and I were a bad influence on Caesar.

"It's been fifteen minutes, bitch! Where the hell are you!"

"We had an incident when we arrived—"

"Jesus Fucking Christ! Did Cara shoot you again?" The speaker screeched at Tiffany's volume.

"For once, no. But I wish I could swear and not have fucking archangels show up in Caesar's living room," I grumbled.

"There was an archangel in my living room?" Caesar's expression matched the perturbed one my husband wore when I'd fucked up.

I held up my hands. "Just the Angel of Death, and he was only here for a minute."

"I may not technically be the firstborn of Egypt, but your statement doesn't exactly make me comfortable, Samantha." From the way the master vampire's eyes glowed neon yellow and his cotton-sweet scent, he wasn't lying.

Or maybe he was teasing me in front of his guests to take me down a peg, but I'd done enough damage to supernatural relations for one night.

Ziva, on the other hand, stood abruptly and crossed to the vampire master's desk. "Give me a piece of paper."

Caesar reached into a drawer for a notepad while Ziva snatched a ballpoint from his pen holder. She scrawled a symbol on the goldenrod legal pad.

"Here." She shoved the pad back to Caesar. "Have Bebe draw this in lamb's blood over your doorways. Make sure the blood is kosher. That will block Azrael from coming into your home."

Caesar held up the pad and considered the symbol, then he smiled at the witch. "Thank you."

"It's not like the angel did anything when Cara tried to shoot him," I grumbled some more.

"Caesar!" The speaker on my phone screeched again. "Are you going to check Torres's memory or not?"

"Yes," he said. "As soon as Anne has finished caring for her bullet wound."

"Cara shot Sam and Torres?" Tiffany said.

"No, I'm fine," I replied. "Thank you for asking."

"Then stop whining about the damn angel, and get your ass back here," Tiffany spat. "It's freezing, and I'm not wasting anymore gas waiting for you. Now, turn off the damn speaker, give your phone to Caesar, and leave the fucking office."

I blinked. What the hell couldn't she say in front of me?

Caesar held out his hand. "John, Ziva, Scott, if you will excuse me for a moment, please?"

Scott shot Ziva a questioning look, but she nodded.

Well, at least I wasn't the only one getting kicked out, but Alex got to stay.

I handed the vampire master my phone, pivoted and charged out of the room. John laughed as he followed me to the kitchen.

Somehow, I managed not to smack the swinging door off the hinges when I entered the kitchen. Constanza and Anne sat at the kitchen table, mugs in their hands.

The newborn had been cleaned up. From the spice and sandalwood scent, Anne had scrounged the black t-shirt for Constanza from my husband's spare wardrobe he kept at the mansion. The cotton emphasized her full breasts. I swam in his shirts. The flare of envy only added to my pissy mood.

The former sergeant downed the last of her blood and pushed back from the kitchen table. "I'm ready."

"Sit back down. Caesar isn't ready for you. Tiffany's narcing on us about something."

"That's not fair, Sam."

I pivoted slowly at Ziva's words. "So you're saying Tiffany isn't tattling?"

Her salt-and-pepper eyebrow rose over the rim of her cat's eyes glasses. "Have you changed that little over the last several years you see nothing beyond your own petty self-interests?"

I towered over the diminutive grandmother in the Day-Glo orange track suit. "I'm trying to find my niece—"

"That's the problem." She shook her head and her eyeglass chain rattled. "Ellie isn't just your niece. She is Tiffany's daughter, and Max is Tiffany's husband. Can't you see? Tiffany is terrified she will lose the only family she has ever known."

"Duncan and Phil—"

Ziva stepped closer and poked my breastbone. "Are surrogates. Yes, they care about her, but with Max and Ellie, she feels like she belongs." She poked me again. "And I thought when you defended them at their wedding, and you rescued Max from Baron Samedi, you understood how important their bond was." She crossed her arms over her ample breasts. "Or are you simply taking your marital problems out on Tiffany instead of dealing with Duncan?"

A hint of ozone mixed with her ginger scent and her floral perfume. "Then there's the total irresponsibility of summoning the Angel of Death into my granddaughter's home. Goddess, what were you thinking?"

I matched her posture. "I wasn't, but I don't need a lecture from you—"

"Maybe you do." Her arms dropped back to her sides. "He was nearby, Samantha. Has it occurred to you that he's in Los Angeles for a reason tonight?"

My lungs froze at her rhetorical question. Or was it really that rhetorical?

Caesar entered the kitchen. That's when I realized the two female vampires and John had vacated the room. I must have gone all glowy-eyed and silver-skinned to scare the alpha were out of watching Ziva chew me a new one.

The vampire master handed my phone back to me. "Thank you for letting me speak with Tiffany privately."

Ziva's lecture poked at my conscience. "Have you heard if Max's condition has improved?"

He regarded me in a way that I didn't need telepathy to tell he was considering whether or not to inform me of the latest prognosis. "Not since Tiffany called Duncan a couple of hours ago," he finally said.

"What?" Disbelief coursed through me. My sister-in-law hadn't peeped when she'd climbed back into the SUV at the gas station in Orange County.

"She should have told you." His expression said he didn't want to be the one to tell me either. "Max suffered a seizure shortly before she and Duncan spoke. If the medical team can't get the brain swelling down, well—" He cleared his throat. "Tiffany asked for my reassurance that Max's wishes would be followed, assuming the worst-case scenario. But I don't think that's really what she wanted."

A chill ran through me. "She's hoping you'll defy his medical directive?"

He nodded. "I believe so."

"You wouldn't possibly—" Ziva started.

"No, I wouldn't," Caesar stated firmly. "However, that doesn't mean, in her fear and grief, Tiffany won't do something stupid. Sam needs to know my enforcer's mental state if they are going into an obvious trap."

He turned back to me. "Buy us that time, and with Ziva and Scott's help, we'll see what knowledge we can retrieve from our newest coven member." He held up a hand. "Call us after you've triggered the trap and you're both safe. I don't want to alert the demons if they can detect electromagnetic signals like you can by calling or texting you."

I nodded. "Anything else before I head back?"

Caesar smiled. "Stay intact and keep Tiffany alive."

"Yes, sir." I saluted before I flicked out a thought and jumped.

Chapter 25

Tiffany

It had been nearly ten minutes since I got off the phone with Caesar. I had just started the SUV engine again when my ears popped. Sam appeared in the passenger seat.

I glared at her. "Five-minute trip, my ass." I threw the gear into drive and pulled back onto the pavement. "Is Torres okay?"

"Yeah, Cara only nicked her ear. I think John's putting that bitch up to shooting me."

"You're paranoid," I said.

"It's not paranoia when they're really shooting you," she muttered.

"So all we're going to do is set off this trap?"

"Caesar said to buy him and the witches some time to retrieve Constanza's memories." Sam's hesitation said there was more to their conversation than the location of the bad guys' secret hideout.

"Now's not the time to be lying to me, bitch." My fingers itched. I needed to shoot something. Stab something. Anything to get the fear and rage out of me.

"Like you did to me?" she said quietly.

My thoughts flipped through my conversation with Caesar, and it clicked in my brain why she was probably pissed. "Not that my or my husband's end-of-life arrangements are really any of your business, but I asked *my* coven master to make sure *my* husband's final wishes are followed."

"I'm talking about you calling Duncan, you know, *my* husband, when we stopped for gas and not telling me."

"You should have done that yourself," I spat back. I wasn't about to admit she was right. Max was—

Is her brother, I corrected myself. But, I'd been working so hard to keep my own shit together. I hadn't been thinking straight at the time.

"And you should have told me about Max's seizure. Not Caesar." Her eyes shone silver, but not enough to compromise my night vision.

"I needed you here," I snapped. "Not running back to the hospital."

The glow dimmed. "Ellie is our priority. I get that, but you still should have told me."

"So you're admitting you can help him?"

"You know I can't." Her voice dropped to a growly quality.

"No. I don't know that."

"Yes, you do."

"Then you need to stop calling yourself a goddess."

Tense silence filled the passenger compartment of my SUV. I'd pushed her too far. I knew I had. I should apologize. Max wasn't just my husband.

Before I could, a demon landed on the hood. This one had a velociraptor's prominent slashing talons. It raised a foreclaw, and I was all-too-aware of what those razor-sharp nails could do from Alex's reports. We'd gotten fucking lucky back in Orange County. Siobhan could have been gutted. Me, too.

I slammed on the brakes and let Sir Isaac Newton take over.

Tires squealed, and the acrid stink of rubber on asphalt filled my head. Those talons dug furrows in the hood of my black beauty, but they didn't stop the demon's momentum. The instant its body broke my hood ornament and it disappeared from sight, I gunned the engine.

Wheels thumped over the body, and the suspension shivered. Like every vehicle owned or used by an Augustine enforcer or Family member, my SUV was armored with bullet-proof glass and reinforced treads. It was specifically designed to withstand most conventional assaults, short of a nuclear device.

The designers, though, never conceived of a dinosaur attack.

However, I had my own version of a nuke. Except for all her powers, Sam couldn't hit the broadside of a barn when it came to firearms. "We need to switch seats," I yelled.

In any action movie I've ever seen, the good guy with gun trading the driver's seat with her sidekick involved complicated maneuvering while the bad guys were trying to kill them. With Sam, I blinked, and I was in the passenger seat with the seatbelt in place.

"Someday, I'll get used to you pulling that shit," I muttered and pulled my gun from my holster.

"Someday, so will I." Sam flicked off both the headlights of the SUV and the interior lights.

"I can't see in the dark—"

"Give your eyes a minute to adjust," she said. "Hold out your gun and ammo clips."

"What? Why?"

Something called out from somewhere off the road to my right. Something else screamed in answer from Sam's side.

"Because Alex needs his ammo," she answered.

Then I realized what she planned to do. I pulled the extra clips from my messenger bag and held them and my sidearm up. She placed her palm on them. Her eyes went from silver to black, and she muttered under her breath. Ozone filled the passenger compartment of my SUV.

"There." Her eyes shifted back to looking like normal human ones again.

I shoved the clips back in my bag. "You sure these will work like Alex's Uka Pacha bullets?"

"We're going to find out real quick," she muttered as she glanced at me.

No, not at me.

My pupils had adjusted, and the desert shadows reformed into rocks, sand, and shapes running beside us. "Why can't these things look like real velociraptors? Where're their feathers?"

"Feathers?"

"Oh, for the love of—" I quelled my initial response. Taking a deity's name in vain when I was in the presence of another god could gain unwanted attention. And I didn't have any magickal sigils on the SUV to guard against such an intrusion. "Don't you read anything actually scientific, or do you gods and demons rely on Steven Spielberg's version of reality? Those things out there are way too big and too naked to be velociraptors."

"You can thank human pop culture for their size and nudity." Sam must have flicked the window control because mine started its downward slide. "Or maybe that's how real velociraptors thought their demons looked."

Something about the demons' behavior didn't seem quite right. "Why are they pacing us?"

"The one you ran over cut the fuel line." Sam made a disgusted sound.

"There's three waiting to jump us, sitting on the rock formation up ahead. You take care of them. I'll deal with the ones planning to pincer us."

The outcropping wasn't very high. If I missed, one of the bastards could potentially get into the cab of my SUV.

Well, then. I couldn't miss. Not when my daughter depended on me staying alive long enough to find her.

I hit the release for my seatbelt. Once it was clear, I leaned out the window to line up the shot. One of the demons pacing us feinted in my direction. The crescent moon and starlight glinted in its eye. I shifted and squeezed the trigger.

The first bullet missed, but the second one didn't. Instead of blasting into dust like Alex described when he used the Uku Pacha bullets, the demon's eyeball exploded into goo, much like Sam's had earlier tonight. But this guy wasn't going to heal from the glimpse I caught of the exit wound.

The body tumbled with its momentum, and one of the dead demon's buddies tripped over the corpse and skidded across the sand and gravel of the desert floor on his face.

I ducked back inside to catch my breath and give my cheeks a chance to thaw. The air had been cold when standing still outside, but the windchill at the speed Sam drove was nearly unbearable.

"How much fuel do we have left?" I asked.

"Not enough to get us home conventionally," she said grimly.

"I hope you're planning on teleporting my baby back to Los Angeles since it was your asinine idea to bring her out here," I said.

Sam glanced at me. "Are we talking about my niece or your vehicle?"

My retort needed to wait. I leaned out the window once more. This was going to be tricky. At least, I didn't have to worry about one of the bastards running right beside me. I caught the image of one via the side mirror, but it was struggling to keep up with us. It was too much to wish it was the demon who'd ungracefully face-planted a mile back.

Focusing on the demons ahead of us, I nailed the first one on the outcropping before it could jump. After I unloaded most of the clip into the second one, it bounced off the hood and dropped out of sight. I wasn't so lucky with the third. My shot missed as it leapt. I jerked back inside and hit the window control.

A massive *thunk* sounded as the same time a dent appeared in the roof. It was immediately followed by an ear-shattering *screech*. I whipped around to check the rear window. Unfortunately, the demon didn't roll off the back.

However, I did see Sam ignite the entire stream of gasoline we'd been leaking. Four of the demons chasing us ignited as well. They thrashed and flamed, but stopped following us.

I hit the release to drop the empty clip and popped in a full one. "We've still got one runner—" A deep *boom* and another dimple appeared in the ceiling. "—on your side, one on mine, and the hitchhiker."

"I thought this thing was armored," she muttered.

"We're damn lucky it is, or we wouldn't be having this conversation," I shot back. "This can't be all of them."

"It won't be." She looked at me. "How attached are you to this particular vehicle?" She sounded like she did when my favorite pair of earrings she'd borrowed had been destroyed in the demon attacks last year in Montana.

"You've got to be shitting me!" I glared at her. "Are you determined to run through my trust find before Ellie makes it to college?"

"Ellie's education is taken care of and you know it," she grumbled. "And I'll repay you for the SUV."

"Like you did my earrings?"

"Actually, I had replacements made for you, plus a matching necklace." She glanced at me. "Merry Christmas?"

I resisted the urge to punch her and looked over my shoulder. This wouldn't be the first vehicle destroyed in the name of my job or other shit with the coven, but—

Nostalgia washed through me. Ellie singing nursery rhymes in the backseat. Our family trip to Disneyland to meet the princesses. Max and I testing the amount of space with the backseats folded down . . .

I swallowed the giant lump in my throat. This hunk of steel and plastic could be replaced. My husband and daughter couldn't.

"What did you have in mind?" I said.

"Well, I was going to wrap them—"

"Sam!" Another blow to the roof punctuated my shout.

"Put your seatbelt back on," she ordered.

This was one of the rare times I actually did what someone told me to and didn't argue. I holstered my gun, because with my luck, it would slide off my lap when Sam pulled some evasive maneuver and discharge. I couldn't die in a stupid avoidable accident. Not when my daughter was out there, somewhere, at the mercy of monsters.

As my seatbelt locked, the demon's third blow punctured the roof. More metal screeching as the damn thing used its super-sized slashing talon as a can opener.

I drew my Glock again and peered through the jagged slash. A yellow eye peered back at me. I could have sworn the damn thing grinned at me as well. I grinned back and drew bead on it.

"Are you insane?" Sam screeched. "Its blood will dissolve you and the SUV."

Then do something about it. Hit the brakes and turn at the same time. I squeezed the trigger.

And immediately knew I'd overloaded Sam when everything flowed in slow motion. The blood spatter from my bullet congealed into one massive glob in mid-air. The rear window shot forward, bending and warping around the black liquid.

She wrenched the steering wheel hard enough the SUV tilted precariously on two tires. The scent of gasoline hit my nostrils, and I realized she'd been telekinetically sealing the break in the fuel line.

I twisted to see the mass of dino demons waiting for us in the middle of the road. Black smeared part way down my passenger window as the demon I'd shot slid off the roof. I could hear the sizzle and pop as its acidic blood ate through the paint and metal of the roof and door.

Then the world outside started spinning.

Except from the teeth-rattling bangs and bumps, it wasn't the world tumbling. Airbags exploded in front and beside me. Pain shot across my chest and hips as the seatbelt attempted to keep me in place. I tightened my grip on my Glock so it wouldn't bounce around the cab and accidentally kill me.

My fucking sister-in-law had rolled my precious SUV.

Chapter 26

Sam

Well, shit.

The last time I'd been in a sideways-rolling vehicle, its destruction hadn't been my fault. However, Max never let me forget it had been his car, and he'd lent it to me while mine was in the shop on the promise I wouldn't get a scratch on it. Ironically, the reason my old Honda had been in the shop was due to the bitch sitting next to me. Tiffany had poured sugar in my gas tank.

That had been nearly five years ago. It seemed like eternity though. Maybe karma was the best revenge.

I took a deep breath and evaluated how to take back control of the situation.

Tiffany was protected by the airbags and seatbelt. Yeah, she'd have a few bumps and bruises, but she kept a firm grip on her firearm despite the jolts as we tumbled across the desert sand and gravel. I didn't have to worry about her accidentally shooting herself.

Or me.

The gasoline I'd tried to conserve splashed all over the place. All it would take was a spark from the SUV's metal hitting a rock, and Tiffany and I would be barbequed.

Not that it would kill me, but it would kill Tiffany, and it would still hurt like hell.

I telekinetically sealed the tank by pinching and folding the metal shut. I'd need the remaining fuel for my plan.

The ball I'd made out of the rear window's safety glass was bouncing around the interior. A glass ball coated with enough demon blood to kill Tiffany if it hit her in the wrong place. We didn't need to deal with acidic third degree burns on our skin in the best-case scenario either. I shot the ball out the back window.

It bounced once before it shattered. The blood wouldn't hurt our pursuers, but I heard the earth itself cry out in agony.

Somehow, the SUV landed right side up. I cast an illusion of Tiffany and I slumped in our seats. Unfortunately, it wasn't too far from the truth where my sister-in-law was concerned.

I took quick stock of what we needed. Her messenger bag with extra clips was already slung over her body, her gun still in her hand. I summoned a couple of water bottles out of the hatch, unlocked our seatbelts, and grabbed Tiffany's arm.

Less than a thought later, I lowered her to a sitting position on an outcrop a mile away. A horde of dino demons surrounded the smoking, steaming vehicle. There were maybe about three dozen but they wouldn't stop moving long enough for me to get an accurate head count. After chittering amongst themselves, they cautiously approached the crumpled body of Tiffany's SUV. I shoved the water bottles into my coat pocket.

"What's—"

Shhh. She listened to my silent shushing. At least I hadn't rattled all of her brain cells out of her head when I rolled her vehicle. I concentrated and pressurized the gasoline inside the SUV's battered tank.

The broken radiator whistled and hissed. The demons whistled and hissed back. In their bizarre language, they debated whether the illusion of me was truly an unconscious me. Finally, the entire horde crept closer.

Goodnight, demons. I snapped my fingers, more for showmanship than necessity, and ignited the precious few gallons of aerosolized gasoline still in the SUV's tank. The size of the explosion would have given Michael Bay an orgasm.

The dying demons screamed, shrieked, and ran around the desert like chickens with their heads burning off. Of course, my stomach decided to gurgle at the delightful stench my nose picked up even from this far away.

Tiffany looked up at me. "Seriously? You're still hungry?"

"Not really."

My stomach contradicted me.

Tiffany wearily waved a hand toward her burning vehicle. "Go eat before we both regret it."

"I'll pass this time. They're all going to taste like gasoline." I sat down next to her and pulled a couple of Twinkies out of my pocket. "Want one?"

"No, thank you." She fished in her messenger bag, pulled out a small white bottle, and popped the top. She glared at the bottle. "I hate swallowing pills dry."

I reached into my other coat pocket for a water bottle and handed it to her. Plastic wrap crinkled loudly when I tore open the Twinkie package, now that the SUV fire had died along with the demons.

"Thanks." She shook out a couple of extra-strength pain killers and tossed them in her mouth before she took a long drink. "The rangers are going to be pissed when they find a burned-out wreck in the middle of Death Valley."

"I know." I took a bite of my snack cake.

"When the National Park Service contacts me about the wreck, I'm going to tell them my sister-in-law borrowed my vehicle. And that if she left my precious in the middle of a national park, she will be paying all fines and fees."

"Of course you will."

"And she will be buying me a goddamn brand-new SUV."

"What have I said about taking a deity's name in vain?"

"I used the non-specific little 'g.'" Tiffany took another long drink of water. She looked at me. "What next now that you've sprung Giovanni's trap?"

"This wasn't the trap. The demons were just the appetizer intended to kill anyone with me." I licked the vanilla crème off my fingers.

She started to shake her head, then obviously thought better of it. "Giovanni can't be thinking of siccing just vamps on you."

I looked over my shoulder toward the road that led into Death Valley. "The dino demons have ways, types of magick, that can trap human gods. They did it before with Ares."

Tiffany took a third swig before she twisted the cap back on the bottle. "I hope you're not planning to walk there. Between twisting my ankle back in Orange County and you rolling my SUV, I don't think I can handle a long hike."

For Tiffany to admit her Normal limits meant she was in a lot more pain than she was letting on.

"I can take you back to Los Angeles."

Instead of the Tiffany-tantrum I expected, she sighed. There was a ton of exhaustion in that sound. "No, if that asshole does have my daughter out here, we need to find her." She didn't dare say anything about Caesar asking us to stall. Not out here where someone, or some thing, could be watching and listening to us.

"Okay." I held out my hand to help her stand. Once she was upright, I didn't let go. "Short 'port. Ready?"

Her eyes narrowed because she knew I didn't do anything halfway. "You're just trying to make me yak."

"Yep." I concentrated. We popped back into reality outside a group of rusty corrugated steel buildings and equally rusty equipment, all part of an abandoned mine site. Despite her accusation, I tried to make the 'port as smooth as silk for her.

However, it didn't stop Tiffany from grabbing my arm when she wobbled for a moment. When she gained her equilibrium, she looked around us. *What are we looking for?*

We were behind an ancient ore conveyor, but that didn't mean the rogues hadn't spotted us yet. I took a deep breath of the night air. No sandalwood, and the slight odor of reptiles could be the normal denizens of the valley. However, the demons could be casting an odor masking spell for all I knew.

Or had shape-shifted into decrepit, rust-coated machinery.

The quiet reassured me that we were right about Giovanni's plans. No coyote cries nearby. No scrabbling of rodents foraging. Between the unnatural silence and the black diamond tracking spell leading here, this had to be a trap. He wanted us chasing our tails while he prepared to sacrifice my niece.

I met Tiffany's gaze. *Not sure. Where would you hide a hostage if you were a dinosaur demon?*

She drew her gun and glared at me simultaneously. *I'm not the one who cast the tracking spell, bitch.*

The spell leads to that building. I pointed to the smallest of the group. It looked like it had been some sort of office. *But just because that's where the DNA trail of the jerk in Orange County ends doesn't mean Ellie or Giovanni are in there.*

Then we split up and search the other buildings before we trigger the trap. Give Caesar as much time as we can. Tiffany started around the conveyor, but I grabbed her arm.

We are not splitting up. Or did you already forget the attack on the road?

She made a soft little snorting sound. *I haven't forgotten you rolled, then blew up, my SUV.*

We're doing this together, I emphasized. *You don't have to worry about any vampires under your protection getting deep-fried when the sun comes up.*

She leaned back and looked at the top of the conveyor. *How soon is sunrise?*

A little over an hour. My attention fell from the rusting piece of steel and rotted belting to Tiffany. *What's your plan?*

She grinned at me. *How good are you at time travelling?*

My cast-iron stomach twisted at the thought. *You can't seriously be serious about this.*

Seriously serious as a heart attack. We've been here for at least a minute. Whoever's here, vampires or demons, have to know we're on site by now. We jump ahead to sunrise. You blow down the building to fry the rogues. I'll shoot any demons that come out.

I threw my arms up. "I don't—"

She hissed at me.

I don't even know if time travel is possible. Your foster grandfather had to show me how to teleport. He hasn't said anything about travelling through time.

I'm open to an alternate plan.

I looked back up at the tip of the conveyor. *What if I flush them out of the buildings, and you shoot them?*

That means separating. Amazing how much snide her mental voice could pack.

I glared at her. *I'm not the one who wants to sit on top of a rusting structure that could collapse at any moment.*

Got a better plan?

I didn't, and we both knew it. *Fine. You win.*

Tiffany holstered her sidearm and climbed onto the conveyor. The metal creaked ominously as she made her way up the incline. Her breath steamed in the chill air. Flakes of rust fell from the frame. However, she was right. She'd have a perfect view of most of the old mining complex.

Once she gave me a thumbs up to indicate she was settled, I strode toward the closest building. The padlock on the double doors was as rusty as the corrugated walls. With a thought and an obscene screech of metal, I tore off the doors and tossed them aside.

Nothing inside, and no one came to investigate the noise. What the hell were the bad guys waiting for?

Me to do something really stupid, I answered my internal voice.

Nothing was inside the warehouse besides a couple of piles of stones and a pickax as rusty as every other piece of metal I'd encountered so far. I continued the circuit around the old facility. Some buildings were locked up. Some weren't. Each one had a piece or two of discarded equipment, but no vampires or dino demons could be found. Despite the fact I deliberately dragged my feet, it only took a few minutes to check all the buildings.

All except the one where my tracking spell terminated.

Tiffany's nervousness crackled along the edge of my psyche while I crossed to that last door. Whatever shit Giovanni and his demon buddies planned would start the minute I entered this particular abandoned shop.

I wrenched the doorknob out of its mooring. The hinges groaned as the door swung open. The dry stink of a chicken coop reminded me of the rare summers I spent with my grandmother on her farm in West Virginia. When nothing rushed me, I stepped inside and immediately regretted that decision.

Eggs filled every inch of space on shelves and desks not taken by straw, twigs, and dried grass. They definitely weren't chicken eggs. Hell, they weren't even ostrich eggs. And every single one of them were quivering and cracking.

The demon we had killed in Orange County must have been their daddy. Or their mommy. Even worse, these things were born fully sentient with their demon parent's knowledge and experience at their beck and call. I wasn't going to get lucky they were stupid when hatched.

And a year ago, I'd learned the hard way the babies were just as deadly as their full-grown counterparts.

With one step, I was out the door and pulling it shut behind me. I concentrated. The door glowed red-hot under the spotlights my eyes had become. Unfortunately, there was barely any non-oxidized steel left in the frame. My temporary weld wouldn't hold long.

Sam, what's wrong?

I just became Ellen Ripley. The door shuddered under a blow from inside. It was followed by a glass-shattering scream of pain. We were fucked the minute they found the windows.

How many? Tiffany's voice felt ice cold in my head.

From the smell, over a hundred. I backed away from the office when more thumps and bangs knocked hunks of rust from the outer part of the wall I faced. They knew exactly where I was.

Just like the damn demon fetus inside of Alyson Tribideaux last year had.

Sam, can you heat up the rest of the building? Broil the suckers?

I can, but after what happened at La Brea, my guess is the resurrection spell that was used on the dead one with the bomb has already been cast on these hatchlings. I don't think I can eat them all before they rip me apart.

Tiffany spewed a few colorful phrases out loud, followed by clanking sounds coming from the conveyor. *We need to get out of here.*

We can't let these things run wild. They're too close to Fort Irwin.

She pounded up next to me. "So we warn Colonel Smith on our way back to Los Angeles." She was right. No sense using telepathy since they knew we were here.

"And what if they decide Las Vegas holds better tasting snacks?"

We stared at each other for what seemed like an eternity before she muttered, "Fuck. I've only got four extra clips in my bag."

I laughed, but the sound had a hysterical edge to my own ears. "Even if you shoot half of them, what about the other half when they're finished eating us?"

Tiffany stared at the old office. More dents formed in the corrugated steel. "What's the one thing you can do that they can't?"

The part of me that was still human gibbered in the back of my mind. "Deliver sharp-witted sarcasm?"

"No!" She punched my bicep. I missed the old days when Tiffany hitting me still hurt. "Teleport! Take the whole fucking building and drop it on Pluto!"

I rubbed my chin as I considered her idea. "That may not kill them." The little bastards continued to throw themselves against the front wall, and the door now that it had cooled enough. If I moved from this side of the building, they would discover the windows.

Then we'd really be in trouble.

"It doesn't have to kill them, but they can't eat us from there." Tiffany gestured at the shuddering steel. "The office is constructed on a slab. You have super-strength. Pick it up, and take it to Pluto. Even if they live, they can't get back here and kill anyone."

"I've never 'ported that much mass before," I whispered. The last thing I wanted was to shred myself into atoms. But if I stood here and did nothing—

A ripping talon pried up a corner of an overlapping sheet of corrugated steel. A yellow eye peered through the opening. The just-hatched demon met my gaze, and it screamed instructions at its siblings. Metallic groans and pops filled the night as steel bent and rusted sections broke.

Shit. The building would only last a couple of more seconds.

I turned to Tiffany. "Get back! Now!"

My voice sounded alien to my own ears. Whatever she saw in my face made her listen. She pivoted and ran.

I concentrated and reached out with my power. As I feared, the slab had cracked from the torrential rains that pummeled Death Valley a few years ago. I couldn't simply pick up the slab with my hands. And I didn't have time to draw a blood circle in the sand and gravel around the building to contain the demons.

As Tiffany had suggested, I heated the corrugated steel, but just enough to drive the demons to the center of the slab. I just hoped my telekinesis was strong enough to hold the slab together.

For good luck, I resorted to one of my old tricks of imitating one of my favorite TV characters. I folded my arms over my chest and nodded.

Everything went black, and I screamed as someone drove a railroad spike through my brain.

Chapter 27

Tiffany

When the dust cleared, I turned my phone on, activated the flashlight application, and shone it towards the gap in the buildings. "Sam?"

The desert was as silent as it had been when we first arrived. I shuffled closer. A gigantic crater sat where the office building full of demons and Sam had stood a moment before. Water from a sliced pipe about a foot down from the edge of the pit dribbled into the hole.

Sam will be back for me.

Comforting myself with that sweet little lie, I limped back to the conveyor and sat on the control box. My ears still rung from the massive air displacement. And I really hoped the scream I'd heard right before the building vanished was one of the demons and not my sister-in-law.

I propped up my injured ankle as best as I could on a gear to alleviate the swelling. I'd twisted it pretty good back in Orange County, but it wasn't broken. As much as I wanted to pull my boot off and massage it, I couldn't. I'd never get my boot back on if I did, and the last thing I needed was to be running through one of the hottest deserts on the face of the planet in my socks if more bad guys showed up.

A deep breath helped calm me. If things had gone to shit with Sam, I still had a decent charge on my phone. Grandpa Ares was a tap of the speed-dial away. Or I could call the Las Vegas branch of the coven for a ride in the worst-case scenario.

So I waited until the sun peeked over the eastern mountains before I called Caesar's direct line. Except he wasn't the one who answered his phone.

"Tiffany, are you all right?" Anne's words came in a rush.

"I'm fine—"

I could hear arguing in the background, something clicked, then the tinny voice of Alex on the speaker phone came on the line. "What's your status?"

"We've got a bigger problem. The demons are breeding among themselves, and they had a hundred eggs waiting for us at an office building of an abandoned mine, all primed to hatch as soon as they felt Sam nearby. She thought they had the same resurrection spell on them as the demon at La Brea. Anyway, she teleported the whole kit and caboodle to Pluto, or that was her plan." I really didn't need my boss yelling at me because it had been my suggestion of how to get rid of the little assholes. Sam could tell Alex when she got back.

If she came back.

"Where is she now?" Anne asked.

"Good question." I shaded my eyes to scan around me. "She left roughly an hour ago, and she hasn't returned."

"Are you in any shape to drive back to Los Angeles?" Alex asked.

"I would be if I had a vehicle," I said sourly.

My boss chuckled. "Should we even ask?"

"My darling sister-in-law rolled my SUV and then blew it up."

"Are you sure you're all right?" Concern laced Anne's voice.

"Yes. Why?" I snapped.

"Every other word isn't a curse word," she said dryly.

A muffled pop made me jump, but it wasn't Sam. Grandpa Ares looked at me, frowned, and shook his head. "Oh, Cherry Blossom."

He snatched my phone from me before I could protest. "Alexander, Tiffany has been injured. I'm taking her straight to Doctor Zachary."

His frown deepened at whatever Alex was telling him. "No, I don't sense Samantha anywhere. If she had a problem while disposing of the demon hatchlings, she may be masking herself."

Another pause, then Ares said, "Very well." He handed the phone to me, but Alex had already ended the call from his side.

I glared at my foster grandfather. "When are you ever going to learn to say good-WHOA!"

He'd scooped me into his arms, which I had to admit made a girl feel delicate even when she's married, and 'ported to Good Samaritan Hospital before I could finish my sentence.

Bebe yelped and jumped up from the CCU waiting room couch where she'd obviously been talking with Uncle Duncan and Max's parents, Ted and Elizabeth. They all stood as well.

"Alexander was supposed to call you—" Bebe's personal cell ringing interrupted Ares.

The doctor shook her head, rolled her eyes, and thumbed the icon to answer. "I know. They just arrived." A pause, and Bebe's eyes narrowed. "Let me check Tiffany. If she shows up here, I'll call."

Duncan's eyes glowed neon green. "Samantha was supposed to be with you."

The pressure building inside me since I got home and found Max beaten unconscious didn't just crack. It exploded my soul into tiny bits. "I'm sorry I lost your wife! But my husband's in a fucking coma and my daughter's about to be sacrificed, so excuse me if she's not my number one priority at the moment!"

Displaced air popped behind us. Ares still held me and turned so fast it made me dizzy.

Sam swayed next to the soda machine. She'd lost the elastic band for her ponytail, and her hair looked like she'd stuck her head in a blender. Or a hurricane. Frost covered every inch of her. "Tiffany didn't lose me."

The voice coming from her throat sounded like a certain cartoon female rodent I'd heard too much of thanks to Ellie and the Disney Channel. Sam slapped her hands over her mouth. The motion must have been too much for her damaged equilibrium. She started to fall.

Duncan rushed over to catch her, but the instant he touched her, he cried out and jerked away. They both collapsed to the tile.

A wave of household cleaner fumes hit me, and my eyes watered. Duncan started coughing and choking, leaving no doubt my sister-in-law was the source of the awful stench. Bebe and Ted charged forward, hooked their arms under Duncan's, and dragged him away from Sam. The doctor knelt beside my uncle and checked his hands.

"The demons started magickally fighting my containment sphere—" Sam squeaked as she pushed herself into a sitting position. The ice crystals on her hair, skin, and clothes vaporized and sent another blast of the ammonia smell through the waiting room. "Aw, fuck! Why do I sound like fucking Minnie Mouse?"

"Samantha!" Elizabeth snapped. "Stop swearing!"

"'Fuck' is the only word I can use without summoning another supernatural deity," Sam squeaked indignantly. She was right. She sounded exactly like Minnie Mouse.

"You can say 'shit,'" I volunteered. Everyone gave me dirty looks. Everyone except Ares who laughed his ass off.

"Where'd you leave the demons, Sam?" I said.

"I was passing Jupiter when I lost my grip on them," she said. "I got dragged into the planetary atmosphere. Last I saw them, the demons were still falling towards the core." Her voice didn't have quite the ear-splitting, high-pitched quality it had a minute ago.

"Keep taking deep breaths and exhaling as much as you can," I said. "When Kuiper Explorer did its flyby a couple of years ago, it confirmed Jupiter's upper atmosphere had a higher helium content than NASA originally thought. You've been breathing it, hydrogen, and from your smell, a bit of methane and ammonia as well."

Ted poked at his glasses, the same gesture I'd seen Max do a million times. "That should have killed her."

"Samantha is no longer human, Theodore," Ares said softly.

The expression that crossed my father-in-law's face was a mix of horror and sadness. Reality had finally sunk in. The little girl he doted on was gone.

I looked down at Bebe, who was checking Duncan's hands. "Is his frostbite healing?"

"Yes," Bebe muttered. She eyed Duncan. "You're going to need blood."

"Come on, son." Ted helped my uncle to his feet. "Elizabeth and I will take you down to the cafeteria." He gave Bebe a pointed look.

The doctor's expression shifted to worry. She rose and wouldn't meet my gaze. "Sam?"

My sister-in-law waved at me. "Tiffany's the one who's injured. She went down hard on her ankle in Orange County, and she was in her SUV when I rolled it. I'll be fine once I warm up." She rubbed her breast bone. "And once my internal organs are no longer Jell-o."

Ares crossed to a wheelchair parked in a corner and gently set me on the vinyl seat. "Doctor Zachary, while you take care of Tiffany, I will watch Samantha and guard Maxwell."

Bebe stiffened. The family had backed her into a corner, and she didn't like it one bit. My heart sank. It meant Max had taken a turn for the worse.

It also meant Ares was telling Sam the bad news because he was in a better position to mitigate anything she might do accidentally out of rage or grief.

Without a word, Bebe grabbed the handles of the wheelchair and pushed me toward the elevator. She pressed the button. I counted to thirty before the indicator dinged, and the doors parted.

She stayed behind me the entire time. Once the doors closed and we started moving, I stared at the doors and said, "How bad?"

"We don't know. It hasn't been twelve hours yet." There was so much pain in her voice. If I looked at her, I'd start bawling, and I'd be no use to Max or Ellie. So I let her lie go.

For now.

"My ankle's sprained, not broken," I said. "I just need a painkiller, and I'll be out of your hair so you can focus on Max." The elevator dinged again and the doors parted.

"How about I do the medical analysis, Doctor Stephens?" She pushed me out of the elevator and into the too-familiar ER section of this wing.

Technically, this wasn't the official emergency and trauma area of Good Samaritan Hospital. On paper, it was the Laura Lannigan Cancer Center. Siobhan's mom had died of the disease back before the supernaturals had any organized medicine. No one was sure why or how a werewolf managed to contract cancer in the first place. Bebe had pushed and nagged the vampires, witches, and weres into a joint service. The amount of money the covens and pack dumped into the so-called cancer center meant the hospital's board of directors didn't ask too many questions about what Bebe and the other supernatural and Family doctors did here.

And no one at the LLCC called conventional law enforcement for gunshot wounds and other reportable shit either. Because, really, what could the LAPD do when they were up against stuff like rabid werewolves, rogue vampires, and dino demons?

Bebe wheeled me into an examination room. Despite her protest, I got out of the chair and onto the examination table under my own power. Having my foster grandfather carry me was one thing. Having an Augustine member or one of the Lannigan Pack haul me around bodily was another.

Bebe checked my vitals and a sweet radiology tech named Alisha took pictures of my ankle. After Alisha rolled her equipment away, Bebe's step-grandfather Benjamin Epstein entered the room. From the white fringe framing his shiny bald spot to the dress shoes he always wore, he was the quintessential retired Jewish doctor. But he was a healer within the Los Angeles witch coven, whereas Bebe, for all her magickal power and surgical talent, had to rely on conventional medicine.

I held up my right index finger and waggled it at him. "No."

He gave me the stern grandpa look that Ares would never accomplish in a million years. "Young lady, this is not a time to argue—"

"Old man, you need to be helping my husband." I smacked Bebe's hands away from me before I turned my eyes and finger back to Ben. "And I need to find my daughter, which means I need a painkiller for my ankle, and I'll be on my way."

Bebe crossed her arms over her way-more-ample-than-mine chest. "When was the last time you ate and slept?"

"Denny's after the rogues blew up La Brea and napped in my SUV on the way to Death Valley."

"Then here's the deal." Bebe's eyes narrowed. "Either you let Grandpa heal you, or I'll give you more than just a painkiller for that ankle."

The first two fingers of her right hand curled and twitched. From the corner of my eye, a hypodermic needle rose from an instrument tray and hovered over my arm.

"You wouldn't," I growled.

The corner of her mouth curved up. "Your grandfather will be the first to tell you I don't bluff."

By now, every supernatural had heard the story of my foster grandfather's wandering hands and Doctor Zachary's retaliation. And she was right. She didn't bluff. So I considered my very few options.

I exhaled and met Ben's gaze. "Just tell me why you aren't with my husband right now, and then I'll let you do your mojo."

"I can't roll back time, Tiffany." His raspy voice carried too much weight. "Neither can any other witch. He was unattended for nearly a half hour. I healed his skull fracture, but I can't stop his body from reacting to the original trauma. I can't stop his brain from swelling, and that's our current problem."

My eyes threatened to overflow anyway, and I swiped at them hard. "I should have been there."

"No." Bebe grabbed my arm. Her fingernails dug into my muscles, but it was just another ache in a whole catalog. "It's a good thing you weren't. Ellie can't—" She pursed her lips and reconsidered her words. "Ellie needs you. Let us help you help her."

Bebe was right. And I was letting my fear for Max get in the way. The situation had to be considered as if it were any other retrieval job. I sucked in a deep breath and nodded. The hypodermic floated back to its place on the rolling medical equipment tray.

Once I'd ditched my jacket and equipment, Ben had me lie down on the table. I hated healing spells. Maybe it's different for the supernaturals, but intimate magick felt like an army of ants crawled under my skin. It took all my willpower not to wiggle. If I did, Bebe really would shoot me full of sedatives, and I didn't have the time.

Ellie didn't have the time.

"Tiffany?" Bebe's voice, and she was shaking me.

I blinked. Somehow, I'd fallen asleep. "You better not have drugged me, bitch."

"You did this one on your own." Her fingers pressed against my wrist. "A half-hour power nap wasn't going to hurt you." She released me. "How do you feel?"

I stretched. A little fatigue still plagued my muscles, but the aches and pain from earlier this morning were gone. "Better."

"Where did you get that knife?" She nodded towards my equipment.

"Ares gave it to me to kill demons. Why?"

Bebe nodded as if my answer confirmed something she suspected. "When my grandfather started his healing spell, the knife started feeding energy to the spell itself."

My heartbeat jumped. "It didn't harm Ben, did it?"

"No." She clasped my hand and pulled me to a sitting position. "It was almost like it was sentient and trying to help him heal you. I just hope it's not..."

I waited but she didn't finish her thought. "Sucking out my soul, or the souls of those I kill?"

Her cheeks flamed dark rose. "My grandfather wouldn't give me a questionable magick object."

"You're just jealous because my grandpa is sexier than your grandpa." I stuck my tongue out at Bebe.

She rolled her eyes. "There's no appropriate comeback to that statement."

"Then I win."

"Just be careful with that thing."

"Only killing demons with it." I jumped off the exam table. No pain in my ankle. Not even a bit of tenderness. I jogged in place and did a few jumping jacks to test it.

"Go to your gym if you're going to work out," Bebe growled. "Or at least stop by the cafeteria before you and Sam head out again."

"Yes, ma'am." I immediately sobered. "Keep him alive. Just until I get my baby back. I can't lose them both. Not today."

"I'll do my best," Bebe said quietly.

"Thanks." It was all I could ask of her, and probably more than she could deliver, but I'd take any little favor I could get at the moment.

After grabbing my jacket and gear, I headed down the hallway, but hesitated at the elevator. Seeing Max broken in his hospital bed would break me, too, but maybe what people said about hearing their loved ones while in a coma was true. He needed to know he hadn't failed our daughter, and that I was working on getting her back.

I jabbed the button, and the bell instantly dinged. Two floors later, the doors opened into an empty CCU waiting room. I pushed the swinging doors leading to the unit. The night shift's head RN, one of Caesar's multitude of Normal nieces, nodded as I passed the nurses' station. Thankfully, she didn't say anything.

"M. Howell" was written in neat script on a white board under the room number of the first door I reached. I sucked in a deep breath before I entered my husband's room. Grandpa Ares sat in the guest chair, holding a magazine.

"To contour your cheek bones, start with a medium brush and the darker hue of blush—"

"What the hell are you reading to him?" I muttered.

"*Cosmopolitan.* Elizabeth left it here." Ares frowned and shrugged. "Duncan was reading Maxwell the article on ten techniques to keep a man happy in bed—"

That spurred a half-hearted chuckle from me. "No, he wasn't."

"But it made you laugh, Cherry Blossom." Ares's smile didn't quite reach his eyes. "And where there's laughter, there's life."

"Where's Sam?"

"She went down to the cafeteria." He turned and set the women's magazine on the rolling stand parked behind his chair. When his gaze met mine again, he was totally serious. "I suggest you take her to Caesar's to ingest more demon meat before you confront your foes."

"All right." I wanted him with me, but the gods had their stupid rules, especially when it came to the Old Ones. And he couldn't interfere because this whole mess with the dino demons over the last year was part of Sam's rite of passage as a new death goddess, or some other such bullshit. We needed to find a way around the stupid rule. We needed the help.

I needed the help.

I needed my daughter back.

I needed my husband whole.

I beat down the pain that threatened to erupt inside me. "You'll stay here with him, right?"

"No one else will inflict more harm to Maxwell, Cherry Blossom." He rose and kissed my forehead. "Spend some time with your husband. I'll be outside until you are done." The door silently closed behind Ares.

For the first time, I took a good look at Max. Tubes came out of nearly every natural orifice, and a few unnatural ones. The medical team had shaved his head from the bits of scalp showing between the bandages. He'd be pissed when he woke up though he'd never admit his receding hairline bothered him.

The click-hiss of the ventilator sounded obscenely loud. Scrapes and bruises still cover his skin because the witches had focused their spells in his major injuries. I gently stroked a spot on his bicep that wasn't discolored.

"Hey, sweetie, it's me." I swallowed the hard lump in my throat. "I'm sorry I haven't been here with you. We're still looking for Ellie. We captured one of Giovanni's rogues. Caesar's questioning her now. You know I won't give up until our baby is home safe."

I wished he'd wake up, and make a joke about him being the damsel in distress. Even just wink at me. "I love you, and I'm proud of you. And I know you fought to save our little girl. Otherwise, you wouldn't be here in the hospital right now."

The lump came back and threatened to choke me. "But I need you to get better, Maxwell Theodore Howell. You're the one who said we had to raise Ellie together. I'm holding you to that because I *will* bring her home." I blinked.

The water running down my face was not tears. I couldn't let them be tears. Ellie didn't have time for her mother to cry.

I sniffed and wiped the offending moisture away. "Hang on, Max. Tomorrow is Ellie's birthday, and you *will not die* on her birthday. You hear me, Max?"

His eyelids fluttered. Hope fluttered with them, but his action was probably involuntary.

I gently squeezed the undamaged spot on his arm. "Your mom and dad will be back soon. Bebe made them go get something to eat. Ares and Duncan are both here, too. I'll be back as soon as I can." I stood and rushed out of the hospital room.

If I didn't, I would die along with my husband and my daughter.

Chapter 28

Max

I'm here! I hear you! I love you! Max screamed in his head.

But his wife couldn't hear him. Hell, not even Bebe and Duncan with all their vaunted telepathic talents could hear him.

Max listened to Tiffany's bootsteps fade away. His head wasn't as fuzzy as before, but he still couldn't move. God knew he'd tried while she'd been sitting beside him.

Why had she come to the hospital? She'd be the first in line to torture the assholes who had taken Ellie. Unless Caesar and Alex had kicked her out for losing control.

And when it came to Ellie, Max could definitely see his wife losing control. If the vampires wanted to interrogate the rogue, he or she needed to be alive to answer those questions. The last thing anyone wanted was Sam resurrecting a vampire.

Except . . .

Why weren't Ares and Duncan in on the hunt for Ellie? There wasn't a thing either man wouldn't do for Tiffany. Or Ellie for that matter. But they were here, guarding him. And Mom and Dad hadn't left the hospital either.

Which meant things were far worse than his family were revealing in their bedside confessionals to him.

He may not be able to do much in his barely functioning body, but Tiffany was right. He couldn't die on Ellie's birthday. That kind of shit would haunt his daughter for the rest of her life.

No, he couldn't do that to either Ellie or Tiffany. All he had to do was hold on until they rescued his daughter. And if they found her in time, all he had to do was hang on until November.

Two days.

He could make it two days.

Chapter 29

Sam

When I entered the cafeteria, I wasn't as upset about the turn in Max's condition as I was with Mom's stupidity. Ares wasn't afraid of her, which was why he narced. No one else in the coven would have told me what she planned or what she'd done.

Not even my own husband, even though Ares had pointed out Duncan had told Mom he wouldn't do it. Did she even understand how much her wanting him to Turn my brother would have hurt Duncan?

Why couldn't she have stopped the damage there?

I marched over to the table where my parents sat with my husband. A good chunk of the hospital's first shift decided that whatever odor, vibe, or eye color I gave off wasn't worth sticking around for food. Only a handful of hungry weres and the kitchen staff decided to risk their lives for breakfast and a little pre-work entertainment.

"One of your children being a freak wasn't enough, Mom?" I snarled.

Her haughty, noveau riche expression appeared on her Botoxed face. "I have no idea what you are blathering about, Samantha. Sit down or leave, but quit making a scene." But her quick glance at Duncan confirmed Ares's story.

I clenched my fists to keep from giving in to the urge to slap her holier-than-thou attitude out of her. I'd kill her if I hit her now.

Maybe that wasn't a bad thing.

"Duncan didn't tell me, Mom. He didn't have to. Did you really think you could hide anything from me or Ares?"

"Samantha, neither I nor anyone else in the coven will ignore Max's wishes in this matter," Duncan said quietly.

"Except Mother Dearest here didn't stop with you, honey." I glared at her. "Did you?"

Dad's mouth opened and closed a couple of times before he choked out, "What did you do, Elizabeth?"

Mom's attention dropped to the paper napkin she was folding and unfolding. "It was nothing."

"It was not nothing!" I whirled and glared at the remaining bystanders. "Get out!"

You know shit's bad when even werewolves run.

I turned back to her, yanked her chair away from the table, curled my palms around the back of her chair, and got in her face. "Tell them, Mom. Tell Dad and Duncan how you put the entire coven in danger."

"I-I only made some phone calls," she murmured.

"To who?" Dad asked.

A neon green glow lit our table area as Duncan did the math. "Did you contact anyone other than the other United States coven masters?"

"No," Mom whispered. Her full attention was on me. Whites ringed her blue irises, and the ashy scent of fear rolled off her body.

"Like we don't have enough shit to deal with while we're looking for Ellie." The plastic chair back cracked under my grip. "Do you even understand what you did, Mom? How many people could die besides Max because all you could think about was yourself?"

I pushed away from Mom and hugged myself before I could crack her like I did the chair. When Caesar took me in after what the mad scientists at Mallory Labs had done to me, I agreed to abide by the Vampire Nation's rules. The vamps were sticklers about their rules for this very reason. And Caesar had been dancing on the edge of an all-out civil war for seven years, thanks to his twin sister's machinations.

The same machinations that had created me and endangered the lives of Max and Ellie now.

"B-but there's an alliance." Dad's incredulous look shifted from Mom to me, then Duncan, looking for some reassurance.

"Not if it appears that Caesar cannot control his own people," Duncan said. "Elizabeth, I suggest you not be in my presence for a while. Go to Ares."

Mom stood and smoothed her skirt. Her mouth opened, but a dirty look from me changed her mind about whatever stupid thing she was about to say.

Once she was gone, I took the seat next to Duncan and reached for his hand. A little relief seeped into me when his fingers curled around mine.

"How did—" Dad cleared his throat. "How did you know, Sam?" In other words, had I invaded Mom's mind, and would I do it to him?

"Ares overheard her on the phone." I squeezed Duncan's hand when I looked at him. "By the way, he wasn't trying to piss you off or leave you out. He thought it would be better if I dealt with her."

"Because you would be gentler in correcting her?"

I blew a raspberry. "Puh-lease! We both know that's not the case, but I am going to have to tell Caesar." My words were for Dad's benefit, not my husband's.

"What will Master Augustine do?" Dad's demeanor was a weird combination of worried and hopeful.

"Normal Family members are required to obey the same laws as we are," Duncan said. "You and Elizabeth agreed to those laws in return for not having your memories wiped after the zombie incident in your own backyard. By contacting the other masters behind Caesar's back, and especially by asking for a non-consenting Normal to be Turned, Elizabeth is technically guilty of treason."

The blood drained from Dad's face. Good. At least, one of my parents understood the ramifications of Mom's actions.

"Maybe I should take her home," he muttered.

"You must not," Duncan said. "We cannot spare any resources to watch your house right now. Giovanni wishes to finish his grandmother's work and wipe out my mortal line. The dino demons desire the same thing for Samantha's family. While we are both furious with Elizabeth, we do not wish her or you dead."

"Speak for yourself," I muttered.

When both Dad and Duncan gave me shocked looks, I amended my statement. "Only in Mom's case, not yours, Dad."

"I'll pretend I didn't hear that, young lady." He ran a hand over his bald spot. "I suppose we should have taken her phone away from her."

I sighed. "Taken care of already, Dad. Just please don't let her use your phone."

"You lifted her phone?" Duncan looked impressed.

Now, I wish I'd thought of that first. "No. I blew the electronics when I yelled at her."

"Then I'd best get back to CCU so she's not harassing the nurses." Dad rose and a couple of his vertebrae popped. "Does the cafeteria staff have permission to come back in so I can get more coffee, or is the lack of caffeine part of my punishment?"

My stomach chose that moment to rumble. "Send them back in before I start eating the patients."

He rounded the table, bent, and kissed me on my forehead. I watched his stooped form shuffle out of the room.

"When did my dad get old?" I whispered.

Duncan pulled me close and held me. "I tried to explain this to you."

"I know," I mumbled against his suit jacket. "Sorry about the frostbite." I closed my eyes and enjoyed the simplicity of this moment.

His chuckle vibrated against my cheek. "I should learn to check if it is safe before I touch you. I wasn't expecting your temperature to be near absolute zero."

Pots and pans banged in the background. Voices were muted, supernaturals afraid to disturb the monster in their presence.

"I'm sorry for acting like an obsessed bitch over the last year."

Duncan squeezed my shoulder. "We will discuss our relationship once you find Ellie. She is your priority at the moment."

A tray clattered on our table, and I opened my eyes. Tiffany plopped down on the chair Dad had vacated. The odor of her bacon and spinach omelet and English muffin set off my stomach again. But she no longer had the faint bitter herb scent of physical pain.

Even without the miasma of emotional pain surrounding her, I knew she'd been crying, but I wasn't about to mention the tear stains on her cheeks. If it wasn't for my rewritten DNA, I wouldn't have been able to see the salt crystals. She must have gone up to see Max after Bebe had one of the healers work on her ankle.

Tiffany pointed her table knife at me. "I know you're not going to like this, but Ares suggested another snack of cola meat before we take our next step." She sliced into her omelet. "Duncan, is the carcass collected in the O.C. at our usual repository?"

"If Alex followed procedure, then yes."

I swallowed the laughter at the edge of my throat at my husband's irritation at her insinuation he hadn't trained his successor as chief enforcer properly.

She forked a huge bite into her mouth. "Give me a chance to scarf breakfast, and we'll head out," she said as she chewed.

"Ack!" I held my hand over my eyes. "Not in the mood for a see-food diet." My stomach rumbled even louder than the last time.

"Maybe you should eat something as well, darling," Duncan said.

Tiffany swallowed before she added, "Just to take the edge off."

The problem was they were both right, and I didn't relish Ares's suggested alternative. After I'd incinerated a demon when it had shoved a tentacle down my throat last year, I should have suspected what would satiate my incredible appetite. Maybe absolute denial was the last human trait I had left.

The witch manning the omelet station watched me warily as I approached, but once I gave her my order, she was a total professional. She didn't even think about spitting in my food.

Just as she handed the tray to me, Tiffany hollered across the cafeteria. "Sam! Make it to go! We got the call!"

Chapter 30

Tiffany

Despite my impatience after Anne's update, Sam insisted I eat my breakfast while she ate hers. At least, I had the excuse and experience of rushing through my meal from being a parent of a small child, not an undead, insatiable appetite.

"Sam, has it occurred to you that your insane hunger might go away after you battle Big Daddy Dino God?" I took a drink of my orange juice.

She paused in mid-bite of her toast. "What makes you say that?"

"I know the idea makes you queasy." I waved my fork. "Hell, my stomach rebelled after what happened in Orange County. But if a few bites from the supernatural-demon crossbreeds can keep you full for nearly twelve hours, think about what a dinosaur god could do for you?"

She laid down her utensils on her third empty plate and shoved it aside as Duncan arrived at our table with another full tray. Sam stared at the plates he set in front of her a moment before her attention returned to me.

She lowered her voice. "Has it occurred to you that the reason I was full is because supernaturals are human beings, and the last full-blood dino demon has crossbred with them?"

I stacked my plate on her empties and leaned back in my chair. No wonder she freaked out last night after she consumed that slice of demon flesh.

My eyes met Duncan's as he resumed his seat, and I saw my own worry reflected in them.

"Unfortunately, we do not have an original full-blood demon to test either of your theories," Duncan said.

I wiped my mouth before I laid my bombshell on them. "That's not exactly true."

"What do you mean?" Sam frowned. "I destroyed the body in Montana."

"After Alex and Bebe took samples." They'd sworn me to secrecy. It had been one of the few truths Alex had admitted to me concerning the incident in Tuttle Creek. And since Sam hadn't been around much over the last year, she hadn't read my mind. Last night, she'd been too busy grossing herself out to pay attention to my thoughts. However, she was right. We needed to test our theories.

From the tickle inside my skull, Sam was reading my mind. She stared at me in horror.

Duncan leaned forward. *I am assuming some of the samples are still here.*

A couple of techs sat down next to us. When I glanced at them, I recognized Alisha, the x-ray gal from earlier. She waved, and I smiled and nodded in return. The were she was with simply scowled at us. He must have been why my uncle had switched to telepathy.

Bebe's research lab, I thought.

Sam jabbed at her French toast. "Is it worth eating this if I'm only going to throw it up?"

"When was the last time you actually vomited? You kept down *all* of last night's barbeque," I said pointedly. From the queasy expression on Duncan's face, Alex had informed him of Sam's post-bomb demon disposal.

She sighed and tore into the fried bread dipped in eggs just like I knew she would.

Ten minutes later in front of the secured biohazard labs, I crossed my arms, tapped the toe of my boot, and glared at my sister-in-law. "I can hack the system."

"I can 'port us in now I know where the lab is." Sam glared back.

"You can blindly teleport to other planets but you can't—"

"How about I simply enter my access code?" Duncan eyed us with a perturbed expression. His index finger hovered over the keypad, which now blinked green. The door hissed as it slid open. "Get inside, you lot."

I threw up my hands. "You could have said you had clearance." I stomped through the door.

"What Goth Girl said." Sam followed me inside.

"Shut up, bitch," I said over my shoulder.

Duncan made a growly sound low in his throat, but didn't say or transmit anything as he entered the lab behind us.

I headed down to the vault and waited for Duncan. It helps when your uncle is the number two vampire in the coven. Once again, he punched in his access code.

When the vault door swung open, I didn't have to point out the correct containers. Sam made a beeline for the dozen wide-mouthed plastic vials on the furthest shelf.

She stopped and stared at them for a long moment before she looked over her shoulder at us. "Maybe you two should wait outside."

I rolled my eyes. "It's not like I'm watching you carve up the demon I just killed."

"Wait. There was a second demon last night?" Duncan's attention flicked from me to Sam and back again.

"A lot more than two if you count the dozen or so that ambushed us at the entrance to Death Valley," I said.

"And that's before you add in the eggs waiting for us inside the park itself," Sam added.

A muscle in Duncan's cheek twitched. "I was not informed about these events."

With his marriage on the fritz, it would be best if I took the brunt of his hurt feelings. "Get your panties out of a wad. You decided to accept the position in Las Vegas, which means you are no longer my boss. Right now, Alex, as our chief enforcer, is doing his job by chasing down leads on Ellie. Our *master* is doing his job, trying to extract more information from the only member of Giovanni's merry band of assholes we've managed to capture alive. If you're going to pull a Selene—"

His posture stiffened more than normal, as I knew it would with the mention of his maker.

"—then stop acting like a whiny nymph and do what you're supposed to. Which is guarding my husband in case Giovanni decides to send in someone to finish the job he started in my home." I jabbed Duncan's chest with my forefinger. "So cut it the fuck out!"

"What are the three of you doing in here?"

I'd like to say we all jumped at Bebe's voice, but only I did. I whirled around to face the witch. "We need to do an experiment before Sam has a nervous breakdown and I shoot my uncle full of silver bullets for acting like a dick."

Bebe's scowl smoothed into concern, but she still had a hand in her lab coat pocket. From the outline, it wasn't a trank gun. "What kind of experiment?"

I faced Sam. "Tell her, or I will." I eased back a step for some clearance and placed my hand on the handle of Ares's knife. Had I just conned Duncan into giving a demon in disguise entrance to Bebe's research? Giovanni would do more than kill for the crap the doc had in here.

"I ate demons tonight." Sam sucked in and blew out a huge breath, and I caught a faint whiff of ammonia. "And Tiffany, if I were a demon in disguise, I would have killed you long before now. Why don't you think it's Duncan or Bebe?"

I shrugged and released my hold on the knife. "They knew the codes." Before I could blink, both Bebe and Duncan had guns pointed at me.

"As much as I would enjoy seeing you two shoot Tiffany, she's clean." Sam pushed the barrel of my uncle's Glock down. "Though it's good you remembered Alex's lecture on not biting dino demons, sweetie."

"How can you be sure?" Bebe's stance didn't relax. "She was out of our sight for a good fifteen minutes."

Sam stepped between us. "She's got Ares's knife, and you're the one who noticed it's bonded with her. While the dino demons may be able to wield a god's weapon, I doubt they can do this kind of link. Lizard Girl sure couldn't with my Incan counterpart's tumi."

Bebe finally relaxed and flicked on the safety. "Alex, told me what happened at La Brea with the resurrected demon, but you're saying there was more than one?"

Sam gave her the rundown of what happened in Orange County, a more thorough account of Death Valley, and the suspicions she laid out at breakfast.

Bebe didn't look too surprised. "I've been wondering some of the same things myself. You sure you want to try this now?"

Sam's big blue eyes were somber. "If it keeps my appetite under control until we find Ellie, yes."

Bebe released a pent-up breath and her shoulders sagged. "Fine. But not in here."

Sam grabbed one of the plastic jars with a section of dino demon flesh, and we trooped out of the refrigerated storage unit. Bebe made my sister-in-law go into the special containment unit built specifically for her. We'd found out the hard way that when her energy became too depleted and she lost control, not even the oldest and strongest of vampires could hold her. Her three baby zombies could control her as long as they had plenty of junk food, but I always wondered if Sam merely recognized them as her creations, and therefore not edible.

Once the door to the unit was secured, we watched Sam through the special window that consisted of five insulated layers of bulletproof glass. She grimaced as she unscrewed the cap.

"It smells like roadkill," she whined.

I leaned closer to the microphone. "It's the only way you'll know for sure."

She pinched off a section of grayish brown meat, closed her eyes and tossed it in her mouth. She made a couple of gagging faces, but she swallowed the hunk and wiped her lips on her coat sleeve.

"That was worse than roadkill," she bitched. "And I love the smell and taste of roadkill!"

"How do you feel?" Bebe asked.

Sam swallowed a couple of times. "Other than needing something to wash down the taste of roadkill marinated in flat Seven-Up, I feel okay."

Bebe made us wait another fifteen minutes before she released the electromagnetic lock and let out Sam. Duncan pulled her into his arms and stroked her hair.

His actions made me keenly aware that my own husband lay upstairs on the cusp between life and death. The stupid throat lump was back. "I need some coffee while you check her out, Doc."

I fled the lab section while trying to look like I wasn't actually running. A breeze warned me before Duncan appeared at my side.

"Tiffany, I want to say thank you."

I stopped in mid-stride and stared at him. "For what?"

"For—" His focus was somewhere else for a long moment. "Maybe this is not the best time."

I crossed my arms. "For having a fucked-up life so your wife will act human a little bit longer."

His face glowed red, a feat he wasn't normally capable of if he hadn't drunk blood recently. "Yes."

I glared at him. "Stop treating her like an incompetent imbecile, and maybe you wouldn't have anything to worry about."

"I do not—" He huffed, but I couldn't deal with his stupid relationship problems anymore. Not today anyway.

"Yes, you do. I know because you've done the same thing to me for nearly a quarter of a century." I shook my head. "It may not be long for you timewise, but for me, it's my entire freakin' life."

I took a step closer and poked his breastbone again. "And while we're at it, you need to listen to her without having a spaz attack. She's still doesn't know what she'll be like once everything is said and done and battled. She needs a little support from you because you know she sure as hell won't get it from Ted and Elizabeth.

"And by the way, you're making the same idiotic mistake my husband makes. Sam's not asking you to fix her problems. She just needs someone to listen without judging."

"I do not judge her—"

"Yeah, you do, Duncan." I scrubbed my hands across my scratchy eyes. Heaven help me, I really needed that coffee. "Just like you judged me for years for not being a good little Elizabethan girl like Grandma Margaret."

A myriad of emotions floated across his face until resignation settled in place. "When did you become your mother?"

His question pleased me and terrified me at the same time. Mom had been my age when she and Dad were murdered. "Probably when I became a parent myself," I answered quietly. "Go be with your wife. I really do need coffee before we head over to Caesar's."

Duncan kissed the top of my head. Air whistled and his form was a blur as he raced up the hallway.

I headed toward the cafeteria, but there wasn't enough double raspberry mochas in the world to reassure me I wouldn't be a widow and childless before this was all over.

Chapter 31

Sam

This time, I teleported to the poolside patio behind Caesar's mansion, instead of the living room. Tiffany immediately dropped to the concrete, which was a good thing because a bullet whizzed toward my head.

I held up my hand. The offending piece of silver and steel halted in mid-air roughly a foot from my left eye. Metal gleamed as it floated under the morning California sunshine. I glared at the werewolf. "Really? Cara? I had to grow back this eye once already in the last twelve hours."

"You're the reason why they banished me outside," the were wailed. "Why didn't you materialize inside the house?"

"Because after the morning I've had so far, I didn't need to get shot," I said.

"This wasn't my fault!" Tears welled and trickled down the girl's suddenly hairy face. She had to be the wimpiest werewolf I'd ever met.

"Please, go home." I rubbed the spot between my eyes. Thanks to the nanites and my rewritten DNA, I didn't get headaches anymore. The sensation was like a phantom itch in my regrown brain that wanted to be a stress headache when it grew up. When she didn't move, I added, "For the love of everything you hold dear in your misbegotten life, Cara Lannigan, go home before I curse you with the fleas from hell."

She whirled and ran for the garage.

Tiffany climbed to her feet. Somehow, she managed not to spill a drop of her double-shot raspberry mocha. She took a sip before she said, "John really needs to find another position for his niece. She's too flighty to be an enforcer."

"She's too flighty to be a fucking were. If I'd known fleas were her kryptonite, I would have threatened her with them earlier." I clapped my hands together. "Shall we see what Master Augustine dug out of my protégé's muck of a mind?"

"You need to stop," Tiffany snapped.

"Stop what?" I feigned innocence. Narcing on Duncan and his "suggestion" to take it easy on Tiffany wouldn't win me any brownie points. He'd noticed the tear tracks on her cheeks as I had.

"Stop with the fake cheerfulness." She had to shade her eyes when she looked up at me. "I don't need telepathy to know Duncan put you up to it, but if you don't return to your normal sarcastic attitude, so help me, I will shoot out your other eye."

"Yes, Master Stephens," I bit out.

"Better." She marched to the French doors and pulled the right side open.

Anne stood way back in the shadows so she wouldn't burst into flames. "I called nearly an hour ago. Where have you two been?"

"You called in the middle of one of my feeding frenzies." I pulled the door shut behind me. So much for the glorious sunshine, but the specially-treated glass kept the vampires from bursting into flames from the UV radiation. I grinned at Anne. "Unless you want me to start snacking on the staff and the household guards."

She sighed and clasped her hands in front of her snow-white apron that mostly covered her black calf-length skirt, probably to keep herself from smacking the shit out of me. "Master Augustine is in the conservatory." She pivoted and led the way.

It wasn't like we didn't know where the conservatory, aka Bebe's magick room, was. Hell, Tiffany had practically grown up in Caesar's Brentwood mansion. But when Anne flaunted her super manners as head of the coven master's household guard, it usually meant a dignitary was here.

Well, that and her sai were tucked in her apron strings. As a habit, the Amish-raised vampire normally refused to carry weapons. This was not good. And it would be terribly rude of me to reach out with my powers and find out who was here before a proper introduction was made.

So of course, I did it anyway. A bit of relief and a bit of worry mixed and trickled down my spine at the presence of Jean-Pierre Rousseau, the vampire master of the Southeastern United States Coven, and his eclectic witch, Yvonne Head. Despite the fact, Yvonne's baby brother tried to kill me, my family and my friends, I could actually call her a—friendly acquaintance. Especially after I had revealed to her the dino gods and their demons had manipulated David into attacking me.

However, their visit meant Mom had caused ripples in the supernatural community by calling the other U.S. vampires masters. Exactly what I feared. I telepathically told Tiffany who was with Caesar.

She let off a stream of silent profanities.

Okay, not that silent from the ugly scowl Anne shot us both. It made me want to rip out the conservative bun she wore.

Anne dropped her right hand to the handle of one of her sai. *Touch me, and you'll find how fast I can lose my non-violence philosophy.*

When even little Anne Levy was this on edge, things were about to go seriously sideways.

"They are here, Master Augustine," she said as we entered the conservatory. Her unspoken "finally" hung in the air longer than pot smoke.

The two vampire masters sat with Yvonne and Ziva at a table just off the carpet that covered the giant silver and marble pentacle in the center of the room. Jean-Pierre's own chief enforcer, a huge man who could pass for a Ving Rhames look-alike if not for the fangs and glowing gold eyes, stood off to the side, a position where he could keep an eye on everyone and still be within reach of his master.

Slumped in another chair between Caesar and Ziva, Constanza looked tired, but grinned when she saw us. Siobhan stood by the double doors. She'd showered, but still wore the standard uniform she and Tiffany shared, jeans, t-shirt, and boots. She was also openly armed, which wasn't at all like her, but with dino demons running around, she couldn't rely on teeth and claws like she normally would. Scott stood in the back of the room, next to the bookcases. A frown and dark circles under his eyes marred his features.

Caesar, Jean-Pierre and Yvonne rose.

Our boss dressed in business casual, a polo shirt and khakis, not the suit he'd worn last night. I didn't blame him for wanting to be semi-comfortable while poking through another vampire's mind.

Yvonne's clothes were even more casual than Caesar's, a flowing green skirt in tie-dyed gauze and a pale green peasant blouse. A white scarf tied back her multitude of braids. Each braid was capped with beads of stone, bone, or metal. Green power sparked in my eyesight, the visual confirmation of the spells each bead contained.

Jean-Pierre's wardrobe was formal, a double-breasted forest green suit with a matching vest, a starched white dress shirt, and a cloth-of-gold tie.

Like his eclectic, his shoulder-length braids ended in beads, but they were all gold or onyx. And unlike Yvonne's beads, they were primarily protection charms.

Ziva had obviously been here all night. She still wore her Day-Glo orange track suit.

Jean-Pierre bowed. "Lady Samantha. Enforcer Stephens." Now that the supernatural rumor mill had spread the story I was a god, not just a zombie or a Frankenstein's monster like everyone had originally thought, most of the supers were at the very least tolerably polite to me. As a former pirate of the Caribbean, Jean-Pierre oozed the same old world charm Caesar usually did.

Compared to the other coven master's neutral manners, Caesar looked ready to rip someone a new asshole. And back in his day, the Romans would have done that quite literally.

"We were discussing your mother, Sam. Have you spoken with her today?"

"Yes, Master Augustine. Lord Ares made me aware of the situation," I said, trying to keep my expression as bland as possible as I turned to Jean-Pierre. "Master Rousseau, I beg forgiveness for my mother's behavior. I hope you and I can agree to a form of recompense that doesn't involve separating her head from her body."

"And what happens if I don't agree, Lady Samantha?" he asked.

Before my temper could ignite, Yvonne jammed her elbow into his ribs.

Instead of anger, he grinned affectionately at the witch. "On our way here, my eclectic pointed out neither you nor Master Augustine claimed recompense after the events surrounding Ms. Stephens's first wedding. Shall we consider my dismissal of your mother's ill-conceived actions as a notation on my debt to you?"

I inclined my head. "Thank you for your generosity, Master Rousseau."

"I would not call it generosity. I'm simply not insane enough to want to collect Master Augustine's problems as well as his property." He stroked his moustache. "However, to warn you, Lady Samantha, I doubt Master Dare will match my actions."

Great. Yet another piece on my pile of shit.

I sat down at the table and the vampire masters, Yvonne, and Tiffany followed suit.

My sister-in-law's anxious desire to learn what Caesar and Ziva managed to scrape out of Constanza's brain itched against my psyche. Well, I'd been playing "Let's Make a Deal" all night. One more wasn't going to hurt. "How long do I have before she will make a play for Caesar's territory?"

Jean-Pierre shrugged. "If what Master Augustine has been telling me is true, we may all be dead by the time she can put her strategy into action."

I stared at Caesar. "You told him the end of the world was nigh?" Hey, I'd worked in the news business long enough to know information was power, but I was a little surprised since he usually played things pretty close to the vest.

"It seemed ridiculous to get into a pissing contest over Elizabeth's behavior given the circumstances." Caesar's wry smile reassured me Rousseau took the threat of the dino demons seriously.

"Can we please talk about the location of my daughter now?" Apparently, Goth Girl's double-espresso raspberry mocha accelerated her bad mood.

Not that I blamed her.

"Therein lies our problem." Caesar leaned his elbows on the table and steepled his fingertips. "Ziva and I have been trying to retrieve Ms. Torres's memories since Sam brought her back here last night with no luck."

So that was the source of his brimstone scent. For him not to be able to retrieve Ellie's location from Constanza's mind had to irk the hell out of him.

I glanced at the Silver Bear high priestess. Ziva appeared sad and upset. Her deep, dark circles under her eyes were even more pronounced than Scott's.

"Ms. Head has offered to try," Caesar continued while he regarded me. "However, I pointed out Torres is Sam's responsibility."

Again, I looked at Ziva. Her coral lipstick had long since been chewed off, and her mouth formed a grim, tight line. She didn't protest Yvonne's offer. For a coven high priestess to tacitly admit an eclectic could do something she couldn't was unheard of, but I wasn't about to turn away a good faith offer of help.

"It's not like we haven't been in each other's heads before. What if she and I do it together?" I eyed Yvonne. "You've got the finesse, but I can give you the power boost."

She smiled. "That's perfectly acceptable."

I turned to Constanza. "You sure you're up to this right now, Sergeant Torres? You look like you've been through the wringer."

The newborn vampire cocked her head. "We don't have a choice. We need to find Tiffany's daughter before it's too late."

I had to give the woman credit. I had seriously flipped out when I entered the supernatural world, and the consequences weren't nearly as dire as they were at this moment. Add in all of Giovanni's lies Caesar and Anne had probably spent the night correcting, and it was a wonder Constanza wasn't catatonic.

"I'm glad someone's looking out for Ellie," Tiffany grumbled.

Rummaging through Constanza's mind should have been easy for Caesar and Ziva. Is that why my personal undead spidey-sense was going off like a five-alarm fire?

I rose and strode to the huge red Persian rug covering Bebe's pentacle. "We should do this in a proper circle."

Yvonne joined me. "Are you concerned about outside interference?"

"Normally, no, but this situation isn't normal," I muttered. "How pissy are you going to get with me if I cast a blood circle?"

The witch's eyes widened slightly, but she inhaled deeply to settle her jumping pulse. There was a reason her people had a prohibition against blood magick, but if I set the protective circle using blood, only another death god could possibly break it. "Only if you plan to use a blood bag from the vampires' lunch supply."

"Of course." I grinned. "Besides, my sacrificial goats are on back order."

"Chickens work better," she said.

I slapped my forehead. "That's what I've been doing wrong. Now, if you supernatural enforcers are finished glaring at each other, can you help us roll up this rug?"

Anne and Siobhan stepped forward, but when the vampire knelt to deal with the fine Persian wool, the werewolf just kept walking across the damn rug.

"Dammit, Siobhan! I've had enough shit from Cara—" My words died as I realized her gun pointed at me and she'd started to shift.

Except her grin was too wide with too many teeth to be a wolf.

A woman who wasn't the Lannigan pack's beta pulled the trigger.

Chapter 32

Tiffany

I wanted to scream as every fucking supernatural stood there in shock, so I did my job, got between the dino demon and Caesar, and squeezed off two headshots.

Except the demon held up her left hand, and the bullets bounced off an invisible shield.

My actions seemed to jumpstart everyone else.

Yvonne's left arm jerked upward. The marble floor followed her motion and flowed into wall between us and the demon. A bullet from the fake Siobhan pinged off the stone shield.

Jean-Pierre's chief enforcer Wallace tackled his boss to the floor and out of the immediate line of fire. Scott was gentler with Ziva, but not by much. Caesar and Torres grabbed each other and hit the deck.

Sam fell to her knees, cursing under her breath. I counted four shots from the demon before Yvonne raised her wall, but my sister-in-law had simply been in the demon's way when she tried to kill Torres.

The former sergeant jumped up, but Caesar latched onto her arm and dragged her back down with him.

Which left Anne on the same side of the wall as the demon.

"Don't bite her!" I shouted.

Instead, I heard the double doors to the conservatory slam shut.

"Don't worry, sweetheart," Siobhan's voice said. "I'm not planning to leave just yet."

"I'm not the one you should be worried about," Anne answered.

I eased to the edge of Yvonne's makeshift wall and peered around it.

And jerked back as a bullet chipped the edge of the marble.

But my peek had been enough to see Anne crouched, sai in her hands and eyes glowing neon yellow. "Don't fucking engage her, Anne," I hollered.

We needed to buy time. For Sam to recover. For reinforcements to arrive. Why were the demons so desperate to kill Torres before she talked? The one who had taken Siobhan's place didn't give a shit until Sam decided to poke through Torres's brain. Better yet, where was the real Siobhan? And why hadn't the demon gone after Anne?

The third question was easiest to answer. Because one vampire wasn't worth killing, and the demon's plan didn't involve escaping.

"Stupid bitch! You know if you'd just come to me, I would have given you Sam," I yelled.

Sam's eyes turned a solid gunmetal gray as she glared at me from the floor. Her ghost bunnies poked their heads out of her coat.

The coat dripping blood all over Caesar's floor.

Trust me, I mouthed. "Because she's fucking crazy and a danger to my daughter!" I kicked a book closer to me, one that had fallen off the table when Yvonne magicked the floor, and squeezed off a round into the leather.

Sam grunted in fake pain and continued fishing bullets from the demon's gun out of her chest.

"I'll keep her down while you bring my daughter here, and we'll trade," I said.

The demon laughed. "Why bother? I only have to wait until your fake godling loses control and kills you all."

"There's one little problem with that plan. Sam's already eaten a couple of your siblings last night, not to mention some filets of your granddaddy demon for breakfast. So she's kind of full right now."

The demon hissed something in her language I was pretty sure wasn't complimentary.

Everyone else behind the wall stared at Sam. She stood, gathered her ghost bunnies in her arms, and whispered something to them before her eyes met mine and nodded.

Five years were nothing to the vampires, but to Sam and me, it was a good chunk of our lives. We didn't always need telepathy.

I looked at the witches and made the gesture for a shield. Scott and Yvonne nodded in return. Chief Enforcer Wallace shifted to cover the two vampire masters and the high priestess. Caesar may be pissed about not joining in the fight, but he'd get over it.

In a century or two.

My eyes met Sam's again, and I held up three fingers.

Two.

At the silent "one", the rabbits launched themselves through Yvonne's makeshift wall. Sam went over it. I squeezed off two more shots as I dived for another table. I knocked it over for some protection.

Sam had gone all silvery once again, and her fingernails raked black furrows in the demon's skin. The demon screamed every time one of the rabbits raced through her feet. Now, why could they do that with her, but not the fake Giovanni we'd battled?

Anne darted into the fray. Her sai landed with accuracy on what would have been pressure points on a human. Between the four of them, they kept the demon off balance. With the intermix, I didn't dare take another shot.

This demon was fast, but nothing like the one down in Orange County. It seemed to be stuck between demon and human form. No tail, nor did it have the slashing talons similar to velociraptors that the rest seemed to have.

A kick from Anne destroyed the demon's knee. It shrieked and twisted toward her. A blow to its spine from Sam cut its proverbial cords, and the demon flopped to the floor.

I stood up and joined Sam and Anne. Marble popped and sizzled from where demon blood had landed. Massive holes ruined Caesar's priceless antique rug.

The demon still breathed, but its form shifted again. No longer Siobhan or demon. It still had the body of an adult human woman. Constanza's eyes and wild curls dominated its features, but it was the prominent nose of Caesar's line that made the air freeze in my lungs.

"Mami!" It started crying. "Mami!"

Sam, Anne, and I looked at each other.

"Shit," I muttered.

The floor rumbled and shuddered beneath our feet as Yvonne lowered the makeshift wall. When the demon caught sight of Constanza, it cried out, "Mami, please don't let them kill me! Mami!"

"Get Constanza out of here, Master Augustine." I tried to keep my voice level. Neutral. I tried not to think about what those bastards had done to the army sergeant. Tried not to think about my daughter at the mercy of those same monsters.

"No." Constanza jerked away from Caesar. She crept closer to us. "I thought I dreamed you." Pinkish tears oozed down the vampire's cheeks.

"Mami, please," it cried. "Help me."

I stepped between them and holstered my gun. "Constanza, walk away. It's trying to manipulate you." I cupped her cheeks. "It came here to kill you. For the love of—" Somehow I stopped myself from saying a name. We didn't need the attention here and now, and I wasn't about to use Sam's name that way. "Leave the room," I finished lamely. "Please."

Constanza's gaze darted to the demon and back to me. "I know. But if it's a bad Turn, isn't it the responsibility of the sire to deal with the spawn?" She shook beneath my touch.

"You don't have to do this," I whispered.

"Yeah, I do." Her focus was locked on the baby that should never have been. "Just like Sam would do it for me." She took a deep breath. "Can I borrow your grandfather's knife? I need to know it's done right."

I handed her the bronze and bone blade.

"Mami! Don't hurt me!" There was something more to the words than we knew from the way the former sergeant shook. Maybe her childhood. Maybe from her service on the other side of the world. Maybe gut instinct of what Giovanni and his buddies had done to her.

Before her own mind blocked the terror and agony.

When Constanza knelt beside it, the demon screamed and screamed. I closed my eyes. After all the shit I'd seen in my very short life, I couldn't watch this. The very real fear I'd have to do the same thing ate at me.

The wild, incoherent sounds stopped abruptly.

"Tiffany?"

I opened my eyes.

Constanza started to hand Grandpa's knife back to me, but Sam took it.

"The rest of you get out of here. I'll . . . clean up," she muttered.

I recognized the look on my sister-in-law's face. It wasn't the expenditure of energy that drove her hunger this time. It was something far deeper and primeval.

We needed to get Constanza out of the conservatory. She didn't need to see what happened next. I wrapped an arm around her waist. Anne hugged her from the other side, and the newborn let us guide her from the room. I was vaguely aware as the witches and vampires followed us past Sam.

Miko and three other daytime enforcers were in the hallway.

"Close the conservatory doors behind us," I said. "No one goes in until Sam comes out."

"But—" Miko's attention darted to Anne, then to Caesar. I couldn't get mad at her questioning look since I wasn't exactly the ranking enforcer present.

"Do as Enforcer Stephens says, Enforcer Osaka," Caesar ordered.

"Yes, Master."

Even without super powers, I could hear the wet tearing of flesh and the crunch of bones as we walked away. I don't know how Constanza found the will to do what needed to be done.

I didn't think I could do the same if Ellie had been turned into a monster.

Chapter 33

Sam

Flopsy and Peter were my only witnesses as I ate Constanza's daughter. Their little amorphous bodies rubbed against me as I wept afterwards. How the hell could she ever be in the same room with me again, much less trust me?

To stall a little bit longer, I restored most of the marble flooring and its silver-inset pentacle to its original form. There wasn't much I could do about the acidic demon blood holes burnt into the antique carpet and a couple of dozen tiles. Considering the current political climate in the Middle East, I couldn't go shopping by myself. Maybe if I took Max with me to Abu Dhabi—

My gut clenched. I hadn't thought about my brother for hours.

There he was, in a coma, and I was giving myself a pity-party.

Because I just ate my charge's daughter. The same charge who had shot out my brains less than twelve hours ago.

And I couldn't even bitch to a deity about how shitty my life had become.

I tucked my rabbits in their pocket and rose to my feet. A deep breath helped my concentration while I pulled in my god power. My jeans felt good. I needed to be relatively normal for the next step, or I might accidentally short-circuit Yvonne and Constanza's brains.

Assuming the former sergeant would let me anywhere near her.

I opened the door to the conservatory to find Miko and a cleaning crew waiting in the hallway, her service Glock in my face.

Miko cocked her head. "You okay?"

"Yeah." It took me a second to realize it was Ares's knife that made them nervous. It glowed with an orange light. "I'm just returning this to Tiffany. Had to clean it for her."

The daytime enforcer slowly lowered her gun while the cleaning crew drew itchy trigger fingers from their own pieces.

I jabbed a thumb at the room. "I cleaned up the worst of the mess. Can you get me the name of the tile place where Caesar ordered his marble? Once things settle down, I'll swing by Italy and pick up some replacements."

"We already have those covered, Ms. Ridgeway," one of the gentlemen chirped.

Of course, Caesar's staff would be that efficient. I nodded. "That's good, but the carpet is a total loss. I've neutralized the demon blood and wrapped the damaged tiles in the wool, so don't unroll it. I can't make any guarantees if you cut yourself with blood-contaminated marble."

"Yes, ma'am. We'll be careful." He tipped his baseball cap and marched past me. His three minions followed him with their cleaning equipment like ducklings after their mother.

I don't know why I was worried. Working for vampires, these guys had dealt with questionable blood before. They pushed safety goggles and masks into place as they passed. Tyvex overalls and booties already cover their clothes and work shoes. Behind me came the snap of rubber gloves.

Leaving them to their job, I started down the hall. Miko kept pace.

"Everyone's in the Florida room," she said.

"Let me guess. You're supposed to babysit me," I said sourly.

Miko placed a hand on my arm, and I paused. "Mai's worried about you."

I blinked. Out of all the crap happening, her sister wasn't the topic I expected.

I crossed my arms. "Mai's always worried about something."

Miko shrugged. "This is more than her usual shit. There's very few people she cares about on a personal level. You're one of them."

Irritation bubbled to the surface, forced by a healthy dose of guilt about my role in the deaths of the two enforcers' grandfather and his boyfriend. "Why? Because I didn't eat Kensai and Jamal like I just ate Constanza's daughter?"

Miko's normally cheerful expression fell. She released my arm. "She's right. You are losing what's left of your humanity, and I don't mean by eating people." She pivoted and strode around the corner towards the Florida room.

I wanted to kick myself. Miko didn't deserve my bitchiness. No, she deserved an award for not tiptoeing around me. She was one of the few who had the guts to speak my own fear aloud. Something Mai had tried, and I'd cut her off time after time because of my own denial of what I was becoming.

What I had become.

Obviously, I was still human enough to be embarrassed as shit. I listened for Miko to reach the door at the end of the side hall before I followed.

Inside the glass-walled room, everyone but Anne sat or reclined on the wicker furniture. The Amish-born enforcer paced in a semi-circle around Caesar. The scents of blood and caffeine hung in the air. They all turned and stared at me when I entered the room. Well, everyone except Miko.

I cleared my throat before I said, "Has anyone called John and Jorge to let them know Siobhan's missing?"

"Not yet," Caesar said. "I'd like to be able to give her father everything we know when I make the call. It would be best if he told her husband."

"I can't believe that was a demon playing Siobhan the entire time." Tiffany glared at me over the top of her soda can. Crap, she'd already picked up that I had said something stupid to Miko without any telepathy. Those two may be cousins three generations apart, but they were tight growing up without their parents. I'd hear about it once Tiffany had me to herself.

"When has she been alone for the last twenty-four hours?" Jean-Pierre asked.

We all exchanged looks.

Tiffany was the first to say anything. "We had a play date yesterday morning with our kids. The park at ten a.m., then fast food. We left In-N-Out around noon to get the kids home for naps."

I shook my head. "There's no way she could have been replaced before the investigation into Ellie's kidnapping started tonight. Not between the pack, three kids and Jorge."

"She was never alone at my place." Tiffany rubbed her forehead. "And she came with three pack enforcers."

"She and Tobias were separated for a minute or two at La Brea," I added.

"In the conservatory, the imposter couldn't seem to transform all the way into her lizard form." Anne stopped pacing. "When was the last time Siobhan took wolf form?"

Tiffany and I stared at each other. "The house in Orange County," we said at the same time.

"The switch? When she went out the window or when she dealt with our peeping tom?" I said.

"Does it matter?" Tiffany snarled. "I should have known it wasn't Siobhan when she didn't argue about you bringing her back here with Constanza last night."

"We never left Ms. Torres alone since Sam brought her back here," Caesar said. "Nor did the fake Siobhan shift. Her presence is probably the reason Ziva and I couldn't retrieve Ms. Torres's memories."

I rubbed the back of my neck. "There's no guarantee Siobhan is being kept in the same place as Ellie."

"But Torres may know where the demons are keeping their breeding stock," Tiffany said. We turned and looked at the newborn vampire.

Constanza shrugged. "You have to do it, Sam. She—" The vampire swallowed hard. "My daughter was only afraid of you."

In the end, no one left the Florida room. Jean-Pierre and his chief enforcer weren't about to leave Yvonne alone with me thanks to a misunderstanding with Baron Samedi a few years ago. Me eating Constanza's daughter, even if she was part dino demon, hadn't helped that trust.

By the same token, Constanza and I were Caesar's responsibility, and he trusted another vampire master only so far. And between everyone's fear, anxiety, anger and a myriad of other emotions, the smell in the room was damn near unbearable.

We'd borrowed a huge square sheet of plastic from the cleaners, laid it out in the center of the room, and placed a lounge chair on it. As Yvonne settled Constanza on the chair's flowered cushions, Anne slipped me a tiny jar of Vicks Vaporub.

I frowned at the blue glass. "What's this for?"

She smiled. "Put a dab under each nostril. It'll help alleviate the mix of scents."

My rotten strawberry embarrassment added to the noxious concoction. "I'm transmitting again."

"Yes," she said. "It's the first time you've slipped in a long time."

"Only because I haven't been around all of you much for the last year," I grumbled.

Anne's silence on the matter spoke volumes.

Miko returned from the kitchen. "You sure a half cup is enough, Sam?"

I took the Pyrex measuring cup filled with exactly four ounces of cow blood she held out for me. "Yes, thank you. I'm sorry for being a bitch earlier."

The enforcer smiled. "Just don't act like one again. Tiffany says I can shoot out your other eye if you do."

I saluted her with the cup. "Understood."

Time to get this show on the road. I addressed the rest of the room. "Ladies and gentlemen, the edges of the plastic are the splash zone. Nor can I guarantee my shield won't slice off body parts when I activate it."

No one moved.

"Your loss then," I said.

Everyone, but Yvonne and the prone Constanza scurried as far away from me as the glass and wood walls allowed. The witch chuckled and shook her head.

"You two ready for this?" I asked as I crossed to the lounge chair.

Yvonne nodded.

"As ready as I'm going to be," Constanza muttered.

I patted her shoulder. "This won't hurt."

"Not physically anyway," Yvonne added. "It can be emotionally uncomfortable to have all your secrets laid bare, but you need to realize you'll see our memories as well."

"That could be interesting." The former sergeant grinned.

I rolled my eyes. "Not necessarily. Where do you want me, Yvonne?"

She gestured toward Constanza's right. "On the floor okay?" She frowned. "What about the circle?"

I grinned. "Everybody needs to be in place first."

Yvonne lowered herself to the plastic on Constanza's left.

Concentrating on the blood, I started twirling the measuring cup. Centripetal force had the liquid climbing the glass sides. Once I had a decent psychic grip on the rotating fluid, I let it rise out of the cup.

I kept the blood spinning, expanding as it hovered above the lounge chair. When it was wide enough to encompass the three of us and the wicker, I gently lowered the circle and slowed the spin. The blood hit the plastic sheet with a soft, wet *plop*.

Yvonne whistled. "That was . . . different. Why the whole spinning thing?"

I sat and shrugged. "Easiest way I've found to make a perfect circle with the least amount of blood. Who knew I'd actually use something from my high school physics class? Here we go." I reached behind me and touched the ring of blood with my index finger.

A hemisphere of black diamond energy sprang to life around us. The opaque shield meant the folks outside of it couldn't see a whole lot inside, and vice versa. As long as no one panicked and did something incredibly stupid, we'd all be fine.

Yvonne took Constanza's left hand and reached for mine. I took hers and Constanza's right hand.

The witch smiled at the vampire. "Remember. Relax and let us do all the work."

"De nada," Constanza whispered.

Red flashed in my vision. Interesting. When I traipsed through Yvonne and her brother's minds, the flashes were green. I was seeing everything from Constanza's point of view.

She/we crouched behind a boulder as the sun beat down on me. Sand abraded skin in places I didn't want to think about. My hands were putting together a gun I didn't recognize and knew more intimately than any lover I'd had in my twenty-one years.

A voice crackled through my comm. "What's the sit, Torres?"

"In position, sir. Almost ready."

I screwed in the last piece, propped the gun on its tripod, and peered through the scope. "Ready, sir."

"Roger."

My friends, my brothers and sisters, escorted a small supply convoy on the road below my position. The village had been friendly every other time we'd passed though, but God knew alliances changed on a whim in Afghanistan.

I spotted the figure through my scope. A little girl fully covered in the dark robes of the region. Maybe six or seven.

Something was wrong. She was too round. These people were on the edge of starvation. I saved the candy my abuelita sent in her monthly care packages to hand out to children like this little girl because even a bit of sugar was better than nothing to eat.

"Lieutenant, possible hostile. Two o'clock," I reported.

A man appeared behind her. He started throwing rocks at the child. She ran.

Straight for the convoy.

My heart choked me. My finger wouldn't move. I'd killed since I came to this godforsaken place, but she—

The little girl stumbled and fell under the lead vehicle. The explosion tore the cab open. A burst of flames followed by roiling black smoke.

Gunfire echoed off the bluffs in staccato bursts. Training kicked in. I picked off targets on the rooftops. In the streets. The opposing ridge.

When everything went silent, cold seeped through my uniform and armor despite the bright, hot sun.

A red flash, and I sat in an office. I sat and lied to the army psychologist. I said all the right things. All the things about how well I was doing. No, I didn't need any more anti-depressants. How I was going to stay with my abuelita during my leave. I said everything with a smile.

I'd see my abuelita soon.

My beloved abuelita because I was as cold and dead as she was.

A red flash.

My skin puckered with the chill desert air, but I didn't really feel it as I sat on my bedroll. The same bedroll that had been tucked in my pack the day everyone died.

But my sidearm was warm in my grip. One in the chamber. That's all I needed. I lifted the barrel to my lips.

"Don't."

I blinked. Someone sat on the other side of my campfire. A man. I'd been jumping at shadows for the last couple of months, but I hadn't seen him approach. Maybe I didn't want to see him. Was I so far gone that I wanted a stranger to rape and kill me in the middle of nowhere?

"Do you want to talk about it?"

I lowered my gun. "No."

He could have been any hiker in the valley the way he dressed. Dark curling hair. Full lips. The nose was prominent and aquiline, but instead of detracting, it gave him an air of authority.

"What if I could take away your pain?" he asked.

A bitter laugh erupted from my gut. "Not interested in anything you have in a baggie."

"I'm not talking about recreational pharmaceuticals." His eyes glowed gold. My fucked-up head now had me seeing things. "Sometimes, what we need is another person."

I sighed. "I kill everyone I care about. Sure you want to take that chance?"

"If I can convince you to live, then yes, I'll take that chance. And I'm far more difficult to kill than you think."

"Really?" I aimed at him.

"First of all, by your own rule, you can't kill me because you don't care for me. Yet." He smiled. "And you do want to live if you're willing to waste your one bullet on me."

My arm sagged to my lap, the weight of the entire world in the metal of that firearm. My thoughts were fuzzy even though I hadn't had a drop of alcohol for the last three days. I'd decided I didn't want to die in a drunken stupor, but the lack of numbness had brought my mistakes into razor-sharp clarity.

"You should go back to your camp," I said quietly.

"I will," he answered. "If you come with me, and you leave the gun here."

I looked down at my sidearm in my lap. "All right." If he was going to take me out into the night to kill me, well . . .

I deserved it for fucking up in Afghanistan. I deserved it for leaving my abuelita so she died alone of the heart attack. I—

"Need to have the power to make things right," the stranger said. "I lost my grandmother, too. She was murdered by the man she loved. And he got away with it."

"What do you want from me?" I whispered.

"If I give you peace and strength, would you help me get justice?"

"Yes."

This wasn't a flash of red. It was maelstrom of scarlet and pink and burgundy that knocked me out of Constanza's memories. Razor-sharp wind lashed at me.

"Yvonne!"

"I'm here."

I whirled around. A twining black and green cord connected us. Yvonne was . . . beautiful.

Not in the conventional sense. I mean, she was definitely hot by a hetero male standard. This though . . .

This was different. Yvonne was literally made of green light. She resembled Azrael in his true form, not the human guise he wore when he was around me.

Then it hit me. This was her soul. I was looking at her fucking soul.

"What is this crap?" I waved at the maelstrom around us. "It almost feels like the Great Red Spot on Jupiter."

Yvonne cocked her head. "How would you know that?"

"I dropped a bunch of demons into it earlier this morning." I held up a hand. "Not on purpose. I was taking them to Pluto, but the little assholes fought me, we dropped into Jupiter's atmosphere, and I lost my grip on them."

"O-o-o-o-kay." Obviously deciding to let the subject go, Yvonne looked around us. "This is a deliberate memory block mixed in with a Turn fever, but I've never experienced anything this powerful."

"Could Fake Siobhan have been reinforcing it while she was at Caesar's with Constanza?"

"That would be my guess." Yvonne folded her fingers together and deliberately cracked her knuckles. "Sometimes a light memory block is necessary when the injuries necessitating the Turn are too traumatic for the newborn to cope with, but I think you're right. This block is for another reason entirely, and it needs to be removed." She smiled at me. "But that's why you're my tank."

"Your 'tank'?"

Yvonne laughed. "You don't game much, do you?"

"Try never." I rolled my eyes. "I have a real life."

She laughed even harder, and I realized my faux pas. Every witch I'd met saw my aura as black, and the only time an aura on a human goes black is when they die.

"Shut up, and tell me what to do."

"If this is similar to an extraterrestrial hurricane, how good are you at controlling the weather?"

I jammed my fists on my hips. "You have got to be shitting me. I can barely keep from transmitting my thoughts to everyone on this planet."

She shrugged. "How'd you get out of the Great Red Spot?"

I held out my arms. "Better hang on tight because I don't want to drop you, and this ride will be rough."

"You get us out, and I'll see what I can do to untangle this mess." Yvonne wrapped her arms around my waist without question. I wasn't sure what I'd done to earn her trust after everything that went down between her brother and me.

"You could have killed him and you didn't," she whispered in my ear.

Dammit. With this close of a link, of course she could hear every stray thought.

I hugged Yvonne tight. The electrical discharges in the Jupiter hurricane nearly fried my sixth sense, but knowing the demons, the energy in this soup was probably Constanza's own neurons, their firing pattern bent into this twisted hell. I'd lobotomize her if I forced my way through like I had this morning.

Disparate things clicked in my mind, like they used to when I chased down a story for *The National Scoop*. Back when I still had a real job. Back when I was still human.

Something the wanagamesak pointed out years ago when the Native American spirit had shown me how to untangle fairy magick. Patterns. Everything had a pattern. And according to modern physicists, even chaos had a pattern. We need to find the end thread of this spell.

Assuming there was one.

There had to be if they were using Constanza's own mind against her. I watched the energy surge and ebb around us. There!

Holding tight to Yvonne, I flew into the gap. Then another. Pause. Charge ahead. Dodge. Up. Sideways. It was a wonder that Yvonne's soul hadn't puked ectoplasm on me.

It was a wonder I hadn't puked either. But Tiffany was right. I hadn't been sick since the day I died.

"Got it!" Yvonne's triumphant yell surrounded me, penetrated me.

As we flew through the free spaces, the emotional winds faded, then died. Stars shone scarlet above us, and Earth's lovely mix of nitrogen and oxygen caressed our skin. I touched down on the desert sand and gravel and carefully set Yvonne on her feet. In her hand was what looked like a huge pulsing ball of angry red yarn.

A tent stood in front of us. I could hear male voices though I couldn't see anyone. I turned in a slow circle. Still no one.

"If you removed the memory block, why didn't we jump right into Constanza's memories like before?"

Yvonne shook her head, appearing as confused as I felt. "I don't know. We should have."

"Maybe it's because of my shame," a feminine voice said behind us.

We turned to find Constanza. She glowed, a deep scarlet that spread and covered this world. Instead of Yvonne's flowing dress though, she wore medieval-style chainmail over leathers with bloody vambraces and greaves. The handle of a sword peeked over each shoulder.

"It wasn't your fault," Yvonne said. "They manipulated and deceived you."

"That's just it." Constanza stared at the tent. "I should have known Marcus was too good to be true. He was right. I didn't want to die that night, but I felt I needed to be punished."

"For what?" I tossed my hands in the air. "For not shooting a little girl? Constanza, even if you had, there was no fucking way you could have stopped what happened!"

Her attention settled on me. "Because I'm not a goddess?"

"We could spend the rest of eternity listing all of my screw-ups, both before and after the assholes at Mallory Labs injected nanites into me." I stepped closer to her and grabbed her shoulders. "You couldn't save that little girl in Afghanistan, but you can make a difference here and now. Please help me save my niece."

"I couldn't even save my own daughter." A sob punctuated her statement.

"I know, but please don't punish an innocent child because of our mistakes. Please make things right." I held my breath, or at least my imaginary breath in Constanza's mind. If she didn't cooperate, I'd have to tear my way through to find what we needed, and I'd destroy a damaged woman who'd done nothing to deserve my wrath other than to be in the wrong place at the wrong time.

Yvonne shifted to face us both, but she addressed Constanza. "Cheré, we need to see where they took you after Death Valley. That's all." She glanced at the tent. "The punishment you inflict on yourself is far worse than anything we could devise."

Constanza swallowed hard. "What about Duke Miller?" She stared into my eyes. "Would he—" She swallowed hard. "Would he do what needed to be done?"

Yvonne gasped and covered her mouth with her hands, but I stared back at the vampire. "Yes."

A red flash.

Agony wrenched my abdomen, and I screamed. I lay in the back seat of a sedan, my fists beating on the upholstery.

"If I lose her—" a familiar voice snarled. Marcus, Marcus . . .

Crap. He'd never told me his last name.

Giovanni, something whispered inside me.

"We'll find you another plaything." The female was familiar, too, but another wave of pain overwhelmed any chance at recognition. I clutched at my stomach and screamed again at the huge bulge.

I couldn't be pregnant. No, I couldn't be this far along after twenty-four hours.

"She has the skills I need for—" Marcus growled.

"For your vengeance of your grandmother's death by her spawn, blah, blah, blah," the woman in the front seat said. "Don't you get tired of your evil minion monologue? By my gods, I sure do."

"Please, take me to a hospital. This isn't right!" I clawed my way upright in the seat. Where were we? Where the hell were they taking me?

"We're taking you someplace safe, Connie. I won't let anything hurt you," Marcus crooned. Just like the same nothings the bastard had murmured when he was fucking me in his sleeping bag.

My t-shirt no longer covered the bulge protruding from my abdomen. Bare skin extended, and I would have sworn I saw the silhouette of a lizard head.

I needed help. I reached for the door handle, but nothing happened. Goddamn childproof locks!

The street seemed familiar. I'd never been here before but somehow, I'd seen it at night, not during the day. We approached someone walking a dog. I beat on the rear passenger window to get her attention.

The woman in the front of the car turned around. I never seen her before, but a part of me trilled in anger. Maddy, the last person unaccounted for from the Sunshine Believers ranch at Tuttle Creek, Montana.

She backhanded me so hard my head bounced off the window. I collapsed to the backseat. I must have blacked out then because the next thing I heard was the low rumble of a garage door closing.

Marcus yanked open the back door and lifted me out. Another wave of pain wracked my belly.

Pay attention, Torres. My old sarge's voice. *Learn the terrain.* I forced my eyes open. I needed to find a way out of this insane asylum. I caught a glimpse of the backyard from the huge windows in the breakfast nook. Rich people's home from the crystal blue pool. The neighboring house past the fence had beige siding with dark brown trim, but the upstairs picture window was intact. I'd seen that house before from a different angle.

Marcus turned left and opened a door. The basement.

Another red flash.

The basement again. I instinctively wrapped my arms around a dark-haired, weeping little girl, and she buried her head in my shoulder. "Dammit, Marcus! You told me we were going after a god that wants to destroy the world."

Maddy grinned. "Of course, we are. She's the bait we need to get Ridgeway's attention." I didn't trust the bitch any farther than I could throw her. And these days, I could throw someone through a wall.

Marcus reached out and caressed my cheek. "I promise we're not going to hurt her, Constanza."

We both knew he had just lied to me, but I needed to go along until I could find a way to extract myself and the little girl.

"What's your name?" I whispered.

"E-ellie," she choked out between sobs.

Everything stopped.

Thank you, Constanza.

I blinked. Coming out of that deep of a telepathic read felt like waking up from an incredibly heavy sleep. But the proof of what really occurred sat on Yvonne's lap.

A pulsing ball of angry red energy.

My circle still held. I released Yvonne's hand. She blinked and stretched as well.

Constanza's eyes remained closed, but tears leaked from under her lids.

I stroked her hand. "Constanza?"

"I remember now," she whispered.

"I'm so sorry."

"It wasn't your fault." She sniffed before she pulled free from Yvonne and me and swiped at her face. "Like you said, it needed to be done."

I nodded at the ball in Yvonne's lap. "What do we do with that?"

"Destroy it." Green fire danced along her dark skin. She picked up the ball, pressed her hands together, and crushed that nasty little piece of work. A few embers flew into the air before the ball disappeared between her palms.

I whistled. The woman could give Bebe or Sarah Goldstein a run for their money. "Remind me never to piss you off."

The witch chuckled. "We long past that, Ms. Ridgeway."

"You ready to face the world, Sergeant?"

Constanza sat up and blew out a deep breath. "Not really, but we do need to save it."

I concentrated. The glittering black diamond hemisphere disappeared.

Jean-Pierre rushed forward and pulled Yvonne upright, searching for any scratch or bruise.

She playfully pushed at him. "I'm fine, just tired."

Caesar hovered over me as I stood. "Well?"

"We've got the location." I was too tired myself to even be pissed at the way Giovanni and the demons had fucked with me.

Tiffany stepped to Caesar's side. "If you tell me it's that perv's house in Orange County—"

I shrugged to ease the tightness along my shoulders. "Of course, it's the perv's house in Orange County."

Tiffany released a blistering tirade that left a couple of former pirates' mouths hanging open and made an Army sniper blush.

Chapter 34

Tiffany

Our first battle against the demons was actually waged in Caesar's Florida room.

"We need to go now while we have the daylight advantage." I smacked my hand against a tiki wood end table for emphasis.

"That will only give you an advantage against the rogue vampires, little one," Rousseau said.

I yanked out a yellow number two pencil from my pants pocket. "Call me 'little one' on more time, asshat."

Caesar stepped between me and the other vampire master. "Stand down, Stephens."

I took a deep, shuddering breath, but I didn't stow the pencil. "The longer we wait, the longer we argue, the closer we get to midnight. Do you really want to take the chance they manage to summon an Old One on Halloween?" I tried very hard not to think about how they planned to summon the dinosaur god. Not think of Giovanni slitting my baby's throat. Not think about her blood burbling out and smearing her pale skin as her life drained away.

I shoved the obscene image away. Focus and work the problem at hand. "If Sam has to take an Old One on here and now, the battle will destroy most of the Los Angeles metropolitan area. Hundreds of thousands of people will die. The earlier we take the offensive, the better chance we have of stopping them."

I hesitated a moment. The last thing I wanted to do alienate our biggest offensive weapon. "And there's no guarantee Sam will win right now."

"Hey!" My sister-in-law scowled at me. "Low blow, bitch."

"Tiffany's right," Torres said. "Whatever you all did around the time I was Turned worries the hell out of Marcus and the head demons."

I snorted. "Yeah, except it wasn't Sam who did it. Alyson Tribideaux, the New Orleans pack princess, was the one who whacked the head off the last of the original dino demons."

"But she didn't kill him," Torres stated.

We all stared at the sniper.

"What are you talking about?" Sam's eyes went neon blue. The eyes of every other vampire in the room glowed as well.

Torres shrugged. "All I know is bits and pieces I've overheard. He transferred his consciousness to another hybrid before his original body was destroyed. He's still running things. They bring him to the safe house in Orange County for the breeding of women who don't know they're part supernatural, but Marcus always made sure I wasn't there. I can't give you a description of him."

I couldn't believe what I was hearing. "You were okay with what they were doing to those women after what they did to you?"

Torres made a visible effort not to lunge at me, or maybe Sam held her in place. The vampire's jaw throbbed before she said, "They made sure I didn't remember what they did to me or the others. And I'm not excusing what they or I have done. I'm telling you what I remember now."

"Besides, these things shapeshift," Sam said. "Daddy demon made himself look like Giovanni to get into Constanza's pants. And he's been doing his daughters and granddaughters as well. That's the only way they could get enough eggs to attack me in Death Valley."

Torres must have decided to ignore both me and Sam because she focused on Caesar. "Odds are they haven't had a chance to move all the weres they were holding in the basement for breeding. A beta like Siobhan would be a major prize for the demons."

"Caesar, if you absolutely need a vampire on site, have Alex call the plays from a protected van," Sam interjected. "And we're not as short-handed as you'd like to think as long as Ziva and John don't get pissy about territory." She eyed the high priestess, who held up her hands.

"You're not getting any arguments from me, dear."

"What do you mean?" Caesar said.

Sam rose from the foot of Constanza's lounge chair. "You've got three tanks as Yvonne would say." A wry grin tilted her mouth. "Me, Ares, and Phillippa. We call in the Warners and both Polk packs. Alyson's another beta who wouldn't mind a little payback against the demons. Not to mention George, Emily, and Logan won't pass up a chance at taking down Giovanni."

Caesar cocked an eyebrow. "And witches?"

Sam glanced at Scott. "How's enforcer training coming with Sarah Goldstein?"

For the first time today, a wisp of a smile ghosted across his face. "She's taught us more than a few tricks since she arrived here in January. Not to mention, she's a powerhouse in her own right."

"And she was the only witch survivor of Selene's house of horrors," I added. "She'll want in, too."

Caesar stiffened at my words, but the man really needed to accept his twin sister was a psychotic bitch and move on.

I eyed Sam. "What about White Rose, Golden Eagle and Blue Hawk on top of whoever Silver Bear can scramble?" I glanced at Ziva, who nodded. "You can get them here the fastest."

"Luckily, we have someone who can pull rank with the San Francisco coven. And we can count on Quinn and his people, but—"

"You want to hold the Seattle folks in reserve," I guessed.

"Yeah." She regarded Yvonne. "You in?"

The witch's eyes narrowed. "After those bastards tricked my brother into attacking you? Of course."

Jean-Pierre grabbed her arm. "You are my eclectic. You owe your loyalty to me."

"Who do you think will stop them if the demons succeed in bringing one of their gods into this world?" She shook her head, and her beads clicked an uneven rhythm. "What if Constanza is right, and they want to catch Sam before she's ready?"

He cupped her cheek. "I'm not ready to lose you."

I tried not to let my mouth fall open. Big tough pirate vampire was madly in love with his eclectic. I looked at Sam, inclined my head toward the pair, and mouthed, "Did you know?"

She glared at me. *Yes. Now shut the fuck up.*

Of course, she did. I forgot about her mind meld with Yvonne the day after my aborted wedding at my in-laws' house. I glanced at Caesar, but his glare was equally dire. Was it because Bebe was about to get pulled into this battle and he wouldn't be there to protect the love of his life either?

Whatever else Jean-Pierre and Yvonne said to each other was silent.

Sometimes I envied the vampire and witch telepathic abilities. Could a Normal ever really share such a perfect intimacy?

Did Max understand how much I truly loved him?

Even if we managed to get Ellie back in the next few hours, my husband may never wake up from his coma. And in my wallowing, I realized something else.

I cleared the sudden lump from my throat. "I know the rest of you with superpowers are gonna object, but you're forgetting a major resource." Every eye in the room focused on me. "Normal law enforcement who happen to be Family."

"LAPD and the LA County Sheriff's Department don't have jurisdiction in Orange County," Caesar said. "That could cause more questions—"

"Detective Jorge Sifuentes of the Los Angeles County Sheriff's Office knows who's who within the various departments," I replied. "And he'll want to be the first in line to rescue Siobhan." Actually, the Normal detective could and would put a major crimp in supernatural relations with local law enforcement if he wasn't included in the retrieval of his wife.

Caesar nodded slowly. "All right. See how many he can pull on short notice. We can't take the risk of assembling here. Even if the demons can't track Sam, anyone with a pair of binoculars could see the extra people on the estate."

I turned to Jean-Pierre. "You in with Yvonne or out?"

"I'm in. What do you need?"

"A place to assemble that's not Augustine. Ready to put your money where your mouth is?"

He grinned. "None of my facilities are adequate for the size of the operation you are planning, Ms. Stephens. Not to mention, I wouldn't put it past Giovanni and the demons to have an eye on my people. However, now would be the time to call my markers with the Laveaus."

I groaned at the mention of the New Orleans witch coven. "Geez, Rousseau! Why don't we just kill ourselves and save the demons the trouble?"

Chapter 35

Sam

Despite the multitude of protective spells, I materialized with Jean-Pierre in the foyer of the ancient mansion of one of the most powerful and feared covens in the world. I looked at the reception committee. "Really? I get that this is New Orleans, but you folks can't do better than lame Vincent Price extras?"

A man stood on the first landing of the staircase. Unlike the fake zombies, he dressed in an immaculate charcoal suit with a purple tie. "You will suffer at the hands of the d-d-dead . . ." His glorious speech died as he took a good look at our auras. Or more particularly, mine. The ashy stink of fear filled the space as the rest of the Thriller rejects did the same check.

I leaned closer to Jean-Pierre. "Do you vamps really find the smell of fear appetizing? To me, it's like someone hasn't emptied the ashtray for years."

The vampire master laughed as he pulled down his face mask. He pushed back the hood of the protective cloak he wore. We decided the asbestos outfit was necessary in case my teleport was bounced into a place with sunshine. "Please tell Madame Laveau that Master Rousseau and the Lady Samantha wish an audience with her."

Obviously, our request was the last thing the guy on the stairs or the George Romero cast members expected. One of the female witches in zombie makeup curtsied. "Th-this way, ma'am, Master Rousseau."

She escorted us to a formal parlor. I went in first to check the UV levels. The windows were coated with reflective film, but more to keep prying eyes out rather than radiation deadly to vampires. The woman curtsied again before leaving, closing the doors behind her.

When she was gone, I looked at Jean-Pierre. "I've never met a witch with such old-fashioned manners."

His grin faded. "You're probably the first god she's met."

"But the loa—" I started.

The doors burst open and crashed into the walls. "Do not presume to replace the Creator Himself." The woman who strode in had a gray-streaked updo more reminiscent of the 1950's. Her wide-skirted day dress and sensible heels matched the same period. She looked to be a hair older than Bebe's grandmother Ziva, but I couldn't detect a glamor, which meant Madame Laveau was probably well over one hundred.

She focused her malevolent glare at the vampire. "How dare you bring this abomination into my home, Rousseau."

He inclined his head. "Good afternoon to you as well, Brigitte."

"Leave." She managed to hiss the v-sound.

"I've come to collect on one of the many favors your coven owes me." His voice was incredibly calm, the same intractability I'd heard in Caesar so many times. I wondered who taught the vampire masters that little trick.

She jabbed a finger in my direction. "I will have nothing to do with that abomination."

Jean-Pierre crossed his massive arms. "You owe me, Brigitte, and Sam is staying."

She started chanting. Even though my French sucked, I could tell she was speaking in some patois.

"What's she saying?" I whispered to Jean-Pierre.

"She is summoning Baron Samedi."

I groaned and rubbed the bridge of my nose. The issues between me and the loa had been put to rest years ago. I didn't need some second-rate mamba to resurrect an old feud that had centered on someone else lusting after my husband.

Cigar smoke filled the room. Its stench was only a tad better than the stink of Madame Laveau's fear. The smoke coalesced into a pillar in the middle of the parlor. It resolved into the familiar white suit with a matching top hat and black cane of Baron Samedi.

"Why do you summon me, Brigitte Marie Teresa Laveau!"

"Sorry, dude," I said. He blinked, his only show of surprise at my presence. I waved a hand at Madame Laveau. "Your girl decided an ICBM was needed for an ant."

A black eyebrow crawled up his forehead, and he dropped the stentorian tone. "And why are you here?"

I jabbed a thumb at Jean-Pierre, who bowed to the loa. "Master Rousseau owes me a favor. Madame Laveau owes him one." I shrugged. "Just need to use her property as a meeting place for a couple of hours. No stealing souls. No baby munching. No black magick." I held up my fingers in the Girl Scout salute. "I swear by my Twinkie stash."

Jean-Pierre gave me a funky look, but Samedi didn't appear too happy when he faced Laveau.

"You summoned me here to avoid a debt you owe?"

I swear his already deep voice dropped into Michael Duncan Clark territory.

"The vampire brought her into my home—"

Samedi tapped his cane on the antique oak flooring. "You did not answer my question, woman."

She bowed her head. "My intent in summoning you was not to renege on our debts to Rousseau, but to protect my people."

"Very well." Samedi sat in one of the fan-backed chairs by the fireplace. "I will protect your people during these dangerous negotiations." He smiled. "Then you will owe me a debt as well."

Her lips parted as she finally realized the dilemma she'd put herself in. Sometimes, you just can't save people from their own stupidity.

Jean-Pierre was smart enough not to laugh at her, but I could feel his urge in the back of my head. "We would like to use the empty horse barn on the east side of your north pasture for three hours this afternoon."

"Why?" she asked.

"We'd rather not say," the vampire answered smoothly.

"You will need to answer in this situation, Jean-Pierre Louis Rousseau." Samedi gestured at Madame Laveau. "I must honor her request to protect her people."

"We need a staging area for a raid, some place where the dino demons aren't spying on me," I said. "Since the Laveau Coven is notorious for not cooperating with anyone, their property is the smartest place for us to hide our activities."

Samedi cocked his head and regarded me. "This has something to do with tomorrow being All Souls' Eve and your missing niece, no?"

I hesitated for a moment, wondering if he'd use the truth against me. "Yes."

He nodded. "Tell her all of it."

I laid out everything from Ellie's kidnapping to retrieving Constanza's memory of the demon's base in Orange County, California.

After my recital, Madame Laveau sneered. "Maybe these dinosaur gods would be doing us a favor by destroying you."

Samedi tapped his cane against the floor again. "Really, Brigitte Marie Teresa Laveau? Do you not recognize her description of the Old Ones? Samantha's request does not place an undue burden on you. And you have already bargained for my protection in this regard, and given the circumstances, my protection would include any retaliation by the demons upon you and yours."

"Maybe we're not protected enough," she snarled, shooting me a nasty look.

"Do you question me?" The entire orb of Samedi's eyes turned black.

Madame Laveau shivered. "No, my baron."

The loa looked at me. "Ares of Olympus has been helping you, no?"

I nodded. "He's Ellie's foster great-grandfather."

"Bending the rules, but not breaking them. I like that." Samedi smiled. "You have three hours, starting now."

After Jean-Pierre and I returned to the Brentwood mansion, I chowed on cola meat while the phone calls went out. It took Ares and me roughly another forty-five minutes to transport everyone and everything to the horse barn. The weapons, snacks, and drinks didn't whine about nausea or throw up like the people did, so I "borrowed" three port-a-pottys from a highway construction site on I-10 for everyone to use.

While I hoped the adrenaline rush of the coming raid would prevent a repeat of the various bathroom problems in California, I stopped by several drugstores for Dramamine just in case.

What surprised the rest of the supernaturals was when a couple of pickups pulled up outside. One was full of Laveau witches in light armor, and the other contained members of the Tribideaux pack, including their alpha and his second wife.

Alyson Tribideaux nervously approached her father. As far as I knew, it was the first time she'd seen him since she became Logan Polk's beta. An instant later, René pulled her into a huge hug, and they were both crying.

One of the females from Laveau saluted me. It took me a second to recognize her without her zombie makeup as the girl who had escorted Jean-Pierre and me to Brigitte Laveau's parlor. I returned her salute. She smiled and sauntered over to join the rest of the witches.

What surprised me were the other gods who showed up. None of them were death gods, of course. There was some odd rule about only a human death god could go mano-a-mano with a dinosaur god.

I pulled Ares aside as Alex in his asbestos suit called out assignments. "What the hell is going on?" I inclined my head toward the deities. They kept to their personal space, so I couldn't say they were huddled in a corner. But all the humans, Normal and super, gave them a wide berth.

He grinned. "Do not fear. My sister Athena is with Duncan, guarding your brother. As for my other sister—" He shrugged and glanced at a woman who wore the same fierce expression I'd seen on his face. "Tiffany's family is our family after all."

"That accounts for two of them, but the rest aren't Olympians," I hissed. "And why are they here?"

"*Your* friends volunteered their associates," Ares murmured.

"But the rules . . ."

His grin disappeared. "We can only take on the half-breed demons and any other varieties of humans in the upcoming battle. If your enemies succeed in their mission, you are on your own. However, you have volunteers willing to help, and you should thank them."

I didn't feel like arguing manners with him. These were my friends' relatives who I'd never met, which would make socializing awkward as hell. Trying to quell my nervousness, I followed Ares's advice and crossed to the space where the other gods stood.

I had to give the four of them credit. They appeared human for the sake of the rest of our team. The ladies who'd taken it on themselves to "train" me, Kali, Morrigan, and Hela, had each sent one deity from their pantheon.

"Hi, I'm Sam." I waggled my fingers. "Thank you for coming today."

"A child of our family is in danger," Artemis said. Even if she hadn't spoke,

I would have known who she was from her silver braid and the quiver slung over her shoulder.

"Greetings, Sam." The black-haired woman held out her palm. "I'm Sif." We shook hands. The Asgardian had one heck of a grip.

The tall, blond man held out his hand next. "Lugh." Instead of shaking my hand, he kissed the back. Fairy magick tickled my skin. "Morrigan sent me to keep an eye on a certain bargain."

I smiled, and tried to delicately pull my hand from his. "Constanza's not here, so Morrigan doesn't have to worry on that account. And yes, I will deliver my charge as promised once we retrieve my niece."

The last gentleman stepped forward. "I'm here to give you and your troops a little luck." His sweet smile and dreamy eyes would have any female here swooning.

"I appreciate all the help you can give, Ganesh." Just shaking his hand made me feel a lot better about our chances for getting Ellie back in one piece.

"Sam!" Alex called out.

This was the moment I dreaded. The cowboy had decided I needed to say a few words before we moved out, and no amount of refusal on my part could dissuade him.

I jumped up beside him on the tack box he used for a podium. Having every eye on me sent an icy plume of discomfort through my gut.

"I want to thank everyone for being here today." I sucked in a deep breath. "I'm sorry I don't have a rousing *Braveheart* speech to give you before I lead you into a hopeless battle."

More than a few of the younger Normals and supernaturals laughed.

"But I don't think this is a hopeless battle. I know a lot of us don't get along for a lot of reasons, but the fact that we have each other's back now, that we can cooperate to save innocents, means everything to me. And more than anything I want to shut down these dinosaur bastards once and for all before they crack the barrier and let their gods through. Because if we fail today, it means the end of everything."

An angry, defiant rumble passed through the assemblage. I didn't expect cheers over my stupid speech. The cheers would come when we won.

The other gods helped Ares and I teleport our troops into position. My next-to-last drop left Alex in the command van with Miko and one of the Silver Bear enforcers. Between electronic and telepathic coordination, there wasn't one fucking reason for a demon to escape.

A friend of Jorge's even had a small fleet of military grade drones keeping an eye on our target. None of us asked any questions about which branch the detective's friend belonged or how he managed to liberate so many of the unmanned craft.

I popped back to the last group left in the barn. "Ready?"

"Yes," John Lannigan barked. He was paired with Artemis. Thanks to Constanza's intelligence, they'd sweep the top floor of the demons' house for vampires and work their way down. The Los Angeles alpha wasn't thrilled about not being with me, but if he accidentally shifted, we didn't want him to chomp on a demon.

And I would be the demons' primary target.

"Ready," Ares said. He wrapped an arm around Phillippa's waist. They would keep the defenders on the first floor busy.

I placed my hands on the shoulders of Jorge and Tiffany. We had the basement assignment. Release the prisoners, then teleport them out of the house to waiting ambulances manned by supernatural and Family paramedics.

Alex, we're going in.

Commencing assault on the front of the house, he answered.

I teleported.

And hit something. Hard. It felt like a gong going off inside my head and getting punched by Mike Tyson at the same time. Instead of dark and mildew, I flew through bright California sunshine that sparkled off the crystal clear water below me.

I made the belly flop to end all belly flops. What the hell was it with supernaturals tossing me into pools? At least, I could see through the liquid, and there weren't any fairy zombies waiting for me at the bottom this time.

A few strokes brought me to the surface and into chaos. Demons shifted as they dodged fireballs and other offensive spells. Sif and Lugh beheaded any lizard that got past the witches.

I scanned the madness, but I couldn't find Tiffany or Jorge anywhere.

Holy me, where were they?

Chapter 36

Tiffany

I tumbled across concrete and slammed into a set of steel bars. It was pitch black wherever I was. Maybe we'd counted too much on Sam providing illumination.

My eyes adjusted, and a thin line of light pierced the bottom of the door at the top of a set of steps. A dark form lay near me. Considering the ringing in my head, I didn't think it was my sister-in-law. Whatever hit us blocked her from materializing. Pushing myself upright, I whispered, "Sifuentes? You still with me?"

"Define 'with you,'" he murmured.

Screams and the smell of smoke penetrated the gaps around the basement door.

"It sounds like your relatives are keeping busy," the detective said. "Where's Sam?"

"Don't know. She didn't make it in. Even without her, our mission's the same." We climbed to our feet. New bruises on my body replaced the ones Ben Epstein had healed hours ago.

"Don't know about you, but I can't teleport," he muttered. "How do you plan on getting the hostages out?"

"First, we have to find them." I popped the snap on one of the many pockets on my cargo pants and pulled out my tools and mini-flashlight. "Keep an eye on that basement door."

At the sight of red stains on the concrete on the other side of the bars, my fingers trembled. This wasn't the time to think about what the rogues or the demons had done here. Focus on the mission.

I stuck the flashlight in mouth and worked the lock. Nothing sophisticated, thank goodness. A click, then steel hinges squeaked as the gate swung inward. I stood and shoved everything but the flashlight back in my side pocket. I removed the light from my lips and shined it over the next door.

"I'm not sure whether to be impressed or worried about your skill, Stephens."

"That was child's play. It's the electronic lock that'll be a challenge," I muttered as I entered the space and passed a stainless steel table and trays loaded with tools. More crashing and banging came from the ceiling along with a couple of trickles of dust.

"Shit." He followed me into the room.

I popped the plastic cover and examined the wiring. *Alex?*

No answer.

Grandpa Ares?

Still nothing. If Sam couldn't 'port into the basement, I wasn't surprised when I didn't get a reply. "Check your comm unit, Jorge. This place is shielded from the supers."

"Sifuentes to Osaka." Static crackled. He repeated the call twice more before he tried the backup channel. "Sifuentes to Austin? Rodriguez? Walker?" He spat an obscenity in Spanish I didn't recognize. Or maybe it wasn't in Spanish. "We're on our own down here."

"No shit, Sherlock." I stared at the circuit board and wires. "Too bad this isn't set in plasterboard. Then I'd know how to bypass—"

Fuck. I was overthinking this. I reached into my jacket pocket for my gum. Popping the stick into my mouth, I folded the metallic paper into a long thin strip and attached it to two leads. "Got a knife?"

"What's wrong with the blade you have strapped to your waist?"

"God weapon." I shrugged. "If I overload the system, we're not getting in."

Shadows covered Jorge's face, but I could almost feel his eyeroll. He fished in a pants pocket and handed me an oblong object.

I snapped open the penknife. Hopefully, one of the gods here got a hint of my prayer. I sliced the wire as an explosion rocked the building.

Jorge shielded me with his body. Apparently, I wasn't the only one waiting for the house to collapse into the basement.

"That wasn't us setting off something in the next room, was it?" he whispered.

"I don't think so. It came from above us. Could have been a rocket from one of your friend's drones." I peeked up at the display. The green light blinked. "Try the door."

He yanked on the handle, and it silently swung open.

"Jorge!" Siobhan's voice.

The detective rushed past me. I jumped to my feet, grabbed a tool off a tray, and wedged it between the bottom of the door and the floor to hold the door open. Last thing I wanted was for the rescue party to get trapped down here.

I felt around for a light switch and flipped it on. The lights were a low, sickening red color. Siobhan and Jorge held each other through the bars of her cage. Four other women babbled in four different languages.

"Mommy!"

I ran for the chubby little arm thrust out of the last cage and knelt in front of it. "Hey, baby!" I did my best to hug my little girl through the bars. "Are you okay?"

She nodded as I brushed her hair out of her eyes. "The bad people hurt Daddy!"

I smiled despite my blurry eyes. "I know, baby. Doctor Bebe's taking good care of him. Right now, we need to get you out of here."

The hair on the backs of my hands stood straight up, and I could feel the rest of my skin prickle. Another blast rocked the house. Ellie shrieked, and the lights flickered. A crack appeared on the concrete in the back of her cell.

I leaned back. "Sifuentes! We need the keys!"

"What the fuck is Walker thinking?" he growled. He pulled away from Siobhan and started searching. "He's going to kill us with those drones."

"That wasn't conventional," I shot back. "That was magick interaction. Either the demons have fae allies or they're throwing spells themselves."

Electricity danced along my skin. "Ellie! Under your bed! Now!" She listened and scrambled under the metal cot in her cage.

A third explosion hit us. I covered my head as chunks of plaster and sound-proofing tile rained from the ceiling. The lights finally gave up, and we were plunged into total blackness.

We didn't have any more time. One more blast, conventional or magickal, and we would be buried alive if we didn't get out now. I flicked on my flashlight the same time Jorge turned on his.

A wild idea came to me. I yanked Grandpa Ares's knife out of its sheath. This might work if the demons didn't ward the cell locks. If they had, the interaction would kill both me and my daughter. A quick death was better than suffocating after being buried alive.

I held my breath and slash the bolt. The enchanted bronze passed through the steel like butter. My pent air released with a silent "Thank you" to my foster grandfather.

"Ellie, come on. We're getting out of here." I yanked the cage door open.

She crawled from under the bed and ran to me. We rushed from cell to cell, and I slashed each bolt. It wasn't until the first were I let out said "Thank you" in Swahili that I realized Siobhan was the only American.

In very mangled Spanish, Jorge tried to explain to the petite brunette, who been in the cage next to his wife, not to bite anyone. She and Siobhan pantomimed the instructions to the other women. I hoped to hell they all understood.

A wave of static sparked when I touched a steel bar and the charge zigzagged up my arm. The African were seized Ellie and me, shoved us against the concrete wall, and pressed against us.

Boom!

A dull roar preceded the collapse of the ceiling where Ellie's cell had been. Then everything was swallowed by a cloud of dust as the contents of the first floor poured into the open space.

I waited to die with my daughter, but nothing happened except chunks of debris bouncing off my forearm covering my head. Quiet settled over us.

Coughs punctuated the silence. The rest of the house frame creaked in protest to its treatment. The beam from my flashlight barely penetrated the swirling particles.

"I hope the stairs are intact," Jorge said between coughs. He swung his flashlight toward the doorway. "Let's go, ladies."

"I need a weapon," Siobhan grumbled.

"Here." Jorge yanked his backup out of its ankle holster.

She looked at the tiny pistol in disbelief. "Really? You're giving me the little one?"

"When I get kidnapped, then you can have the bigger one," he shot back as he made his way past debris. I recognized the fake bickering as their coping mechanism. Max and I did the same thing.

I sheathed my knife and swung Ellie onto my hip. We followed Jorge and the first three weres. The African were brought up the rear. I reached the door when she shrieked.

Something yanked Ellie from my grip.

I whirled but I didn't need a flashlight to recognize the neon yellow eyes glaring at me from the dark and dust. Giovanni held Ellie by her delicate little neck. From the healing cuts and dust covering him, he'd fallen through the ceiling.

"Tell your grandmother hello for me, sweetie," he murmured in her ear, but his eyes were locked on me when he sank his fangs into my daughter.

Chapter 37

Sam

A couple of strokes took me to the side of the pool. Lugh held out his hand and pulled me out of the water.

"What happened?" he yelled over the chaos.

"Some kind of shield spell, I think." My skin silvered automatically with the presence of so many demons. And the sunshine reflecting off me definitely attracted their attention.

I pulled Flopsy and Peter out of my pocket. The two ghosts were barely visible in the bright California afternoon, but they took off on their mission. Their effect on younger generations of crossbred demons was instant and obvious. The bastards shrieked as the rabbits froze their toes.

"Move," I yelled at Lugh. We separated as a reptilian tail lashed the place where we had been.

My fingernails extended, and I slashed at the demon's throat. The bastard jerked back, only to impale himself on Lugh's spear. The Tuatha whipped the spear toward the pool, and the corpse slid off and sank to the bottom.

"I need to get inside! Tiffany and Jorge are in the basement alone!"

Lugh nodded. "I'll cover your back." We started for the house.

The demons had other ideas. They focused on me to their detriment. By bunching up, they made themselves attractive targets.

All witches and weres, back off from the rear demon cluster. We have Normal incoming. The way Alex's mental voice echoed in my head, the Silver Bear witch in the command van must have been amplifying it.

"Ah, shit. He's not serious," I muttered.

The scent of honey overwhelmed the dry reptilian smell. Lugh tackled me and threw up a magickal shield at the same time. The drone missile detonated on top of us and sent a bright orange plume into the air.

Part of me wondered how the hell we were going to explain this to the Normal authorities.

My stomach rumbled at the mix of honey and barbeque demon. Lugh's shield collapsed, and a wave of heat hit me. His color was an ashy gray.

"You okay?"

His smile was a fraction of the brilliance it had been. "Too much iron in the elements of the explosive."

"Did any touch you?" I frantically searched his body for injuries.

"If it had, we wouldn't be having this conversation. Though I would not object if you continued your examination of my person." The glint in his green eyes was downright wicked.

"Get to an ambulance."

"Forgive me, m'lady." He disappeared, and air popped as it rushed into the empty space. He must have been feeling really shitty. The male deities I'd met didn't let anything short of decapitation interrupt their flirting.

I jumped to my feet, looking for my next target.

Boom!

The ground shuddered under my boots, but this blast came from the front of the house.

Alex, stop firing rockets at us! I got bounced out of the basement by a demon spell! Tiffany and Jorge are unprotected!

That wasn't us—

Instinct and experience took over. I threw up a shield around me and the two weres who were eliminating the injured demons that survived the missile blast. I could feel Ganesh doing the same for our folks on his side of the estate.

Neither Sif nor the witches with her were fast enough. The backlash of interacting magick rolled over them. The weres guarding their flanks went down, hands clutching ears as they fought not to shift. One of the witches from Las Vegas screamed and clawed at her eyes. The other witches had simply passed out.

I hoped.

The backlash didn't give me a migraine-level headache or blind me like the first time I experienced it. Dropping my shield, I called out, "Sif, can you evacuate the people with you?"

She nodded and mouthed, "Sorry."

Dammit, we were already two gods down. So much for Yvonne's tank theory.

A fireball launched from the second floor toward me. I jumped back. No, not a fireball. The burning vampire hit the grass with an obscene *sploosh*.

Two more vamps arched through the air. Like Constanza's little girl in Afghanistan, there really was no place for them to go. Face Artemis's arrows and John's stakes or jump.

I dodged toward the empty space Sif and her evacuees had left. And tried desperately to ignore the sounds of the bodies landing.

The sharp bark of gunfire echoed through the neighborhood for the first time. It was followed by the screech of tires and a crash. Somebody had tried to make a run for it.

A second explosion rocked the front of the house. I ran for the back patio door. We needed to get our people out before some idiot brought the whole place down on Tiffany and Jorge. Assuming I had actually left them in the basement.

I couldn't think about the alternatives. Not now.

Alex, call for retreat and tell the witches in front to stop throwing fucking spells!

Yvonne says it's not our people. Someone inside is deliberately tossing demon and fae magick together. Alex's frustration over being stuck inside the van crawled like ants through my mind.

The glass in the sliding doors was already fractured. A good kick opened a hole. The action felt pretty good, too.

Phil looked up from the vampire she straddled and obviously just staked since the corpse was intact, and she did a double-take. "Where's Ellie and Siobhan?"

"Probably still in the basement," I snapped.

Phil climbed to her feet. "And you aren't there because?" The dead vampire's flesh liquefied and slid off the skeleton.

A vampire appeared in an interior doorway and charged her from behind. I telekinetically grabbed the fireplace poker and rammed it through the rogue's heart.

"I'll explain it later," I said. The floor shuddered beneath us. "We need to get everyone out now."

I ran toward where the basement door should be based on Constanza's memories, Phil on my heels. Ozone hit my nose. I whirled, yanked Phil close, and threw up a shield.

This explosion rocked the entire foundation. A dull roar vibrated against my shield. Fear whispered in my ear that the house was collapsing on top of my niece.

When everything stilled, I dropped the shield. Dust plumed from the front of the house. Part of the ceiling had collapsed behind us, and a bed tilted precariously on a joist and some plywood.

I'll hold the frame up as long as I can, Ares said. *Get Tiffany and Ellie out of the basement.*

We ran. Racing around a corner, I spotted John Lannigan at the basement entrance, the door open. He stared downward.

"John, have the stairs collapsed?" We would need to figure something out fast if I still couldn't teleport down there.

A shot rang from the basement.

From behind us came a shout. "That's not me!"

The demon pretending to be the werewolf whirled to face us.

Phil and I dove in opposite directions.

A silver arrow and three shots hit the demon before he tumbled into the blackness behind him.

Down into the pit where my family was.

Chapter 38

Tiffany

Light shone from above us and spotlighted the stark reality of our situation. The mother in me howled her anguish. The enforcer in me dropped her flashlight, drew her sidearm and fired. I nailed Giovanni between the eyes.

A head shot wouldn't keep a vampire down permanently. I ran for Ellie who screamed in pain.

More shots were fired from the door at the top of the stairs. I grabbed my injured daughter and darted for the concrete wall beside the doorway, the only cover we had. The African were huddled there, too. She bled profusely from her neck, but the liquid wasn't spurting so Giovanni hadn't hit her carotid.

"Dad!" Siobhan's voice. Then a series of thumps sounding an awful lot like someone falling down the stairs.

"Don't touch him! Demon!" Relief swept through me at Sam's voice.

I peered around the corner. The demon, who looked exactly like the Los Angeles alpha, struggled to his feet, a broken arrow shaft sticking out of his chest. Jorge grabbed for Fake John and yelled when demon blood burned his skin. Unfortunately, the demon was between my little group and the stairs.

Sam raced down the steps, raised her knee, pivoted. I ducked back behind the concrete just in time. The demon flew past me and crashed into the pile of debris.

I jumped up and shoved Ellie in Sam's arms as she strode into the cell room. The beams overhead creaked ominously.

"Go!" I yelled.

For once, my all-powerful, pain-in-the-ass sister-in-law didn't argue. She pivoted and raced up the steps. I helped the African were upright and pushed her in the direction of the stairs.

The building will not hold much longer, Grandpa Ares shouted inside my head.

I glanced behind me. The demon threw something at the pile of rubble and yelled something in her language. Because it was a her now. A red-headed her. In the midst of the house debris, a swirling vortex of sienna light shone. The dust and flashing light cleared to show a stark desert landscape with a bizarre sun.

She bent over, grabbed Giovanni under his shoulders, and jumped into the passage with him. Then something else came through from the other side—another demon.

This one didn't look quite like a velociraptor. More like an orange and purple gecko with way too many teeth.

It charged at me. I fired three rounds before it slammed me into the stairs. Sharp pain burned into my skull and my back. Claws raked the forearm I threw up to protect my eyes. I wrapped my legs around its waist to keep it from gutting me with its slashing talons on its rear feet. The demon swatted my gun away, and my fingers fumbled for a weapon.

Any weapon.

"Do you think you can destroy me with your puny toys? You can't kill eternity—*urp*!"

I shoved Grandpa Ares's knife hard through its tongue to penetrate the soft palate and enter the demon's brain. Black ichor dripped from its mouth and dissolved my t-shirt. I bit back a scream as it started burning through my skin.

Someone grabbed my jacket and yanked me from under the collapsing corpse.

I got her, Ares. Get out. Sam's voice in my head.

The house groaned. This time, the rumble was a hell of a lot louder. The instant we cleared the doorframe at the top of the stairs, the ceiling above me bowed and snapped. Instead of plaster and two-by-fours, gut-wrenching vertigo hit me.

I lay in grass. The skin on my abdomen burned like hell. The roar reached a crescendo, and I turned my head in time to see the house collapse on itself.

And continue collapsing. The hole to the other dimension swallowed the structure falling into it.

"One of the demons opened a portal in the basement," I choked out.

"Shit!" Sam ran for house, her coat flying wildly behind her. Black diamond strands of energy trailed from her fingertips. I couldn't quite make out what she was doing. Maybe it was one of those things beyond human vision or comprehension. Whatever she did must have sealed the breach because water sprayed in a graceful arc over her head from a broken main instead of getting sucked into the basement.

Something cold touched my hand. As long as I didn't look at it directly, I could see the faint outline of a rabbit.

"Ellie?" I tried to roll over, but everything hurt too much. "Where's Ellie?"

"Artemis has taken her and the injured werelion to Doctor Bebe, Cherry Blossom."

I turned my head the other way. Grandpa Ares sprawled on the grass next to me. Dust and a mix of red and black blood coated him.

"You need a healer as well." He lurched to his feet.

Tears trickled down my temples and into the dust and other crap that covered me.

Ellie.

Giovanni had bitten her.

My daughter was doomed because I didn't get her out of that fucking house in time.

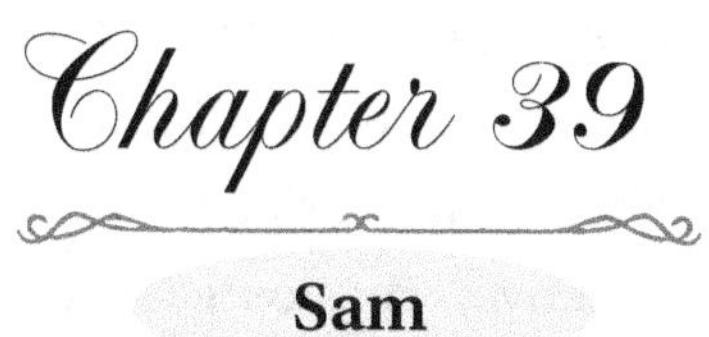

Chapter 39

Sam

After Ares teleported Tiffany to Good Samaritan for burn treatment, I became Alex's eyes and ears while we cleaned up the mess we'd made of the Orange County McMansionville. It kept me busy enough to distract me from my own thoughts and worries. I'd seen the horrible, deep bite on Ellie's shoulder. The matching injuries on the werelion we'd pulled out, too. With her healing factor, the were would survive her injuries. She was damn lucky weres couldn't contract the V-virus.

As a Normal, Ellie . . . would. And infected children never survived.

I tried to focus on the positive. We gotten pretty fucking lucky. One of the Lannigan wolves had died because he'd lost his head in the fight and bitten a demon. The witch who'd scratched out her own eyes had died on the way to the hospital. But overall, our team of rescuers had not only survived, they'd worked damn well together. Even the folks from Rousseau's territory.

But we still had no idea of who had been throwing fae magick from inside the house. Lugh was the only fae-related being on our side, and it sure as hell hadn't been him. Morrigan had already proven she would uphold the fae side of the truce with the vampires. Neither the Summer or Winter queens would be happy about a defector.

I really couldn't see either of them being stupid enough to go behind Morrigan's back and cut a deal with the dino demons. The fae were just as much tasty treats for them as the human race.

While Artemis came back and transported the most severely injured straight to Good Samaritan, Sif and Ganesh had taken the witches and weres, who weren't from the greater Los Angeles metropolitan area, home. No one had heard from Lugh since he had to bug out. As a Tuatha de Danann, he should be fine though. I'd need to consult with Morrigan and the other deities about appropriate recompense. I couldn't call them "Thank you" gifts in front of the fae or the gods. They got rather pissy about things like that.

I hadn't heard directly from Duncan in hours, but he, Caesar, and Alex would be keeping each other updated. Part of me didn't want to call my husband. Didn't want to know if Max's condition had worsened.

When the sun dipped below the horizon, Alex climbed out of the van. He'd stripped off the protective asbestos gear and donned jeans and a button-down shirt.

"I can finish up here, Sam."

"I shouldn't leave." I glanced at the hole in the ground that had been someone's home. "The patch I put on the dimensional rip may not hold. You don't want any of the shit from Otherwhere spilling into our space."

"We will heal the rip, Samantha Marie Ridgeway," a male voice said from behind me. A waft of honey hit me as I turned.

I breathed a little sigh of relief when I saw Lugh. He still didn't look quite right, but he stood straighter and his skin didn't have the gray shade it had after his encounter with the missile.

"What do we need to do?" I asked.

"Not you. Your patch was sufficient for a temporary fix." Lugh's brilliant blue eyes narrowed, and his scent shifted to burnt sugar. "You realize the demons used a fae spell to tear the fabric of the universe."

I nodded.

"Morrigan and others are in Otherwhere."

With his statement, I realized we were surrounded by both Tuatha and fae. Several of the Augustine enforcers edged closer to Alex. Even though the truce had been brokered between the fae and the vampires over my existence four years ago, no one was taking any chances.

"Our magick must heal the tear from both sides," Lugh continued.

"Do you know who's been side-dealing with the dino demons?"

"We will discover the culprit, and Morrigan will call a hunt."

Lugh's statement sent a shiver up my back. I'd read stories during my research into the other pantheons. I'd feel sorry for whoever was the prey of this Wild Hunt if they hadn't been double-crossing us this whole time.

He placed a hand on my shoulder. "Tend to your mortal kin, Samantha Marie Ridgeway. I swear by our mother Danu we will honor our treaty with the vampires, nor will any harm come to the vampires or their Family."

Lugh made a point of pitching his voice so everyone would hear, but the enforcers didn't relax until Alex signaled them to stand down. Being married to a demigoddess, he understood the seriousness of Lugh's oath.

"He's right." Alex's Texas drawl became even more pronounced than normal. "You need to be with our family. Would you mind taking Phil with you?"

"No problem." I turned to collect Tiffany's foster mom.

"Samantha—"

I faced Lugh again.

"The terms of your bargain with Duke Millanthropas—"

"I know." I tried to hold back my irritation with the Tuatha. "I'll make the delivery before dawn."

He gave me a little half-bow before I stalked off to collect Phil. Part of me wanted to scream at the universe. With all these powers, I was more tightly restricted by what I could do than when I was human. It made me want to start breaking rules, but I'd destroy the universe and everyone I loved if I did.

Except if I lost everyone anyway, what was the point of holding back?

Chapter 40

Max

Something penetrated the gray haze cocooning me. A name. A name that meant something.

Ellie.

My daughter was in danger. Someone in the house. They took her. I needed to get her back. Rescue her. A little girl expected her daddy to take care of her.

I struggled and lunged. Something snapped, and I hurtled through space. Or time. Or maybe both. Falling.

Not falling. Flying.

I stood in a hospital room. Ellie lay on the bed, a tiny, pale figure on the stark white sheets. She was asleep. Or maybe sedated. A wad of bandages covered the space between her neck and right shoulder. A drainage tube poked out of the gauze with a flattened plastic bulb attached to the free end. An IV line entered her left hand.

I reached for her forehead, only for my hand to pass through her skin, her skull. I jerked back, but she didn't stir.

What the hell? I held up my right arm. The security lights outside shone through both the window and my flesh and clothes. I tried grabbing the railing on Ellie's bed.

And couldn't. My fingers slid right through the aluminum rod.

Maybe I should have expected the inevitable. Especially after the convocation of the death gods.

But it didn't matter. Tiffany kept her promise. She brought our daughter home.

Something clattered behind me. I jumped and whirled around to face the intruder.

Bebe stared at me, her mouth agape. A clipboard and papers were scattered on the floor. "Max?"

The PA system beeped in the hallway. A nurse's voice announced, "Code blue. We have a code blue in room 1103."

Bebe closed her eyes, leaned her head back, and took a deep breath.

"That's me, isn't it?"

She nodded.

"I have a DNR on file." I didn't have anything against my wife's family. I just didn't want to be like them. From watching them the past few years, immortality wasn't all it was cracked up to be.

A shriek echoed down the hall, then a series of curse words that didn't come from my potty-mouthed little sister or my equally potty-mouthed wife. Mom was fighting the staff. Or the in-laws.

It would be best to ignore the commotion. I looked at my daughter, and my hand hovered over Ellie's hair since I couldn't actually touch her. "What happened to her? The wound must be deep of you need to drain it."

"Giovanni bit her."

I stumbled back and fell through the visitor's chair I tried to sit in. The odds of surviving a vampire virus infection were damn low for a healthy adult. Ellie was too young.

"Before you panic and short out the electronics in your floundering—" Bebe continued dryly. "—she's not infected."

I stared up at the doctor. "How?"

"She's naturally immune." A wry smile tilted her mouth. "Like I am."

"Wait a minute. There's no witch blood in our family—" Understanding swept through him. "If Ellie's immune, I'm immune?"

Bebe nodded. "I just got the lab reports back. I was coming to tell Tiffany, but when I sensed someone else in here with Ellie—"

I managed to climb to my feet without accidentally passing through the floor tiles. "Yeah, I heard it's been a pretty rough—how many days has it been?"

The doctor glanced at the clock on the wall by the TV. "You left our place about twenty-five hours ago."

More shouting came from the hallway. Bebe rolled her eyes. "Let me deal with your family. You stay with Ellie."

"Say my good-byes you mean."

She hesitated a moment. "Are you going to be a problem, Max?"

"No." I looked down at my daughter. I would miss so many things, but

I didn't have a single regret. "I'll wait until Sam comes to get me." My eyes shot back to the doctor. "*Is* she coming to get me?"

Bebe shrugged. "My understanding is that's up to you."

"Okay." I lowered myself gingerly into the chair. It felt a little weird but I figured out how to stay on the surface. "I'll be here."

Bebe pivoted and charged out the door. I distinctly heard Tiffany yelling that time.

Would she be angry with me for leaving her and Ellie? We'd talked about plans and wishes when we learned she was pregnant. She had my life insurance and savings. The house was paid off. Hell, Tiffany had her own multi-million-dollar trust fund that she'd get full control over next year. Financially, she and Ellie would be fine.

But that wouldn't make up for missed ballet recitals and martial arts tournaments. Or my absence for birthdays, anniversaries, and graduation ceremonies.

Okay, maybe there were some regrets.

But I wouldn't change a thing.

Chapter 41

Tiffany

"What the hell were you thinking, you freakazoid!" I'd held back since our wedding that the bitch insisted be held at her estate. *My* wedding. I'd held back over the goddamn ballet lessons she insisted my baby had to have. But this was one interference too many. Especially since I'd lose my daughter on her fourth birthday. "You crossed the line!"

For all my training though, god power still trumped my Normal strength. Sam jerked me backward and wrenched the knife out of my hand. The one I was trying to plunge in my mother-in-law's heart.

Sam tossed the bronze weapon to Grandpa Ares. I took advantage of her slight distraction and twisted until I had her in an armlock. Yanked my Glock from its holster—

And was promptly tackled to the floor by Phil. Her boot landed on my right hand, and my gun slid across the floor.

Rage didn't begin to cover the emotion coursing through me. "Let me shoot the bitch!"

"What the fuck are you people doing in my ward!" Bebe's magickally amplified voice drove a spike through my brain. It was worth my pain to see Elizabeth collapse.

Uncle Duncan could have caught her. From his disgusted expression, he deliberately let her hit the tiled floor.

I think Ted did, too. He only made a half-hearted grab for his wife as she went down.

I couldn't say a word to Bebe because Phil had me in a headlock.

"Chill, or so help me, I *will* choke you out," she whispered in my ear.

I stopped fighting her, but I didn't relax, which was why she didn't release me.

The werewolf who was the duty nurse for the critical care unit stepped forward. "We followed the DNR order for Mr. Howell." She jabbed an index finger at Elizabeth. "She was already performing CPR on him when we entered his room."

"Mom restarted Max's heart." Sam kicked my gun over to Ares who collected it. "Honey, I need your help relocating my dislocated arm."

Duncan snapped his wife's humerus back into her shoulder socket.

Ted pulled his wife off the floor.

Bebe covered her face with both hands.

Grandpa Ares shook his head. "If I wanted to deal with this type of family shit, I would have stayed on Olympus."

Bebe dropped her hands to her sides. "Everyone, take a seat, and if any one of you opens your mouth before I'm done, I'll turn every last fucking one of you into newts."

Not even Sam and Ares argued with the witch. Everyone perched on a chair. Everyone except me.

Phil literally carried me to the couch. Ares sat on my other side. They both had a firm grip on me.

Probably in case I went for another weapon.

"I'm starting with the bad news, which Sam already knows—"

"Doctor Zachary, do you want me to call security?" the nurse asked.

The nasty look Bebe gave the lady were said she was now included on the possible newt list. The nurse slunk back to her station.

Bebe crumpled in a chair herself. "Max died when he coded. I'm sorry."

All of us looked at Sam, who stared at her hands in her lap.

"B-but his heart is beating." Ted's face had turned an ashy gray hue.

Guilt hit me. I wasn't the only one losing a child tonight.

"It's an autonomous reaction. It will stop again. Max is no longer in his body," Bebe said quietly. She turned to me, and a tired smile lit her face. "But we have some damn good news. Ellie's not infected with the V-virus."

Something cracked inside of me. I didn't dare believe her. "Giovanni bit her. Deep. A-and chewed on her to make sure . . ."

"I know." Bebe pulled her chair closer to me. "I'm not saying she's totally out of the woods. She lost a lot of blood when he bit her, but I can bring in a healer tomorrow morning. We're a little short-handed at the moment."

"But I still don't understand how . . ." My words were lost when Caesar and Alex entered the waiting room.

Bebe glanced at them. "Take a seat, boys. I want everyone to hear this at the same time." She turned back to me. "Ellie's immune to the v-virus."

Nothing she said made sense. "That's not possible. There haven't been any witches in our family all the way back to Duncan, Grandma Margaret and Grandpa Kensai."

A light glinted in Bebe's brown eyes. "That's because Ellie's immunity is from Max's side and it's very, very Normal."

"So what are you saying?" Elizabeth looked angry enough to chew nails.

"Max would never have Turned, even if he had agreed to it," Bebe said quietly. "All the trouble you caused between the vampire covens today was for nothing."

Everyone was quiet for a long moment before Caesar said, "Are you saying what I think you're saying, *amora*?" His eyes glowed neon yellow.

"The Howells have the missing blood element I've been searching for." She shook her head. "I should have suspected something a long time ago. Anne always chalked her inability to alter Max's memories to her inexperience." She gestured at my uncle. "But Duncan had difficulty with Sam when she was still Normal, and you couldn't affect Elizabeth."

I could tell Caesar wanted to jump up and race around the hospital with glee. A cure for vampirism was something he'd wanted for over two thousand years. But he glanced at me and squelched the urge.

"What—" I sucked in a deep breath. "What are you going to need from Ellie?"

Bebe's smile turned downright evil. "Not a damn thing. She's too young, and Sam's blood is tainted thanks to the nanites." She stared at my mother-in-law. "As restitution for her treason, Elizabeth will be my donor."

The subject of our discussion jumped out of her chair. "I most certainly will not! That's a violation of my rights! I will not be someone's lab rat!"

"You lost your rights when you violated protocol and contacted the other vampire masters without my consent," Caesar said. His eyes went from yellow to red.

"I'm an American—"

Sam rose to her feet. "Mom. Shut up."

Elizabeth's teeth clicked when her jaw snapped shut.

"There's a plea deal on the table." Sam crossed her arms. "I would advise you to take it, and become Bebe's lab rat for however long she needs. Your alternative is a death sentence, and since you've gone out of your way to antagonize everyone in the coven, there will be a lottery over who gets the right to behead you." Sam stepped closer to her mother. "That's assuming you make it out of this hospital alive tonight."

A whine came from Elizabeth.

"You may speak now." Sam snapped her fingers for show.

"You can't do this," Elizabeth hissed.

Sam shrugged, but said nothing, merely stepped away from her mother. Both Duncan and Alex stood, waiting for a signal from Caesar.

I tried to stand, too, but Phil and Ares maintained their grips on me.

No, Cherry Blossom. If this goes against her, if she makes the wrong choice, you do not want her shade haunting you.

Elizabeth's mouth twisted as if she were sucking lemons. "Fine. I'll be the guinea pig."

Bebe glanced over her shoulder at the nurse's station.

The charge nurse smiled, the evil kind that only a were could pull off. "Randy's on his way up to collect Mrs. Howell."

Elizabeth jerked. "Tonight?"

"Just your first pint," Bebe said mildly. "One of my staff will call you in the morning and schedule your future visits."

The elevator doors slid open, and the med tech who'd been with Alisha in the cafeteria this morning strode out. "Mrs. Howell?" He beckoned her to follow him.

She looked down at Ted. "Aren't you coming?"

"You're a big girl," he said. "You can handle donating a pint by yourself."

"B-but—" She seemed flabbergasted that for once, Ted didn't come running when she called.

"I'll be up here when you're done." The look he gave her could have frozen Lake Tahoe solid. "With my family."

My mother-in-law stood there, stunned, searching for an ally, but she found none. Not today. Maybe not ever again. She pivoted and took three steps when Alex drawled, "And Elizabeth?"

Both the tech and my mother-in-law paused. "What?" she snapped.

"Doctor Zachary will give me a copy of your appointment schedule. An enforcer will escort you to and from each and every appointment."

"And you will make every appointment," Caesar added.

"Because if you don't—" Ares grinned and flames danced in his eye sockets. "—I will find you, and you don't want that."

Elizabeth shuddered, and from the way the med tech wrinkled his nose, she stunk with fear. She backed into the tech before she whirled and ran for the elevator. The tech followed, humming the theme from *Jaws*.

I released the breath I didn't realize I'd been holding. Part of me was hoping my mother-in-law would do something incredibly stupid to earn her execution. I didn't know how Max and Sam survived their childhoods with that selfish bitch.

"Is Max already gone?" I said.

Bebe and Sam exchanged a look before the doctor said, "He's in Ellie's room right now, saying good-bye."

"Does he—did you tell him that she'll be all right."

"Yes," Bebe said.

I was torn between running down the hall and staying glued to the couch.

"Tiffany—" Bebe hesitated. "You're his medical power of attorney. I need your permission to remove the ventilator."

"I-I need to see him first." I tried to stand up and this time, Phil and Ares let me. Everything felt so numb. I was preparing for Ellie's death, then everything went topsy-turvy.

"How—" Duncan cleared his throat. From the twitches of his face muscles, someone told him what I was about to ask.

"Sam, please." I'd only begged for one other thing in my life until today. Tonight would be my hat trick for pleading. "You let me see your rabbits. Please let me see him."

The shoulder I didn't dislocate on her sagged. "All right." She held out her hand.

I crossed the waiting room and grasped her palm. Everything took on a slow-motion quality at that point. The walk to Ellie's room lasted decades. But when I reached the door, I couldn't open it. Couldn't make myself reach out.

Because once I saw Max's ghost, I'd have to face the fact that he was gone.

"You don't have to go inside," Sam murmured close to my ear. "You can go back to Bebe. Deal with the paperwork."

And I'd regret my actions forever if I did. I pushed the door open.

Ellie lay in her bed, asleep. Max sat with her. He almost looked like he'd just gotten home from work with his slacks, button-down shirt, and glasses. He even had all of his hair, and the Bugs Bunny watch I'd bought him for our first anniversary was strapped to his wrist.

Except his body and everything about him was transparent.

I jerked out of Sam's grasp and rushed to him. My arms went through his shade. "You're still here. We can fix this. Sam can—"

"No." Max's hand brushed my cheek, or tried to. All I felt was a wave of cold. "Not this time, Tiffany."

"Yes, she can!" I didn't care if Sam saw me crying. "She did it with the baby zombies!"

"And we promised each other Ellie wouldn't grow up like you did." He tried to pull me close. An icy sensation swept through my gut when his arms went through me. His face reflected my frustration. "You need to stay here. You need to take good care of our little girl."

I whirled to face Sam. "Do something. Put him back."

Except she was staring at the corner of Ellie's room. The hairs rose on the back of my neck. I didn't need her to tell me what or who was there. I drew one of my spare silver knives from its boot sheath, spun, and charged at the blinding white outline of a man with wings.

The blade shattered into a million pieces. He held out a hand and gently caught me against him. I tried every move I knew, but it was like I fought a cloud.

He sang something, notes so agonizingly beautiful I slapped my hands over my ears and fell to my knees. If I didn't block it, my brain would explode.

Sam pulled me away from the angel. She cradled me on the floor while I sobbed like a little baby.

A rush of cold penetrated my bones. "Tiffany, I love you. I will *always* love you." For the briefest of instances, Max's warm, living lips kissed my forehead.

"No! Sam, fix this!"

"Azrael says I can go with Max to the gates," Sam said. "I promise I'll make sure he arrives there."

"No! You can't take him." The words became my mantra. My screaming woke Ellie, and her howls echoed my own.

The door slammed open. Cooler arms replaced Sam's. Duncan's voice crooned in my ear, repeating "It is all right. I have you."

Over and over again.

Phil lowered the railing and cradled Ellie as gently as she could.

"You let that bastard take him, Sam, I'll hate you forever!"

She ignored me. "I'll be back soon, Duncan."

The angel wrapped his wings around Max, and the three of them disappeared.

"Sam! Noooooooooooooo!"

Phil comforted Ellie while Duncan dragged me from my baby's hospital room.

Chapter 42

Sam

"Thank you for letting me accompany my brother," I said.

"You're welcome," Azrael replied. He led us through a gray mist. It was as eerie and disconcerting as the first time I'd entered the transition space.

"This doesn't look like Otherwhere," Max muttered.

"It's not, Maxwell," the angel said.

Rays of sunshine pierced the thinning fog. The ground beneath our feet felt spongey. Azrael strode a little ahead of Max and me, giving what passed for a small amount of privacy. Ziva's words about the Angel of Death from earlier today rang in my head. *Has it occurred to you that he's in Los Angeles for a reason tonight?*

"I'm so sorry, Max. I should have been there."

"Come on, Sam." Max's tired smile crushed my heart. "We both knew the moment Baron Samedi took me to the amphitheater I was fucked. Only death can walk there. Isn't that what SHE told you? I got four wonderful years with my wife and daughter. I can't ask for more."

Shit. Had Max's death been Samedi's plan all along? Was his capitulation four years ago and his cooperation in today's raid been for show?

"You should have had more," I grumbled. "It's not fair."

"Since when has death been fair to either of us." Max chuckled. "When Tiffany gets over her grief and anger, she's going to laugh her ass off over the fact Selene had the cure to the V-virus right in front of her the whole time."

"I don't know about that." One small favor was that my brother didn't hear Tiffany's last thoughts before we left. I really hoped it was her pain talking. She may be Normal, but she had all the makings for an evil genius.

"Give her time." He nudged my shoulder, which made me stumble. I'd forgotten spirits had substance here. "Would you be willing to take one last piece of big brother advice?"

"Depends."

"Quit taking Duncan for granted."

I blinked. "What the hell is that supposed to mean?"

"Look, I get that you two will still be around when the continents become one again. But when you take off without telling him where you're going or when you'll be back? Well, that's just rude."

"He knows what I'm doing," I protested.

"And he knows why, but dammit, Sam! Even Tiffany gives me—gave me that little courtesy."

I sucked in a deep breath and released it. Maybe Max was right. Duncan could be patient as hell, but despite his disease, he was still human.

"All right. I'll try to treat him better."

Max opened his mouth, and I held up a hand. "You quote Yoda, and I'll have your corpse turned into one of those Body World plasticized museum pieces."

He closed his mouth.

One of the fluffy white clouds grew bigger the closer we approached. It resolved into a large wall with—

I stopped and tilted my head. Yep, those were definitely pearly gates. I guesstimated the wall and gates had to be five hundred-feet high.

A man in white robes stood at a podium in front of the gates. A waist-length beard made up for the lack of hair on his head.

Azrael turned to Max and me. "This is where we part ways, Samantha."

I nodded. The inevitable had arrived. I hugged Max. "Take care of yourself, Snotface."

He squeezed me back. "You, too, Pain in the Ass." We parted and he headed for the man at the podium. Max didn't look back.

Azrael turned to me and smiled. "If I may make a suggestion?"

Once again, I nodded, not trusting my voice.

The angel leaned close. "Add a drop of your blood to Ziva's lambs' blood spell, and we won't hear you when you have one of your . . . verbal accidents."

The need to cry warred with the desire to laugh. I settled on returning the angel's smile. "Thank you for the tip."

The gates opened. Max and Azrael entered. I knew I'd never see my brother again, and I found I couldn't go home quite yet.

The entrance to Norman's realm looked like the front of a New England college library. All stone and moss with huge oak doors adorned by ugly brass knockers. I banged one of the knockers to the rhythm of "Shave and a haircut."

The door swung open to the cheerful mien of Norman. Still looking like some liberal arts college professor, he wore an ivory cardigan over a black turtleneck and matching slacks. Add in the horn-rimmed glasses and the shaggy hair and beard. A brandy snifter rested in his right hand.

He held the glass out to me. "Thought you might need this."

I entered what appeared to be a foyer and accepted the glass. "I take it you heard."

He hesitated before he admitted, "Everybody knows."

"And?" I took a sip of the liquor before I followed him into his study. That he let me go straight there was probably a good thing with my state of mind.

Every other time, I had to pass through the halls of souls that ended up in his care. Since those folks who didn't believe in any god, or even a god, ended up with him, he basically ran a soul compost facility. Each soul dissolved in its own little see-through box until it had degraded enough to rejoin the quantum flow of the universe.

I was still human enough to find the process freaky as shit.

His study, on the other hand, looked like the proverbial professor's man cave. A huge fireplace, dark wood, matching leather furniture, and lots and lots of bookshelves completely full of the classics.

Norman gestured for me to take a seat by his fireplace. He sank into the matching chair. "There's no 'and' to it. Would you like me to say that I'm sorry for your loss?"

"No." I set the snifter on a side table. "Why'd Baron Samedi bring my brother to the convocation?"

Norman sighed. He reached for the decanter on the side table next to him and poured a healthy amount into a glass that matched the one he had handed me. He took a long swallow before he leaned back and regarded me.

"You're asking if Max's death is Samedi's fault."

"You mentioned fault, not me."

"The loa are prideful and capricious, but Max's death tonight wasn't their fault." Norman leaned forward. "Any more than it is yours. Our position is unique in the grand scheme of the universe, but we can't alter other beings' free will."

"You mean Giovanni's for initiating last night's attack?"

Norman shrugged and leaned back again. "Or Mallory and Selene's pursuit of a modified V-virus, or even David Head's obsession with Duncan, which if I may point out began long before you met your husband."

I knew when I was being played. "Be straight with me for once. Did Max die tonight because Samedi brought him to the convocation?"

"No." Norman took another swallow of his brandy. "He was supposed to die the night of his wedding. You interfered."

"H-how did I interfere? I wasn't anywhere near him during the zombie attack."

"Quite simply, you were there." Sad, brown eyes stared deep into mine. "You saved most of the attendees by coming back and destroying the zombies."

My heart stopped, and the silence in my head was deafening. "Wh-what do you mean?"

"You should have died at Mallory Labs two months before Max died at his wedding. He would still have met Tiffany, but it would have been through Anne, not you." He stared at his glass a moment before he faced me again. "This is why we emphasize not interfering with mortal matters. We have no way of predicting the effects."

I swallowed hard. "And the people I've killed?"

"Sam, you are still learning. You're going to make mistakes. We all have. The question is whether you will learn from those mistakes."

I'd screwed up enough over the last five years. There was one more thing I needed to do tonight. I pushed myself to my feet. "There's one mistake I won't make. I have a promise I need to honor."

Norman nodded and rose as well. "If you need to talk again, Sam . . ."

I smiled and hugged him. "I'll take you up on that offer, but I need to deal with some things at home first."

When I popped into Caesar's living room, no one shot at me for the first time in years. Colin Fitzgerald, Anne's husband, looked up from his book.

"Where is everybody?" I asked. "Better yet, why are you here?"

"I'm holding down the fort. Anne is supervising the last of the clean-up down in Orange County. I think she was a little tired of babysitting Caesar though she'd never admit it." He carefully marked his place, set aside the book, and rose. "And Alex needed to be with the family. How are you doing?"

"Fine."

"Uh-huh." He crossed his arms. "I've been in your shoes. Wanna try again?"

I blinked, and the tears I held back for the last day and a half came pouring out. "It's all my fault."

Colin didn't give me any fake platitudes. He just held me while I sobbed. If anyone understood how one simple decision changed the course of your life, it would be him. His brother had died because Colin had swerved left instead of right when a truck crossed the highway median and hit his car.

When the tears ebbed, I stepped away from his embrace and wiped my face on my sleeve. "Anyway, I need to talk to Constanza."

"I'm ready to go." She stood in the doorway to the foyer. From the fresh mix of her natural sandalwood and the citrus-scented bath products I'd gotten Anne hooked on, Constanza had washed up in preparation for the payment to Duke Millanthropas.

"You don't have to do this," I repeated for who-knew-how-many times.

"Yes, I do." Her smile was a mix of sadness and wistfulness. "After the last thirty hours, I think I need more than even the fae are capable of dishing out. Besides, I've never welched on a deal. I'm guessing you can't either because of what you are."

I waved toward the duffle slung over her shoulder. "I have to ask what's in the bag."

"Clean clothes for when you pick me up." She grinned. "It'll make him look bad if he returns me to you . . . messy."

I sighed. I didn't like thinking about the position I'd let Constanza put herself in, but she seemed almost . . . enthusiastic about spending time with the fae. "All right. Let's get this over with." I patted Colin's shoulder. "Thanks for letting me use you as a tissue."

"Be careful with them, Sam." He turned to Constanza. "You, too, newbie."

I'd forgotten he had his own bad experiences with the fae. "We will," I said before I crossed to Constanza, placed my hand on her shoulder, and did my genie nod.

We popped back into conventional reality on the street in front of Millanthropas's estate. I waited a second before I approached the dark purple gates, more to give Constanza a chance to catch her balance than to let the fae get a good look at us.

"Samantha Ridgeway and Constanza Torres to see Duke Miller," I called out. "We have an appointment."

Sapphire stepped from the shadows. "I'm surprised you're early." She sniffed. "Begone, Ridgeway. Only Constanza Abril Torres is welcome here."

"Excuse me, bitch?" I cocked my head. "My deal was with Duke Millanthropas, not you. I will deliver Ms. Torres to him, not you. Or shall I tell Morrigan you managed to breach the contract in less than five minutes? Because I'd love to watch her flay you alive. I'd even bring popcorn for the show."

If looks could kill, I'd be incinerated into my composite atoms. But in the end, Sapphire knew I was right, and she let us both enter the grounds.

Millanthropas waited for us in the same receiving room as he had hours before. He rose with his unnatural grace from the loveseat. "A pleasure to see you both again."

"Don't you mean you're disappointed the demons didn't kill me?" I growled.

He held up his hands, fingers spread. "Hardly. I wouldn't be looking forward to an enjoyable time with Constanza Abril Torres if things hadn't worked out for you, Lady Samantha."

"I'll be back in forty-eight hours, and I expect Ms. Torres to be returned to me in the same condition I left her, Millanthropas, otherwise—"

"You can't kill me, Ridgeway." He smirked.

"You're right. I can't kill you—directly." A feral grin stretched my lips. "But I hear Jupiter's a little stormy this millennium."

Once I was past Millanthropas's gates and on the street again, I concentrated to locate Duncan. He was still at Good Samaritan Hospital. Had Ellie's condition deteriorated after the scene in her room?

I teleported to the CCU waiting room. It was empty except for my husband. He was slumped on the couch, his head listing to the side. Sound asleep.

He jerked upright, fangs extended and eyes glowing a brilliant emerald.

I held up my hands. "Hey, it's just me."

Duncan relaxed a little and rubbed his eyes. "I am sorry, darling. I—"

I touched my index finger to his lips. "No excuse necessary. None of us have had much sleep the last couple of days." I sat down beside him. "Is everything okay with Ellie?"

He nodded and reached for my hand. "Phillippa got her back to sleep. I fear she may be having nightmares for the next several months."

"And Tiffany?"

"Tiffany had to be . . . sedated."

I winced. "That's not going to go over well when she wakes up."

"No." He squeezed my fingers. "She will not be happy about many things. Since she was unconscious, and Ted and I were Max's back-up decision-makers, we made the decision to discontinue the life support. It helps to know with absolute certainty that he was gone."

Duncan and Dad.

Because Max didn't trust Mom or me to abide by his wishes.

"I get not having Mom as his medical power of attorney." I swiped at my blurry eyes. "But was he really that afraid I would resurrect him?"

My husband's silence said everything.

"So it's a no-win scenario?" I bit out. "Either Max and the rest of you hate me, or Tiffany carries a grudge for the rest of eternity?"

"I did not want to hurt either of you," Duncan whispered.

So he was in the same position I was. It was a little pathetic that it made me feel better. I cuddled against his shoulder, and he wrapped his arm around me. "Where's everyone else?"

"Ares and Phillippa are with Tiffany and Ellie respectively since we know Giovanni and one of the demons escaped."

I sighed. "That's probably the best arrangement. She'll think twice before she gives her grandfather shit."

Duncan chuckled. "That was the consensus here as well. Alex took Caesar and Bebe home. She has not slept in nearly two days."

"Tell me about—" My gigantic yawn interrupted my train of thought.

Duncan must have picked up my intention before I lost it. "Your parents have been taken to their home. Given your mother's indiscretions, we have had to make alternate arrangements for their protection since only one enforcer volunteered for the duty."

"Such as?"

"Jake, Agnes, and Emerson will be staying with Ted and Elizabeth for the foreseeable future."

I leaned back and stared at my husband for a moment. Nope. He wasn't joking. We both cracked up at the same time.

When I could catch my breath, I wiped my eyes. "Holy shit. That's the start of a really bad joke. Your ex-fiancé, your conspiracy theorist friend, and her cursed werebulldog boyfriend walk into your parents' house . . ."

I took a deep breath and cuddled against Duncan's shoulder again. Of course, Jake was the only volunteer enforcer. While every other member of Augustine's law enforcement arm would want Mom's head separated from her shoulders for betraying Caesar, Jake would step up for Max's sake. I never really understood why the two of them had remained friends after I left Jake.

Or maybe I wanted to believe I was the only thing they had in common.

That wasn't the only uncomfortable thought drifting through my tired brain. "Mom didn't give the lab people much trouble, did she?"

"No." Duncan stiffened beneath my cheek.

"If you think I'll be upset you gave Bebe permission to harvest what she needs from—the corpse, I won't be."

"Actually, it was your father's idea." Duncan's voice softened. "He also recommended that you dispose of Max's body in the sun, so no one will dig up his body once news of your family's immunity gets out."

"Where did he get the idea that I'm Supergirl?"

"When you teleported to this very waiting room, squeaking like Minnie

Mouse after a visit to Jupiter. I told him your heat vision would be sufficient to dispose of the remains."

I was definitely too tired to think straight if I giggled at Dad's idea. The problem was I could generate that kind of heat, and it would be a good idea to incinerate Max's corpse. I'd learned over the years the split between Caesar and Selene was partly due to her fear that Bebe's grandmother would reverse engineer the witches' immunity gene into a super-virus to wipe out the vampires. Last thing we needed was someone else making Psycho Vamp's paranoid fantasy a reality.

"Wait." Another disturbing thought scratched its way through my brain. "If Max carried the immunity through Mom's line, what about Grandma Neel?"

"Ares already sent his sisters to collect her and bring her to Los Angeles. We could not let her stay in Dare territory."

"Shit," I muttered. "I hope she didn't give the ladies too much crap. She's refused to leave West Virginia for the last twenty years."

A bit of my own fear tainted my last question after the way I'd been treating Duncan over the last year. And I really hated admitting my big brother was right. Maybe I should start there.

"I'm sorry for the way I've been acting lately," I whispered.

Duncan nuzzled my hair. "I only want a phone call to let me know you are alive."

"I'll be home more often."

After a long pause, he murmured, "No, you will not."

I jerked out of his hold. "Wh-what are you saying?"

Green eyes stared into mine. "Only that Giovanni and at least one demon hybrid are on the loose. They will be seeking to restart their breeding program in order to destroy you. And you have to find them before they do." He smiled and brushed my hair back. "As I said, I would like a phone call once in a while to know you are alive. Perhaps every three days?"

I relaxed a bit. "I think I can manage that. Um, would you, um, maybe, want to go home now?"

"As much as I truly desire to sleep in our own bed with you, it is better that we stay at the Brentwood mansion. Caesar has asked we attend a meeting at sundown."

I toyed with Duncan's tie. "I can always pop us back in plenty of time."

"There is also the matter of your new dietary requirements, darling."

I groaned. "Don't remind me about the dinosaur sushi." But he had a point. We needed to experiment to find out how much curbed my unnatural appetite. Maybe cook that shit the next time I had to eat it. And I may have to learn how to hunt the damn things for food. A shudder ran through me.

Duncan stood up and pulled me to my feet. "Then let us get some rest, and we will discuss your appetites when we wake."

I tugged on his tie. "Can we not discuss any appetites, food or otherwise, right now? We both need some sleep."

He kissed me soundly. "All right, but I expect you to adhere to my phone call request as recompense."

I smiled. "I think I can accommodate you, Mr. St. James."

"By the way, happy birthday, darling."

I knew he meant well, but his felicitation only added to the ache in my heart. Max's death had probably ruined Halloween and her own birthday for Ellie, even though technically he'd died the day before.

His death had definitely ruined the day for me.

Chapter 43

Tiffany

Caesar insisted I be at this stupid meeting of his even though Ellie was still in the hospital. The healer and Bebe had done their jobs before I woke up this morning, but they wanted my daughter under observation for another twenty-four hours due to her age and the severity and depth of her injuries. Grandpa Ares promised to stay with Ellie while I was gone.

I deliberately ignored *her* when I entered Caesar's study. I also deliberately sat cross-legged on one of the antique end tables that framed the leather couch. I hoped my boots scratched the hell out of the finish.

For the first time ever, Caesar didn't sit behind his desk, the lord of his domain. He leaned against the front of the cherry monstrosity. Bebe perched on the desktop next to him.

Once the coven's entire inner circle was there, Caesar cleared his throat. It wasn't like the boss to be so hesitant. Good. Maybe he felt guilty about using my husband for spare parts.

Maybe that guilt was why Bebe spoke first. "Everyone in here knows that Sam's family is immune to the vampire virus through her mother's line. I've already run some preliminary tests, and the results are promising. We should have a vaccine that will work on both witches and Normals ready for human testing within four to six months."

She took a deep breath. Even I, as the only Normal in the room, could feel the sharp prick of tension.

"We're looking at a potential cure within two years."

"There are those who will want to gain control of the research as my sister tried to, or try to destroy our most critical sources of raw materials," Caesar said, picking up the real reason for this little session. "Which means Elizabeth, Ellie, and Fanny Neel will be at risk for abduction or death, especially once the news gets out." He turned to *her*. "Sam, I know your grandmother is upset about leaving her home, but she cannot go back to Dare territory."

She nodded. "I'll go see her as soon as we're done here. Anne, you're close to Grandma's age. Would you mind coming with me? She's more likely to listen to you."

Anne nodded. "Of course."

Caesar's eyes shifted from brown to gold. "As you all know, I've been searching for a cure for some time. I know not every vampire will rejoice at the news of such. Nor do I want to leave any of the supernaturals or Normals living under the aegis of Augustine Coven at risk from the other members of the Vampire Nation. I want to put together an orderly plan for the transition of power. Therefore, I need to know each of your personal wishes."

He turned to Colin who was the youngest vampire in the room.

Colin laughed. "I haven't celebrated my fifth Turnaversary yet." He glanced at his wife. Anne's eyes glowed a soft gold as well. She took his hand in both of hers, before he returned his attention to Caesar. "We'll take the cure, but we'll wait until things are settled with the coven transition before we do."

"I'm staying vampire," Alex said.

Phil nudged him. "You should tell them why."

A rueful expression crossed the chief enforcer's face. "Bebe and I spoke. She can't guarantee that old health issues won't return." He shoved his hands in his back pockets, his tell that he was uncomfortable as hell. "Back when I was Normal, I suffered from what was then called melancholia. To-day, we'd call it clinical depression. I'm not taking the chance of going back to that hell, and I'm sure not putting Phil through it either."

Duncan eyed *her*. "I will also remain a vampire."

"What the fuck!" I launched myself off the end table and across the room. "You hate being a vampire more than Caesar! You're going to throw away everything you want for that bitch!" I jabbed an index finger in *her* direction.

My uncle actually had the balls to scowl at me. "As you have been telling me since you were twelve—my life, my decision."

"Oh. My. God. You're throwing a teenage temper tantrum in my face!"

Bebe groaned behind me. "I'm so glad I did Granny E.'s spell already."

Duncan straightened to his full six-foot-four, which meant he towered more than a foot over me. "When you are acting like a spoiled brat, then yes."

"Don't try that intimidation shit with me." I poked him in the chest with an index finger. "She'll fuck you over. Just like she did with her own brother. She's no different than Selene."

The silence was deafening. Maybe I'd gotten through to the other members of the coven. But no, they all looked at me like I was the crazy one. Everyone except Phil, who had a disappointed expression on her face.

"I guess you all will have to learn the hard way." I spun on my heel, but I stopped in front of *her*. "Stay away from me. Stay away from my daughter."

I marched out of Caesar's office and out to my rental car. No one tried to stop me.

There had to be a way to kill the bitch for betraying me. And by every god in the universe, I would find it.

Chapter 44

Sam

I teleported into the Bethesda mansion a little after midnight on November 2nd. Like Caesar's Brentwood home did for us, this property acted as the de facto capital of the master of the United States Northeastern Vampire Coven. And as much as I had romanticized the story of Virginia Dare, the first Englishwoman born in the New World, and the missing colony of Roanoke when I was a child, the reality was a totally different story.

When I entered her gigantic study, the clearly marked targets on the map of the states west of the Mississippi on the sixty-inch monitor didn't leave much doubt as to what her intentions were.

John Robbins, her husband and chief enforcer, was the first to notice my presence. He grabbed Virginia and shoved her behind his huge body. An instant later, every eye in the room glowed and thirty-six sets of fangs extended. The reaction made me sad and exhausted. The fairies had finally backed down on wanting to destroy me and were actually cooperating, and now the vampires were getting pissy.

"Master Dare, I understand my mother, Elizabeth Howell, contacted you concerning my brother, Max."

Virginia glared at John, and it was obvious that they were arguing silently. Finally, she stepped away from him. "Yes, she did."

"I have come to discuss recompense for my mother's breach of protocol."

"Who gave in and Turned him?" she spat. If anything, her eyes kicked up their neon blue a notch. "Or did you resurrect him?"

"No one Turned Max." I couldn't cry. Not here. Not now. "None of you could have if you wanted to, which is the other reason I am here."

John's curiosity got the better of him. "What you mean? That you would have stopped us, or that he is immune to the virus as are certain witches?"

"Max *was* immune." I smiled. "As was I when I was Normal. There is a certain irony that Selene Antonius had the cure for the V-virus in front of her and didn't see it."

"No," Virginia growled. "You lie."

"Master Augustine will be petitioning the Vampire Congress in three days with his proposal for vaccinations and distributing the cure." I shrugged. "Given the good working relationship Augustine Coven has had with Dare and Rousseau Covens, he asks to meet with you and Master Rousseau tomorrow at sundown at a place in North America of your choosing."

"What has been done with your brother?" John asked.

"The Angel of Death escorted his soul to his final destination. His funeral was today."

John's eyes narrowed. "And his body?"

"Cremated." Which was true since I'd done it myself, but I wasn't going to admit that to the Dares.

Virginia lifted her chin. "Your mother still broke the law."

"I am not disputing that fact, Master Dare." I folded my fingers together at my waist, emulating Anne's pose in trying to keep my patience. I knew what they were aiming for, but they weren't going to get control of the cure through my family. Caesar hoped for the best, but even Jean-Pierre warned him. "However, she is my mother, which is why I am here to make amends for her atrocious behavior."

The master tossed her long blond curls. "Then give me her head on a platter."

Damn, so this was how it was going to go. Fine. Time to get a little nasty.

I let the power running under the veneer of humanity I still wore seep to the surface. The ashy scent of fear poured from every vampire in the room.

"Under the laws of the Vampire Nation, I have made the offer of recompense. You're correct, Master Dare. You don't have to accept it." I snapped my fingers and the huge monitor exploded into thousands of plastic shards. The coppery scent of blood filled the room. I made sure none of the cuts were lethal though every single vampire was tagged.

"Currently, I'm still a member of the Augustine Coven. Ask yourself if your plans for conquest or the effort to control the cure are worth me killing all of your people. Because I will defend my coven."

Virginia smiled despite her fear. "But you are not a vampire. Augustine's penchant for strays has been an issue among the other masters for some time. I could petition that you be expelled."

"Yes, you could." I returned her smile. "But I agreed to obey the Vampire

Nation's laws as a member. Do you really want to eliminate that token protection?"

John grabbed his wife's arm and hissed something to her in the old Virginia Algonquian language. Whatever he said pissed her off. If I had to guess, he told her not to be stupid here and now.

I reached into my pocket and pulled out six crisp one hundred-dollar bills. "That particular large-screen model is on sale at Target this week." I set the money on a nearby credenza and turned to leave.

"You can't bully people, Ridgeway!"

I faced the vampire master again. "No, Virginia. The issue is that I shouldn't bully people because I can. I find my own husband is a good sounding board. Duncan suggested I *not* melt your faces off a la *Raiders of the Lost Ark* tonight. I recommend you consult with yours before you throw everything away on a half-assed honor quest." I eyed John, and he slowly nodded.

Good. My message had gotten through one of their heads.

I teleported to her lawn where Duncan waited for me.

His attention swung around the yard. "None of her security have noticed we are here."

"I'm getting pretty damn good at veiling spells." I wrapped my arm around his waist, and he pulled me close against him.

"You did not veil their screams while you killed them, did you?"

I rapped him lightly on his chest. "I listened to you." I sighed. "I think John got my message, even if Virginia was ready to slice off Mom's head."

"Would that be such a bad thing?"

I laughed. "Hey, you were the one who said I couldn't melt heads."

"We are not talking about melting your mother's head. Only removing it. With a very sharp object."

We started walking down the drive toward the estate's main gate. Duncan was quiet for a long moment before he added, "Once news of the cure gets out, matters could become quite ugly."

"'Could become'? My darling husband, you have a marvelous gift for understatement." I glanced up at him. "Have you changed your mind about taking it?"

Despite his lower body temperature, the high front pushing through

Maryland tonight was cold enough for his breath to steam. "No. But I do have a request."

I paused, scared of what he'd say next.

"I will remain a vampire, but I want you to do the same for me as you did for Max. When my time comes, let me go."

"Duncan—"

"Samantha, please promise me."

The tears I thought I'd purged after my brother's funeral welled, and my vision blurred. "I-I—"

He cupped my chin and forced me to look at him. "Promise."

All of the other gods' lectures on promises, and how dangerous they were for us and our believers, burst in my head. "I-I'll do what you ask me to do at that point. Don't make me promise something now because you might change your mind. And if you do, we'd both be fucked."

I could almost see the variables rolling through his mind. Finally, he nodded. "Very well. Until the time comes."

We resumed walking. "She'll let go of her anger," he murmured.

I snorted because I knew he wasn't referring to Virginia or Mom. "Duncan, Tiffany stabbed me in the back at Mom and Dad's after the funeral. Literally. As in I'm damned lucky she didn't still have Ares's knife. Jake and Miko had to pull her off me before she went Norman Bates on my ass."

My husband squeezed my shoulders. "Give her some time."

"I can give her the rest of eternity, but I wouldn't get my hopes up if I were you."

Duncan squeezed me again. "Sometimes, hope is all we have."

Big changes are coming to what was the Augustine Vampire Coven, and if there's one thing Mai Osaka can't stand, it's change. Even if it means she and her boyfriend Stan Gryffudd are finally stationed in the same city. But she will need to make some hard choices when she discovers Stan's connection to the rogues' fae allies. Turn the page for a preview of *Reality Bites*!

Reality Bites

Excerpt © 2018 by Suzan Harden

Chapter 1

Mai Osaka waited by the limousine for the small private jet to taxi closer to the Augustine hanger.

St. James hanger, she told herself sternly. She wasn't the only one who'd slipped over appropriate names and conduct the last two weeks. But as the head of security for the Las Vegas branch of the Western United States Vampire Coven, she was expected to set the example.

Even if she was a Normal.

Sharp-edged sunshine bounced off the tarmac and penetrated her standard black pantsuit and boots. Her extra dark sunglasses barely held back the rays. The enforcer standing next to her pulled a white handkerchief from his back pocket and wiped the sweat from his face and neck.

"I don't know how you can stand this heat, Ms. Osaka," Thad Wolford said.

"It's a dry heat." Her standard reply. Personally, she couldn't wait to climb back inside the limo. It was a wonder her sidearm didn't rust with the amount of sweat trickling down her back.

Thad grunted in response. Given that his wife was a werecoyote, non-committal sounds probably kept the peace at home. The former sheriff didn't feel the need to make constant small talk, which was why she brought him instead of one of the were or witch enforcers.

The men standing by the fuel tanker didn't say much either as they waited. But maybe that was more due to the hearing protection they wore.

Engines whined as Mai's younger sister Miko guided the coven jet into an "L" turn and a stop at a safe distance. She waved off the tow vehicle and cut the power. Crap. That meant her little sister couldn't even stay for dinner.

The jet's door swung down creating the staircase to disembark while the workers set about refueling the plane. Mai's heart did a little pitter-pat when Stan Gryffudd ducked his six-six frame through the opening. Brown and green canvas bags were slung over both broad shoulders. A tight scarlet t-shirt covered his torso. Equally tight jeans covered his lower half. His white-blond crewcut literally glowed under the afternoon sun. His long-legged stride made a beeline for the limo.

Thad popped the trunk, met Stan, and offered to carry the bags. The new general manager of the Karnak Hotel and Casino flashed a genial smile and politely refused the offer of assistance.

Unsure of what to do, Thad shot a confused look at Mai. She shrugged, and he backed off. When Duncan St. James had been Normal, he was nobility. Before him, Selene and Ptolemy Antonius had been literal royalty. They all expected a certain amount of deference from the people who served them beyond any other vampire who'd ruled Las Vegas.

Between those three, Grandfather Kensai had been in charge of the coven's interests here for two and a half very short years. But even his Normal status as a military man had carried through with how he expected the staff to behave. Frankly, all the vampires, employees, and Family in Las Vegas were looking at a huge adjustment.

"Getting maudlin in your old age, big sister?" A devilish grin lit Miko's face as she approached.

"No."

"Right." She wrapped her arms around Mai. "I don't need telepathy to tell when you're thinking about Grandfather."

Mai returned her baby sister's hug. "What happened? Vegas was supposed to be your last stop today," she said softly.

Miko released Mai and scowled. "Alex happened. I swear he's getting more paranoid than Duncan ever was as chief enforcer. He scrambled travel plans because he thinks someone leaked the originals." She held up her hands. "So don't ask me where I'm going next. I'm not allowed to tell you."

There was more to the story, but Mai wouldn't press right now. Alex Stanton didn't panic over nothing, and she was fairly certain Stan would tell her later.

"In the meantime, I get to babysit new pilots." She gestured toward the cockpit. A vaguely familiar face looked back at them. The man behind the windshield smiled and waved enthusiastically.

Mai saluted back before turning to her sister. "Who is that?"

"Tom Wellington."

"Who?"

"One of the Billings, Montana, vamps." Miko rolled her eyes. "He's been a bush pilot for a century but I've got to get him up to snuff on jets."

The name finally clicked in Mai's head. "Wait a minute. Doesn't he write romance novels?"

"Yep, with his wife." Miko grimaced. "They're branching out to same sex romance."

"And he's using our need for additional pilots to do a little research?" Mai tamped down on her irritation on her sister's behalf. Even though they'd been raised by their bisexual grandfather and his male partner, Miko still got weird bout being out of the closet herself.

A shadow loomed over them. "You don't have to say anything about your personal life to Tom, Miko." Stan's voice rumbled with his displeasure.

"It's not him. It's me." Miko fidgeted, which wasn't like her at all. Finally, she said, "Brittany and I broke up last night."

Mai cupped her sister's cheeks with both hands. "Why didn't you call me?"

"Because it was a long time coming." Miko sighed. "With the demon craziness the last couple of years, coven matters have taken precedence in my life." She drew Mai's hands from her face and held them. "We'll have a sister night soon. I promise. And I'll tell you everything, but right now, I have a schedule to keep before a certain vampire has a cow."

"All right, but I expect a call in the next two days."

They hugged again before Miko jogged back to the little jet and climbed inside. The fuel truck had already departed. She waved at Mai before she closed the door. A minute later, the engines roared to life, and the plane headed for the line of aircraft awaiting clearance for take-off.

"Mai, would you ride in the back with me?" Stan said.

"Yes, sir." She tried not shiver at his voice. It wasn't his fault he was part fae. Half the time, she didn't think he even realized the effect he had on her.

Thad opened the rear door for them and stiffly held it.

And despite protocol, Stan insisted she climb in first. Mai bit her tongue to keep from chewing him out and wasting even more time. Duncan had to adjust his normal responses when Caesar appointed him the city master of Las Vegas. Her experience with Stan indicated it would take twice as much time to retrain him.

Once they were settled in the back seat, she looked at Stan. "Did something happen?"

He rubbed his temple. "Yeah. A car bombing in Seattle. We're pretty sure the target was Donna Whitefeather."

Thad climbed into the driver's seat. "Is she okay?" Whatever bothered the other enforcer emphasized his slight accent.

Stan reached into the satchel he still carried. "Shrapnel cuts and mild burns. Nothing the V-virus couldn't handle, but one of her Normal nieces and the girl's were boyfriend were killed. Pissed doesn't begin to cover Donna's mood."

"Suspects?" Mai thumbed through the reports. As she suspected, the additional attacks weren't limited to Seattle, or even the western U.S.

"The Vampire Liberation Front is claiming responsibility." Stan shook his head wearily. "Despite Caesar's fears of an all-out civil war, their incidents have been limited to guerilla tactics."

A particular name sent a trill of worry down Mai's back. Her eyes met Stan's. "Dare Coven?"

"What about Dare Coven?" Thad said.

"An explosives-filled van rammed into Virginia's main house in Maryland at twelve-oh-five in the afternoon," Mai answered as she read. "Three daytime enforcers died. Virginia and her inner circle weren't there at the time, and the surviving staff were able to get the two vampires in residence to safety. That doesn't make sense. Virginia's on their side."

"So far she hasn't accused Aug—" Stan sighed. So she wasn't the only one slipping. "She hasn't accused St. James of sponsoring the VLF, but Duncan's concerned that was the terrorists' intent. The DNA of the driver matched one of Caesar's grand-nephews who remained loyal during Selene's rebellion."

"It says here his wife reported him missing two weeks ago," Mai said.

"Yeah, he supposed to pick up his kids from school and never showed." Tension bled off Stan.

"They could have threatened to kill his kids when they nabbed him," Thad offered.

His suggestion sent a chill through Mai. Was that the real reason Miko and her girlfriend had broken up? The possibility of harm coming to the woman she loved might have driven her baby sister to do something stupid.

She frowned as she looked at Stan. "Those kind of stunts will attract too much Normal attention."

"Alex thinks that's their plan," he replied.

"Why out themselves if they want to stay vampires?" Thad said. "That makes no goddamn sense."

Mai sighed. "There's more than a few sadists who enjoy spreading fear on both sides. If they get enough people afraid, no one will take the cure or the vaccine. They can increase their numbers and make a play for world domination."

"And how do we know this Vampire Liberation Front are actually vampires?" Thad asked.

"What are you suggesting?" Stan asked.

"The ones with the most to gain from the collapse of the Vampire Nation are the fairies," Thad bit out.

"Wolford," she snapped.

"I'm just saying what none of you will," he growled back.

"And I will not tolerate racial slurs from any of my staff. Is that understood?" Mai said. Good. Now, she knew where things stood and could take steps.

After a long moment, Thad said. "Yes, ma'am."

"Do have a particular problem with me or just sidhe in general?" Stan asked.

"No one told me you were Unseelie." Thad glared at them in the rearview mirror.

"Ah. You're the former sheriff from Ohio." Stan shifted to look at Mai as well. "Wanna explain to me what's going on?"

There wasn't any tickle in her mind indicating Stan read it, but then, he never needed to resort to those tactics. She shrugged. "I wanted to see how Mr. Wolford would react given his previous encounters."

Thad didn't say anything more until he pulled in front of the Karnak's private entrance and stopped the limo. He turned to glare at her over the driver's seat. "You expected me to shoot the new boss?"

"Given Anne's report of what happened in Millersburg, it was a concern of mine." She returned his glare. "Considering your use of inappropriate language, it seems my concerns were warranted."

Thad sucked on his teeth for a moment before he turned to Stan. "I apologize, Mr. Gryffudd. It won't happen again."

"Good." Stan scowled at the Normal. "I'd hate to start my tenure here by turning you into a mushroom for insubordination."

Mai made a sound low in her throat. She didn't need Stan making his first day here a total disaster.

He shot her a look. "I'm just teasing him."

"I wouldn't go there if I were you, Mr. Gryffudd." Thad smirked. "You need Mai. She's the only one I've met who can keep Sam Ridgeway in line."

"Really?" Stan's left eyebrow quirked upward. "This could be an interesting assignment."

"You have a series of meetings tonight, sir," she reminded him. "You might want to get settled and cleaned up before then."

Thad climbed out of the driver's seat and circled the limo to the right side.

"Slave driver," Stan whispered in her ear.

A shiver ran through her body that she managed to quell before Thad opened the passenger door. She climbed out on unsteady legs. Thankfully, Stan's attention was on his luggage after he followed her out of the vehicle. Maybe she should have Kunal deal with their new boss. Her judgment was too . . . compromised when it came to Stan.

It wasn't exactly either of their faults really. Maybe her cousin Tiffany was right that Murphy was the one true god. Mai swallowed a sigh. Anything that could go wrong had gone wrong in her life.

When Thad drove off to return the limo to the coven's vehicle pool, she led Stan to the private elevator for the penthouse. Sanjay, one of Kunal's Normal cousins, guarded the alcove. He pulled a bronze pin from his lapel.

She held out her hand, and he poked her little finger. Bright red blood welled on her skin, and Sanjay handed her an antiseptic wipe. He repeated the procedure with Stan.

The enforcer inclined his head. "Thank you for your cooperation, Mr. Gryffudd."

"I'm happy you're not poking me with an iron pin," he said dryly.

A wry smile tilted Sanjay's mouth. "According to Ms. Ridgeway, it takes something a little more to detect the dino demons."

Mai headed for the elevator door.

"Have you had any more incidents here?" Stan asked, his long legs keeping pace.

"Not since Master St. James and his wife moved back to Los Angeles."

"So six months, then?"

She didn't want to talk about what had happened. The demon that had gotten into the kitchen still gave her nightmares. "Your biometrics are already encoded for access. Place your hand on the plate." She indicated the black plastic panel on the wall. "And say your name."

She turned to leave when he grabbed her arm. "Who else has access to the penthouse?"

His inquiry only reminded her of her limitations as a Normal. Something she had never questioned until the dinosaur demons had started their campaign against Sam. "Unfortunately, I haven't devised a way to keep out all deities."

He flashed his bright, charming smile. "I meant staff? Security?"

"Only myself, Kunal Saravati, and your executive assistant Staci Warner. One of us has to authorize access for anyone from another department such as housekeeping or room service. The enforcer on duty checks everyone who goes upstairs." At his odd expression, she added. "St. James is the only coven looking for dinosaur demons. They're not bothering anyone else."

"I'm aware. But maybe you should come up?" Another grin. "To make sure I understand all the security measures. I'd hate to set off a false alarm by brushing my teeth."

Her back stiffened. "I adhere to the standards set by our chief enforcer."

Stan glanced around and lowered his voice. "C'mon, Mai. No one's going to suspect anything by you showing me around."

She could feel her resolve melt. They'd never been assigned to the same city, so things between them had slipped under everyone's radar for years. But Stan Gryffudd had become her private addiction, and she didn't know how she'd deal with their new status.

And if she asked for a transfer, Duncan would want to know why since she was the highest-ranked enforcer within the Las Vegas branch of the coven. Hell, she had five years of seniority on Kunal, who'd been perfectly content with his string of drycleaners in Houston until Selene's rebellion.

"Please?" His pale blue eyes didn't glow like a vamp's, but they held a different kind of intensity. One that dissolved the rest of her control into a massive puddle.

She mutely nodded.

He slapped his palm on the panel and said his name. With a *ding*, the doors parted, and they stepped inside the car. He pressed the "PH" button and glanced upward, no doubt noticing the security cameras.

"Guess I'm not sneaking a woman up here without you knowing."

She didn't take his bait. "There's a facility outside of the city that caters to supernatural clientele." She couldn't suppress her grimace. "It's my understanding Selene made frequent use of their services."

"Are you equating me with that bitch?"

Mai suppressed a smile at his aggrieved tone. "Of course not, sir."

He frowned at the panel. "Is 'L3' the old safehouse vault?"

"Yes."

"Maybe we should clear it out. We may need it if we catch one of these VLF bastards."

She chuckled. "Unfortunately, we cannot at this time."

"Why not?"

"Sam's storing some . . . courtship presents from previous suitors that she cannot exactly return. We don't have any other adequate facility to put them."

Stan groaned. "Should I ask?"

"The worst is a rosebush Ares gave her. It drinks blood, and has a tendency to wander around if it's not locked up."

"And she didn't take it with her to L.A. because . . . ?"

Mai looked up at Stan. "Do you really have to ask that?"

He rubbed his forehead. "Forget I said that. No interfering in other people's marriages. I blame jetlag."

The elevator doors slid open. Mai was pleased Staci had followed her suggestions. Greenery filled the penthouse living room. Compared to Duncan's minimalist tastes, it almost felt crowded with the multitude and variety of potted plants.

His gaze swept the area. "Did you do this?"

"Not in my job description, but since you couldn't bring your greenhouse with you—"

Stan dropped his bags, grabbed her and pressed her against the wall. His warm mouth covered hers. And she willingly gave in to him.

She was breathless when his attention turned to her neck.

"Morrigan, help me," he murmured against her skin. "You have no idea how much I've missed you."

She chuckled. "I can guess." It didn't help that his huge hands cupped her ass, and her legs were now wrapped around his waist.

"A quickie is not what I had mind the next time I saw you—"

Mai's walkie-talkie crackled to life. "Ms. Osaka, we need you in holding." Mike Warner's voice. Despite the werecoyote's youth, he didn't call her unless it was a real problem. Hell, he'd been the one to realize the new busboy wasn't remotely humanoid.

Her forehead fell to Stan's shoulder. "And we're not even going to get that."

He lowered her back to the floor, making a point of sliding her body down his length. Like she wasn't frustrated enough already.

She unclipped her radio from her belt. "What's the issue, Mike?"

"We have a player from Marley's roulette table who was a little too lucky. She smelled ozone."

Mai groaned. Last thing they needed was a cheating witch in the middle of all the Karnak's other problems. But Marley had been running roulette nearly eighty years ago when she'd been Normal, and she had an eye for the scammers.

"I'll go down with you," Stan said. "A witch won't randomly fling spells if I'm there."

Mai pressed the response button. "We're on our way." She released the button before she said, "And they'll be fucking lucky if I don't stick them in the vault with the blood-sucking rose plant."

Reality Bites **is available at your favorite online retailer.**

Acknowledgements

It's hard to believe I started writing this series fourteen years ago. The publishing industry was a totally different animal back then. The changes that have enveloped both writers and readers have been amazing. I can carry my entire personal library on my phone. I can write an entire book on my phone. Any time. Anywhere.

But there are some things that haven't changed. No writer does this all by herself. To the following:

Many thanks to Jaye Manus of QA Productions and Elaina Lee of For the Muse Design, who have been my companions for a good chunk of this road. Your talents make me look good.

Love beyond words for my husband, who has provided the emotional support for the last twenty-four years.

Admiration for my son, who is now a young man starting on his own journey.

Appreciation to my friends Ro, Becky, and Kat, who have encouraged and cheered me.

And most of all, gratitude to my readers who have read and loved these characters as much as I do.

About the Author

Suzan Harden transitioned from writing information technology manuals for companies and legal articles for a law enforcement magazine to her first love, fantasy and science fiction in all their forms. She's the author of the Millersburg Magick Mysteries, the Soccer Moms of the Apocalypse series, and the Books of Apep series.

Contact Suzan Harden
Facebook: Suzan Harden
Email: suzan@suzanharden.com
Website: www.suzanharden.com

Sign up for Suzan's mailing list